W9-CQK-111

MCMXCVi
Descartes gammes, gainansche dachs.

Necessity

Necessity

a novel

Mark Ticao

Copyright© 2024 Mark Ticao
All rights reserved.
HTG MCMXCVI
Uddevalla, Sweden

cover layout & illustration©
Tina Marie Ticao
Frances Grace Ticao Abañes
Helna Pettersson

ISBN 978-91-531-0964-8

This is a work of fiction, purely a product of the author's imagination. Any resemblance to names of people, living or dead, or events is purely coincidental. Names of local establishments and some names of certain places have been changed.

*To my mother, Eda Arias Cordero Ticao,
and to all mothers who place their
children above anyone else.*

1

*n*ecessity is the mother of Jeremy Ilaya and Anthony Berano. Necessity is gone, so she actually was their mother, if one is to strictly adhere to the universally, but nevertheless morosely established notion that people are forever gone after they've passed away, to the effect that everything they cause to stir ought to belong to the past tense, even if it means memories of them that are still powerful enough to move continental plates in the present. Some people come into one's life and they never leave, they seem to linger in one's finite mind indefinitely, whether one thinks hard or exert no effort at all in thinking. To Anthony, his mother is never gone, he invokes the spirit of his literary hero George Eliot when he makes the case that no one is dead until one is forgotten. And so at least to one person, Necessity is not dead. She is his mother, not was.

To Anthony, she is still there, always lurking, the first figure to steal scenes in his thoughts in times of jubilation and good fortune, as she plays the role of an entity who ought to receive the happy news ahead of anyone else. It is also the same figure to appear in harrowing, desperate and unsettling moments when he cannot trust even the sweetest of his dreams, when he turns his back on them and tries to walk away. She'll surely be there, and she'll tell him, No, you're going the wrong way! She's gone though.

Jeremy Ilaya and Anthony Berano are full brothers, actually. However, due to his profound disdain for his father, Anthony prefers to be called Anthony Berano. Berano was Necessity's maiden family name. Anthony is aware that he cannot use Berano officially without an Ilaya attached to it, so whenever he's asked his name in circumstances when the official name is not expressly required, he seizes the chance and calls himself Anthony Berano. It did not bother Necessity in her lifetime, she understood and felt for Anthony, and in fact, there had been many instances while he was growing up when it felt like it was a necessity not to reveal his true family name.

Born in 1947 in one of the most deeply Roman Catholic alcoves of the Philippines, Necessity had all the odds against her in matters of getting that unusual, rather bizarre name. The baptismal certificate was then the most powerful document in the land, and priests had all the authority to reject any proposed name if they deemed the name awkward or odd enough to place children in the position of being bullied, or if it was too foul that it may cause filial hatred sometime during crucial periods of growth, or if they simply thought the name was somewhat close to that of the devil's. A few years earlier, in the same town where Necessity was born, a couple was chastised and ordered to fast and abstain from eating meat for half a year for attempting to name their son Lucifer, the devil himself.

Oddly, in the rainy month of May 1947, Necessity was baptized as Necessity Berano y Baydadong at the old church of Saints Bartholomew and Barnabas in the coastal town of Burog, Iloilo. Her mother was one of the town's first native school teachers, she taught English, arithmetic, and good manners and right conduct, and so she was so fond of all sorts of English words, common or odd, sweet or foul. English was introduced to the country by the American colonizers just less than half a century before, and to be able to speak a neat English phrase was considered a tag of the privileged.

And so Alicia Berano, Necessity's mother, the most admired school teacher in town, thought that an English word for a name was like a leap to royalty, as she herself came from a less privileged family. She initially considered Felicity, but then it did not give her peace, as the name was becoming all too common, and there had been three prostitutes in the surrounding towns named Felicity, all belonging to three different successive generations.

So Alicia dropped Felicity halfway thru the pregnancy, just the name, not the baby, and came up with Necessity, if it was a girl. Had it been a boy, she'd have given him the name Abundance, Renaissance or Resentment. She had no doubt all the skills to teach English - grammar, composition, reading and all, but the language was still new to the land, and so words were often used and applied clumsily, even by teachers, or sometimes used as names, especially by teachers themselves.

Armando Berano, Necessity's father, was a great grandson, a grandson, a son of a fisherman and was a fisherman himself, he was from a small village in the outskirts of Burog, at the coastal side. This long line of fishermen had squatted a on a few sturdy rocks by the shore and always thought that their descendants would remain there to fish the seemingly inexhaustible Burog Bay, and that the line would be unbroken for all eternity. Armando must have understood a few English, but obstinately refused to speak it, except, for reasons unknown, the word Help!

Unlike many others in town, he held no deep grudge against what many would call their colonizers, he just thought their language was too intimidating, and that his tongue and the tongues of his entire bloodline were not naturally made to speak it. But when Alicia suggested the name Necessity, he had no objections. Though he did not know what it meant, he too, thought it sounded like royalty, and he was quite comfortable with and grateful to the idea, as such a name would compel him to speak another English word on a daily basis, aside from Help! When he uttered the word Necessity for the first time, his heart pounded in tumult, he got soaked in sweat and almost passed out. What he felt after that moment though was complete relief, it was like a long-awaited liberation. Necessity- it was the first English word he uttered after the one, the only one he learned to speak early in the American occupation - Help!

Jose Baydadong, Alicia's father and thus the grandfather of Necessity, was a great grandson, a grandson, and a son of a fisherman, but an extreme fear of the deep seas compelled him to move inland and work as a farmhand. His mother was from the hinterland town of Calinog, which explained why his middle name did not begin with a letter B, as almost every family name did in Burog then, it began with the letter C - Cañosi.

Jose Cañosi Baydadong, in contrast to many in his line and in his village, loved to speak English. However, he spoke it in a manner that was understood neither by speakers nor non-speakers of the language. His favorite line was, Night for life and good for all morning! Whatever he meant by that, the Japanese army during The Second World War thought it was good English and so he became an instant suspect American loyalist and informer. He was captured and tortured, beaten and water-boarded several times during the war, but he was saved and released every time, thanks to the Japanese Army's interpreters in English who swore it was not English he was uttering, to them it sounded like a lost language of one of the extinct Asian tribes. He for his part deeply despised the Japanese invaders, not because of the physical torture, but because he thought they were a hopeless lot who would never get to understand English. His English.

Jose Cañosi Baydadong loved anything American, making him an object of resentment among the nationalists in town. When the Americans landed on Panay Island towards the end

4

of the Second World War, he was among the first to rush to the shores of Tigbauan at the southern part of the island to greet them as liberators, temporarily forgetting his fear of the seas. He was initially picked by his liberators as some native guide, American soldiers gave him a ride, asked him for directions and information but all he could say was, Hey Joe! Chocolate Joe! He was considered a liability and was dropped off the army jeep after barely a mile's ride from the beach.

Nevertheless, he loved his country dearly, and he too, wanted an independent Philippines, though he wanted America to be around like an omnipresent babysitter. He wanted the new Philippine Republic to keep playing The Star Spangled Banner on official events, he enjoyed the attention during the long American era, as his name, Jose Cañosi Baydadong, sounded to local ears like the first line of The Star-Spangled Banner. Oblivious to perceptible ridicule, he felt like the spotlights were on him each time it was played or sung. It was in fact, what made him love everything about that foreign power which made his country its colony.

He was a teenager when America took over the country from Spain at the turn of the century. He'd never been to school as it was not required in the Spanish era. Initially, he didn't care much about which superpower was in charge, he never understood government structures and what The Philippine Revolution was all about at that time, his thoughts were that simple. One day, when he was already a young adult, one of his friends told him as some sort of a prank, Hey Jose, you ought to go to the flag raising ceremony on the last Monday of the month, they sing your name there!

There was a flag raising ceremony at the municipal hall every Monday for government employees and soldiers, and at that time, The United States hadn't decided anything yet apropos their national anthem, so they alternated Hail Columbia!, My Country 'Tis of Thee, America the Beautiful and The Star Spangled Banner every week. Curious, Jose Cañosi Baydadong attended the flag raising ceremony one

Monday in late April 1910, The Star Spangled Banner was sung, he was so moved upon hearing what he believed was his name, his collar and his sleeves were all soaked with tears. It was more than he could digest. There he was, in tattered farmhand's clothes, broken sandals separated his muddy feet from the earth, he even had flecks of mud on his face, his right hand which was placed on his chest during the singing left mud stains with a shape of a palm on his shirt, yet this rising superpower nation was celebrating his name in an anthem, so he thought. He was a fixture there every last Monday of the month, his friends went there too, to have a good laugh indulging in jeers, but he took it for cheers.

In March 1931, President Hoover signed the bill officially declaring The Star Spangled Banner as the National Anthem of the United States. News reached Burog more than a month later, and upon hearing this, Jose Cañosi Baydadong went wild. He snatched a cow tail from the butcher's, ran around town in a frenzy waving the tail like Archimedes running around Syracuse screaming Eureka! Only he was screaming America, and he had his clothes on. He became a fixture every Monday at the municipal hall flag raising ceremony, never missing it, rain or shine, drought or flood, even when he was sick. To his dismay, there came a major change just a year after the war ended as the Lupang Hinirang supplanted The Star-Spangled Banner when the Philippine Republic was inaugurated, and that made him pine for the erstwhile American era for the remainder of his life.

Alicia got her school teacher's degree at the Normal School in Iloilo City after the war, she had to attend classes in makeshift nipa huts in her final year in school as the campus buildings were virtually pulverized by incendiary bombs. She was her father's greatest pride as she was the only one among nine siblings who could speak English. She spent many years in school, as it was interrupted by the war, and halfway thru her schooling her father began conversing with her in English, and they frequently talked for hours, though each was not quite able to figure out what the other was saying, as it was like a clash of two completely unrelated monologues. Their talks were nevertheless warm, hearty, and quite mystifyingly, never once had a tone of conflict.

When Alicia revealed to her father that the child's name was to be Necessity, Jose Cañosi Baydadong went delirious out of sheer delight, he felt like he was lifted out of himself up to heaven, and when he came back to earth he was never the same, he did not speak better English though, but in every way he was not the same, everyone thought so at least. It was his logical reasoning that changed for the worse, and it was already quite bad before. It was not his first grandchild, but she was the first to have an English name, or rather, an English word for a name. He loved the word, he adored it, he bragged about it all over town day and night, but just like Armando Berano, the father of the child, he did not really know what Necessity meant. To have that name was for him like being a citizen of Kingdom Come, as that was how he referred to Heaven, and he thought that the child bearing that name would lift the entire clan beyond the ranks of nobility. He suspected however, or was near-certain, that Holy Mother the Church was herself to be the lone but insurmountable obstacle to the name Necessity being ever written on a baptismal certificate, so he thought of a plan.

Father Antonio Poral was the first Filipino secular parish priest of the town and had held the post for nearly twenty years by the time Necessity was to be baptized. He had fended off proposed odd names like Palito, which means matchstick, Pilato, the local term for Pilate, Uyog, meaning to shake, Tay-og, meaning to shake harder, Belzeebul, that is, Lucifer's spawn, and then recently, Lucifer. Father Poral was conservative, reserved and pious when sober, but was rash, absent-minded, and quite progressive when he'd had enough tubâ, a native palm wine, in his blood.

7

He and Jose Cañosi Baydadong became like brothers in blood during the war. Father Poral was quite lucky that the Japanese regiment stationed in town tolerated church activities to some extent. In other towns, some clergymen reportedly lost their heads, literally, especially the caucasian-looking ones, that was why stories of apparitions of headless priests had become a relentlessly redundant piece of folklore.

Father Poral managed to undergo many years of horror and uncertainty during the war with his head intact, though he played a vital role in saving the lives of many guerrilla men in the coastal towns. Countless of times he interceded to the Japanese to spare the lives of captured guerrilla men, offering in exchange proceeds from Sunday collections and whatever ornament there was in the church, like expensive chandeliers and candleholders and even his own bejeweled chalice. Jose Cañosi Baydadong was his runner during the war, and those years of working together in dreadful circumstances had forged them to stick together like brothers, that and their nearly nightly sessions of imbibing tubâ. Tubâ was the commodity in town that was least affected by the catastrophic war, it flowed into jars no matter how extensive the destruction was.

The ethyl in tubâ may be most short-lived among all boozes. It is a sweet, potent wine from coconut sap which is collected in the late afternoon, but it quickly turns to vinegar by dawn. Still, during its short lifespan it does wonders to the mind, though it causes blunders too - it makes people talk, it makes them sing, dance, tell the truth, and make bad decisions. It made Jose Cañosi Baydadong talk in his native tongue without any attempt in English, thus making him more intelligible than usual, even though it made him slur. It made Father Poral relax which could be a good thing, but it also caused him to be a little foolhardy and unstable in his decisions, a side-effect that usually lasted for several days after the last ingestion.

It was a rainy Friday evening in late May, barely two years after the war ended, the old grandfather clock had just struck 8 and the old priest had just finished saying his evening vespers. There came a familiar knock at the rectory's gigantic mahogany door, it sure sounded like the good old times, the horrible war time but somehow, in at least a diluted manner, the good old times for the two rather old men.

There came three light raps in rapid succession, then two harder ones with a couple of seconds' interval, then again four lighter, rapid ones. It could be no other than Jose Cañosi Baydadong! Father Poral thought. The priest went down to the rectory's main entrance, he lifted the big iron bar that served as a sort of a diagonal lock, the door opened sluggishly, making an unearthly screeching sound.

The lone street lamp from the plaza across the church brought about by the doorstep a silhouette of a man, quite tall, plump in the belly and the buttocks but gaunt in the limbs, he had hairs only at the sides of his head, the top shone as it reflected the faint light from the street lamp. The man was almost 60, but it was hard to tell if one did not know him, by his posture one might think he was 80. The priest could not see his face clearly, but he knew he was grinning, because his grin was always paired with that thing he was carrying - a couple of five-gallon tin containers which the guerrilla men used to store crude oil and gasoline during the war, only this time, they contained tubâ.

Jose Cañosi Baydadong said, Good evening, Padrecito! I brought you three months' supply of vinegar! Light shone on his cheeks, indicating he was widely grinning.

Father Poral replied, Bless you, brother, and may the good Lord bestow upon us moderation, that some of it may see the light of dawn as vinegar!

Jose Cañosi Baydadong said, Excellent! Such an unwavering keenness in your sense of smell! You know it is still tubâ and not yet vinegar even when it is inside a tight container! I too, pray for moderation, that you may indeed have three months' supply of vinegar!

Father Poral replied while he himself was almost on the brink of grinning, You knew I'd be having seven baptisms tomorrow morning, didn't you?

Though he did not say it, the priest according to how Jose Cañosi Baydadong read it, sounded more like saying, I wish you'd come with your tubâ another night, but if you are here with those containers right now, it would be tragic to say no and turn all of it to vinegar by daybreak.

Jose Cañosi Baydadong said, How can I not know about those baptisms? My granddaughter is one of them! I think you know!

The old priest feigned surprise, appeared to gawk at him for a while, then finally chuckled and made a subtle nodding of his head with a little wink like saying, Come in, and let's get on with it!

They went upstairs to the old rectory's living room after traversing a short hallway and a flight of stairs studded with bat droppings. By 11 pm they were done with the first gallon, they were both struggling to sit upright by the rectory's long, antique dining table made of acacia lumber.

They talked and sang, they had to raise their voices as the heavy rains drowned every sound. By that time, Jose Cañosi Baydadong was slurring like some venomous viper had bitten him in the mouth, and his eyes were fixed on the ceiling most of the time, he said, It's a wonderful name, Padre! Heavenly! Heavenly! And as holy as can be!

The good priest was also slurring, he talked slowly, interrupted by short chuckles. He said, No doubt, it's a beautiful, though unusual name, but don't you think she'll be a little alone in this God-chosen land with that name?

Jose Cañosi Baydadong raised his arms with open hands as if to protest, he said, But Padre, this is the American age, in the entire world! The name will be a classic in the future! It will be immortal! In a decade everyone will be speaking English, every other girl in this land will bear that name, I assure you!

Father Poral replied in a tone like he was retracting, Oh yes, yes…perhaps. I just thought for a while it sounded more like a functional, pragmatic kind of word!

I don't know what you mean, Padre, said Jose Cañosi Baydadong as he rose from his chair, he then walked towards the large window to breathe some fresh air. The priest said the very words functional and pragmatic in English, not in the local Hiligaynon, so Jose Cañosi Baydadong was being precise in saying he did not know what the former meant. He did not know what Necessity meant either.

The priest cleared his throat and said with much caution, I mean.. Then he paused and chuckled, and went on, I mean, you know what it means, right? That word necessity?

Jose Cañosi Baydadong replied, Not exactly, but it's American, and it's brand new!

The priest said, Well, to give you a clue, you know the Spanish word necesidad? It's been in the country's vocabulary for three hundred years now, surely…

Jose Cañosi Baydadong interrupted him, raising his voice, Well, that word is Spanish, Padre! I know what it means, it's not as beautiful as Necessity, it's Spanish! The Spaniards were losers! God bless America!

Father Poral, slurring, said, Well, both words exactly mean the same thing, I mean, even in the Spanish era no one was ever called Necesidad, I've never baptized anyone with that name, at least, and…

But you were ordained after the Spanish era! The now irate Jose Cañosi Baydadong replied, raising his voice even an octave higher, practically squeaking.

The old priest said, Alright, alright! There! There! But I have to tell you, I administered a lot of funeral rites too, to elderly people born in the zenith of the Spanish era, I have never sent anyone to heaven with names like Necesidad, Habilidad or Calamidad, neither to hell!

Jose Cañosi Baydadong replied this time in a lower, calmer tone, he said, Well, it's different Padre, completely different! One is Spanish and the other is American, it's the sound that counts! We are talking of baptisms and the future! Like what I said, in three decades every other girl in town will be named Necessity! My granddaughter will be the proud flag-bearer of that name, she will speak English as good as any American, and she will go to America, she will have her office on top of that Emperor Building and Americans will serve her, they'll bring her what she wants! She'll ring the bell once, someone comes in with a glass of water for her, she rings the bell twice, someone comes in to shine her shoes!

Father Poral replied while scratching his sparsely bearded chin, Aah, you mean The Empire State Building? New York City, that's a long way from here...

Jose Cañosi Baydadong replied, It's in America, Padre, not in Yoyork, wherever that town of perdition is! And nothing's too far for someone named Necessity! I have a picture of that Emperor Building, it was given to me by a sergeant of the U.S. Army who joined our guerrilla forces, and I told him that one of my descendants will sit on top of that building and will give orders to everyone! I think the chosen one has come!

The priest asked, And what did that sergeant say?

Jose Cañosi Baydadong replied, I don't know, he didn't say anything, he seemed not able to comprehend, he must have been drunk!

Father Poral said, Too big dreams for a girl, don't you think? She's a girl, Jose, you might have forgotten, her place is in the house to serve and honor her husband!

The proud grandfather replied, Not with the name Necessity! She will be breaking norms with that name! She can hurdle any obstacle! Times have changed! Even women can be on top of the world! Haven't you heard of Allanor Rose-belt and Amelia Air-heart?

The old priest replied, I have, though the names sounded a little bit different...

As the night wore on, they chuckled more than they talked. By 3 a.m. they were snoring with their heads rested on the antique wooden table, three glasses were broken to pieces, three more were sprawled between them, tubâ was dripping to the floor from several focal points on the woodworm-infested table. Fr. Poral officiated the Saturday morning mass at 6 a.m., still chuckling. His sermon was not like the usual in which he picked out a specific sin, expounded on it and declared who was next to go to hell. This time he talked more on how to enjoy and live life to the full, he said life should be like a dry run of the eternal bliss in heaven. Parishioners knew him too well, they knew what was behind his words, they called it the Tubâ Gospel.

At 10 a.m. that day, Father Antonio Poral, still hungover, baptized Necessity in the Name of the Father, and of the Son, and of the Holy Ghost, chuckling after mentioning each Person of The Trinity. A calf, two hogs and a flock of chickens were slaughtered for the occasion and though no invitations were sent, almost the entire town came for the baptismal feast that followed at the humble Berano home, as it was understood that everyone could invite themselves, as was in the case of each and every baptism.

The rain stopped shortly before the banquet, guests came in waves, they ate while standing on damp, soggy soil outside the small house of the Beranos which squatted on a mango grove that belonged to Jose Cañosi Baydadong's landlord. During the feast, the very proud grandfather passed around the black and white picture of that famous landmark of New York City which he called The Emperor Building, in his thoughts he flattered himself that all were impressed, but the guests barely listened or glanced at the picture, they just ate, drank, packed sizable portions of food in paper bags, and left. Most were not able to recall the child's name, it was too novel, too awkward, and a four-syllable colonial word for a name was too much to retain.

The day of reckoning came for Father Poral in January the following year. He received a letter from the archdiocesan chancellor Monsignor Valdemar Valdez, known to fellow priests in the diocese as Val-Val, sounding like bal-bal, a Hiligaynon term for someone who can beat you badly. Msgr. Val-Val summoned Fr. Poral to the Archbishop's Palace in Jaro in Iloilo City, some 30 miles south of his parish. Msgr. Val-Val's job was, among others, to see to it that the tithes summed up right and all who got married the previous year and all who were to be married that year were eligible, and that the names of the newly baptized sounded more or less like the usual. An unusual name caught his eye.

Msgr. Val-Val was furious, he yelled, What in the name of John the Baptist were you thinking, Padre Poral? What name is this? The chancellor was smoking a Tabacalera cigar, his favorite brand, and when he was really angry he never puffed out the smoke.

Fr. Poral was shuddering, and he stammered as he said, It's, it's Necessity, Monsignor...

Msgr. Val-Val said, Yes I know, I can read! What I want to know is why, why such...word? Why such a name? In a couple of decades she'll bear a child, and when she names her child Invention I'm sure the likes of you would go rogue and approve it!

The poor old priest was nervous, apart from having been struck by the thought that he'd be dead in a couple of decades long before anyone could ever invent the name Invention, he dreaded confrontation by his superiors. He could handle the Japanese occupation forces but he trembled to the foundations of his soul the moment a superior frowned at him.

He kept on plucking the little of what was left of the goatee on his chin, he replied, still stammering, Monsignor, when I heard the name I saw a ray of light from my right, a bright, shimmering light, and I thought, at least I believed, that it was a sign!

14

Msgr. Val-Val, tittering and trying his best to display perceptible sarcasm, asked, A sign? And did you have a headache right after that?

Fr. Poral was genuinely surprised by how his superior could know, he gawked, this time not faking it, and said, Why, yes Monsignor, exactly! An excruciating one on my right temple, like something was forcing its way into my skull, very painful, I think it was the Spirit taking over!

Msgr. Val-Val deliberately set his eyeballs rolling and said, I've had that one too, Padre, my doctor says it's called migraine, if I took every bout of it as a sign from heaven then every other child in this diocese would have been named Tabacalera!

The alarmed Father Poral asked, My grain? Is there a grain in my head?

Msgr. Val-Val replied, this time really laughing, It's migraine, it's a new term! You like novel terms don't you, Padre? Like Necessity? Try and baptize anyone with the name Migraine and I'll send the bishop a note of recommendation for your excommunication! Now go and have your glasses checked, and stay away from that tubâ!

Alicia Berano had another child the following year, and another word topped the list of possible names, a favorite word from any local school teacher's glossary - Lackadaisical, be it a boy or a girl. Jose Cañosi Baydadong was ecstatic. Lackadaisical - an even more complicated five-syllable English word the meaning of which he would never know. Armando Berano however, was desperate, he wondered if he could ever manage to call his second child by his or her first name if that was the case. Father Poral, fearing excommunication, had forewarned that no one could ever become a member of The One, Holy, Catholic and Apostolic Church with the name Lackadaisical, but so as not to displease his blood buddy Jose Cañosi Baydadong, he conferred first with Msgr. Val-Val this time, and both agreed that the baptizable options instead were

Daisy, if it was a girl, and Darius, if it was a boy. The family agreed, though Jose Cañosi Baydadong grumbled.

It was a girl, so she was to be called Daisy. Daisy however, never made it it to the formal baptism. Within a day of her birth she turned blue, and by daybreak the following day she was gone. Fr. Poral made it just in time to pour water on her head naming her Daisy in the name of the Father, and of the Son, and of the Holy Ghost. This time he was not chuckling.

The household was grief-stricken, nobody could fathom what had happened, she was so strong at the moment of birth, everyone thought her cry was louder than the church bells. She was so lively and vigorous then all of a sudden she turned lackadaisical. Dr. Juanico from the nearby town of Ajuy thought it was her heart, that it was not formed to last a day outside Alicia Berano's womb.

The enraged grandfather Jose Cañosi Baydadong however, thought it was the craft of Purita, an old hermit who lived by the outskirts of the the inland side of Burog and who had been tagged for decades by village folks as a witch. Purita was young when she was widowed at the turn of the century, her husband was slain in one of the early skirmishes of the Philippine-American War, people claimed she tormented and killed Americans through evil spells, as a form of vengeance, that she kept dolls made out of coconut husks in her hut, each doll was tagged with an American name, the names of her victims, and at night when the moon was full she'd make a ritual, burning incense and herbs and chanting oracles in half-Latin, half-Kinaray-a, and she'd skewer the dolls thru the chest to complete the execution of the spell.

People even spread the tallest of tales that she caused the disability, and eventually, the death of President Franklin Delano Roosevelt. Nobody actually saw her doing such things, but whatever was believed to be true by two or three among the townsfolk was most likely to be held as true by the entire town.

Jose Cañosi Baydadong concluded without a speck of doubt that Purita was the culprit because he thought she resented the baby's American name. He went berserk in the afternoon following Daisy's death, he rushed to Purita's hut and tried to kick the front door open, and because the door was made of nipa leaves, his foot just went thru it. The rest of the hut was made of nipa leaves too, so he could have just kicked through anywhere. Then he turned around, and with his sharpened bolo he cut down dozens of papaya shrubs that Purita had planted around the hut. He yelled, threatening to chop Purita into pieces if she did not get out of her hut.

He stayed there for hours, screaming incessantly. Why he did not break in no one knew. Some said he caught sight of a spider web by the door, and he was dead-scared of spiders. Then night fell, not a sight of Purita, nothing stirred inside the hut. He then began to recall stories about her turning into half-human, half- horse at night, and that she charged at people with the strength of an elephant and devoured their livers and sucked their blood. It was then that Jose Cañosi Baydadong began to feel his feet getting cold and shaky, then his legs, then his belly, then his chest, then his neck, then all of him, and so he retreated, scampering through the vast rice fields homewards.

Every year on the 12th of June the family offered mass for Little Daisy in Limbo, they said they'd make sure that the practice was passed on to every generation, because they believed that after the 99th mass Daisy would be released from Limbo and taken to heaven. However, the tradition flickered away after some twenty years even though the date was not hard to forget, as the 12th of June was later on declared as the official Philippine Independence Day. Fr. Poral claimed on the other hand that Daisy was still breathing when he administered the emergency baptism, and so he was certain she was going to bypass Limbo and was already an angel. Jose Cañosi Baydadong didn't care much where Daisy was, he just wanted Purita to go to hell as soon as possible.

Alicia Berano herself did not really believe it was Purita, but she opted to harbor the thought, because she thought that some form of defiance to what people believed to be witchcraft was some kind of a driving force for her to have more children with American names, it was her conscious fantasy, to spite Purita or anyone who resented her fondness of the English language.

The following year she gave birth to a son and called him Arthur Douglas, loosely after the popular general who liberated the Philippines from the Japanese, a feat that culminated in an iconic landing in Leyte. She thought it would amuse her father Jose Cañosi Baydadong extremely, but it was not to be, he maintained that nothing could beat the names Necessity and Lackadaisical, and that Arthur and Douglas already sounded too common. He actually suggested the name Artillery, and he went sour because it was not even remotely considered by Alicia.

Two years later, another son was born, Jose Cañosi Baydadong wanted to call him Ride, as he always cherished that moment when American soldiers picked him up on an army jeep by the beaches of Tigbauan shortly after they landed to liberate the island of Panay. One soldier called out to him, Hey, Pop, wanna' ride? He ecstatically obliged. Luckily, he had completely forgotten how they offloaded him in a case of need after barely a mile's ride because they could neither stand nor understand his babbling. The same soldier who picked him up shooed him and told him, Fuck off! He didn't know what that meant. He adored the word Ride, fortunately the only new English word he could recall from that day.

Father Poral and the Msgr. Val-Val again stood in the way, and the boy was baptized Percivale. A third son was born a year later, and while Jose Cañosi Baydadong was still busy looking up the newspapers and the dictionary for another odd name, they had the baby hurriedly baptized as Lancelot. Jose Cañosi Baydadong was actually brooding over the names Derelict and Dividend. Because he didn't get things his way, he always thought that these boys, who got their names from Camelot and not from a list of English words which he couldn't understand, would never amount to anything. Necessity was his undisputed favorite.

Jose Cañosi Baydadong died of tuberculosis in 1957, at the hour of his death he summoned the ten year old Necessity to his bedside. He showed her that black and white picture of The Empire State Building. He was frail and seemed to be perpetually coughing, but he gathered the last of his strength to talk to her. He said, See this, my Necessity? This is the Emperor Building, tallest in the world, on top of this is an office space, you will have a very big desk there, you will be the boss of Americans, just sound a bell and they will come and bring to you whatever you want, a glass of water, pens, paper, ice, just say it!

Before he expired, Jose Cañosi Baydadong said one last phrase in English to Necessity, the big apple of his eye. In a feeble, trembling voice, he said, Life, still like flowers, run sunshine bright!

Whatever he meant by that, he must have wished Necessity only the best.

2

*G*ive me some water please! Necessity called out. She had
a mild but clear tone of impatience in her voice. She was
a grown woman now in her early forties, already she had
visible gray hairs on her temples and ripples of fine
wrinkles on the outer edges of her eyes. She waited, but
nothing happened, so she raised her pitch a little to indicate
that she had no time to lose, she said, I need some water,
please, now!

Anthony obligingly came to the scene, carrying a bucket of
murky, light-brown water. The bucket was a light red plastic
one, it had a long crack through almost the entire diameter of
its base, making it leak water by some hundred drops every
second.

Necessity, with clearer urgency, once again called out, The
faster you move the less water you'll spill!

I'm trying, Mama! said the distressed Anthony. He
couldn't be blamed for not being fast enough, he had to fetch
water from a large tin container where they collected rain

water, it stood beside the house, and though the outdoor privy where Necessity was was just barely twenty feet away, one would have to walk through spongy stones of uneven heights, and these stones were studded with sharp, prehistoric barnacles.

Necessity needed the water to flush the small porcelain latrine in that makeshift outdoor privy. It was a small one, an average adult would only need to stretch both elbows, and that was all with the width. Necessity was not tall, she stood five foot three, when she sat on the toilet seat her knees were flexed just comfortably enough, and when she stood her head was just a couple of inches from hitting the ceiling. The walls of the privy were made of used plywood which she found drifting after a typhoon, and the roof was made of zinc plates which she salvaged from a junkyard. She waited for Anthony, she sat and crouched there like a snail in her shell.

The top observation floor of The Empire State Building might just be as tight, but she was not there, she was in the same village where her untraceable paternal line had fished for a living for centuries, on the coastal edges of Burog. The village stood on rocks which protruded from the shore bed, the rocks clearly looked like they had once been underwater long before the dawn of mankind, as they bore ample areas covered with fossilized corals. Where the rock was not that porous stood shanties on stilts, most of them were made of bamboo and nipa leaves, some were of any material that villagers found floating after storms, like fragments of billboards, plywood, zinc plates, and even erstwhile wooden walls of neighbors. It did not look all that shabby, the village. At dusk when the sunlight is dimmed and the yellow lamps were lit, the decrepit materials were not that visible, and one might actually want to sit by the opposite side of the cove to paint it, like a classic fishermen's village, though no one ever did that.

The village is called Sitio Putak, it had been renamed about six times in the past decades, because each time a new set of municipal councilors took office, which was about two to four years, they made a move to change the name of every village, to add to the list of their accomplishments. Strangely enough, in the late 1970's, just after the village was named Sitio Putak, a name which the villagers abhorred, the politicians stopped the practice, and so it was to be called Sitio Putak, perhaps forever. The villagers squatted in the area, they did not own any piece of rock where their houses stood, but since everyone believed that these fishing folk had been there longer than there had been fishes on the bay, they were tolerated. To evict fishing villagers was political suicide. But the officials put rules, like no latrine was to be installed nearer than a dozen feet from the waters. Only the few who had latrines knew of this rule, the rest used the great Burog Bay, and to that effect, the entire Iloilo Strait and the Pacific Ocean, as one giant latrine, and they couldn't care less.

Necessity's privy stood exactly a dozen feet from the waters of Burog Bay. One could safely say she followed the rules, she respected the sea like it had a soul. Burog Bay bore the fattest oysters, shrimps and fish in the long Iloilo Strait and it sustained her ancestors for what she believed a hundred generations before the Spaniards arrived in the archipelago. Though she herself did not fish for a living, she believed the sea pumped life into her soul, and she would not do anything foul, not even as little as to spit on the waters. About twenty feet from the latrine was a tiny blue wooden hut where she raised her two boys, Jeremy and Anthony.

Her house was quite isolated from the rest of the village, the nearest cluster of houses was some hundred feet away, and it gave her peace, though they had to pay the price of treading thru those uneven, rocky, barnacled grounds before getting into and after leaving the house. There used to stand a hut made of crumbling bamboo and nipa leaves at the very same spot, they actually lived in that hut for a year when they moved to the village many years before, but it was too wobbly a house, it appeared to want to fly away even long before a typhoon made landfall. When they were not home one day, a mild gale actually blew it away, and Necessity, ever defiant of all manners of adversity, managed to buy some materials to build their snug and petite house - plywood for the walls, bamboo for the floors and zinc plates for the roof.

In school she had learned about Burano in Italy, how fishermen painted their houses with bright pastel colors so it would be easier for them to find the village on their way back home from the seas on foggy mornings. So she painted the entire house bright blue, except for the roof, which she painted mustard. It was a fine little place for a struggling, single mother who was trying to keep her chin afloat on the surface of poverty line, it shone and stood among the houses in the village. It had three rooms - one for her, one for the boys, and one where they ate and received people. The kitchen was virtually outside of the house, with only a little roofing and no walls, it had a makeshift stove made out of an old automobile hood, and they used firewood to cook. The house was most pretty in late May when it was surrounded by white daffodils with hues of pale purple that bloomed when the rains came after a long dry spell, they looked like balls of pastels with youthful energy eagerly protruding out of a bed of nonchalant senile rocks.

At dusk, Necessity would sit by the bamboo bench in front of her house, she would gaze at the golden sparkles which the weak sun concocted in connivance with the sleepy sea. She wondered if the sea on any spot on earth could be any lovelier than it was at Burog Bay at dusk. She was aware that she was far away from the New York Harbor where her grandfather Jose Cañosi Baydadong wanted her to be, and she thought about it everyday, every time she brooded over the sea, but it did not seem to bother her much.

She and the boys fondly called their house The Blue Cottage.The fishermen, who indeed found the bright blue house useful when visibility was poor, referred to it as The American House. The villagers called her The American Girl, and for any outsider, the reason was not so clear - she looked like the rest of the villagers, she dressed just as shabbily, she had all ways of a fisherman's wife, or widow for that matter, and she had never been to America. However, she spoke neat English when she had to, and that happened about once every three years when some tourists would pass by the area by chance and ask for directions.

Townsfolk, most of them, also called her The American Girl, and it was in every manner derogatory and disdainful. The dream of the poor pseudo-English speaking farmhand Jose Cañosi Baydadong that his granddaughter, who bore a name which barely half the town could pronounce, would be served like a queen by Americans on top of The Empire State Building was something townsfolk loved to hate and talk about. For some, or many, it was a relief to see Necessity in her situation, which was no better than theirs, it was like being reassured that not dreaming big did not bring much harm at all.

When she was done with her privy visit, Necessity saw Anthony sitting by the crumbling old bamboo bench outside The Blue Cottage. It was deep in the afternoon. His head was bowed low, his eyes were on the ground and he was purposelessly kicking a few loose pebbles. She could sense that he was into some kind of distress, so she sat beside him and stroked his hair gently.

You'll find new friends, I'm sure about that, said Necessity, then she kissed his forehead lightly.

Creases became visible instead on his forehead, he asked, Will my new teacher be as nice?

She replied, I cannot guarantee a lot of things, but if you play nice and try to be diligent with your schoolwork, I'm quite sure she'll play nice too.

There was a short stretch of silence, then Anthony made a deep sigh and said, But I'm in love with Carla! Then he blurted out a faint, Whew, like he could not believe he just said it to his mother. Then he turned red like a shrimp that just got exposed to high heat.

Necessity broke into laughter, tried to say something but could not let out a syllable of intelligible sound. Finally, she was able to say, Are you sure about that? You're barely ten years old!

Anthony tried to show her the best he could how unamused he was by the way she laughed, he gave her that stare, like telling her he meant business. He said, I've been in love with her since I was eight!

Tears were already spewing out of Necessity's eyes, out of sheer amusement, then she stopped abruptly, then cleared her throat, and said, Alright, I believe you, you're in love. Is she in love with you too?

I think so, he said.

She bent and turned to look him in the eyes, and asked, How do you know?

He replied, My friends said so! Her face turned red when I tried to talk to her, my friends said when a girl's face turns red when talking to you it means she is in love with you!

Necessity tried to hold back laughter the best she could, then said, Carla, hmm, was she not the girl we talked about during last year's PTA, the one who had allergy to acacia pollen?

He asked, What's allergy?

She replied, It's when some substances like food and flowers and animal hairs make you feel itchy and turn your skin red, without falling in love!

He said, Oh that! I know that, but Jeremy said it's energy!

Oh don't you mind what your brother says, she said. Remember his English teacher summoned me twice last year?

Anthony could only shake his head, he then asked, So what's with the acacia?

She replied, Well, her parents said the acacia pollen makes her turn red and makes her feel itchy, so you can't tell when she is in or out of love...

He raised his voice a bit in protest, saying, But Mama, there is not an acacia tree anywhere near Santa Helena!

Oh well, there's a blooming kalachuchi tree near the school's rectory, I saw one!

He protested further, That's no acacia!

Alright, alright, she said. But it has pollen though!

Anthony was still crustacean-red on the face, he blew cold air to his forehead, determined not to end the conversation appearing defeated. He said, If you want proof weightier than her getting red on the face, you ought to know that Leo and Chaz sneaked into her bag and managed to read her diary! There you go, they read it, there is not an entry in her diary where my name isn't written! And remember last year on my birthday she gave me a whole bunch of Butterfinger and Mars bars?

Necessity paused, turned a little serious and pensive, and it made Anthony wonder. He was the best person when it came to reading the message on his mother's face, he could tell she turned sad, quite all of a sudden.

He asked, Are you alright?

She was looking straight to the sea's horizon, she then spoke in a low tone that sounded like she was embarrassed, she said, Okay, she's in love with you, I give in, but look, her father owns that store which delivers television to almost every household in Iloilo City, right?

Anthony said, That's right, everybody knows that!

She said, You know it, good! Now, have we owned a TV set, ever?

He thought hard for a moment and said, We had that black and white TV when I was about five or so, I remember that!

She scoffed and said, Your father stole that one from a family in Ajuy, it was never ours, he dropped it many times as he tried to bring it here so it worked for just over a week!

Anthony now realized what his mother was driving at, but tried not to sound defeated. He said, Alright Mama. That means, without owning any TV, I made Carla fall in love with me?

She looked at him, stroked his hair again and said, Apparently you did! But no matter how round this world may appear, it has lines and margins, making life feel rather like square. There are lines that are better left uncrossed!

By this time a weight of sadness had clearly fallen on Necessity's face, and anyone, not just Anthony would have been able to read it. She felt silly about herself, on how a seemingly petty chat with a boy who was quite far away from pre-puberty but was already in-love could make her feel like a big parcel containing heavy, callous reality was being delivered right in front of her.

Anthony was silent for a while, he kept on kicking some loose pebbles, then said, I don't think I'll ever forget Carla!

She replied, Oh yes you will, you will find another girl in town just as pretty, someone within your reach!

Her words hurt him, she could tell, and she regretted it instantly, but did not know how to take it back. There was a long stretch of silence, both had their gazes fixed on the rocks where dozens of gulls perched. It was a sweltering, humid afternoon, it made the birds too languid to fly. Necessity was aware that her words were harsh, but she tried to justify it, she thought somehow she needed to make her son aware of the commonly understood gaps in society, she thought he'd be hurt further in the future if he did not have a grasp of it that early.

She broke silence and spoke first, she said, I think the boys in town will be nicer to you, no one will call you Arupi anymore, you ought to miss your name Anthony by now!

Anthony got amused, unexpectedly. In reply he gave her a playful look with a funny pout of his lips and hit her lightly on her right flank with his elbow.

The year before that, shortly after the start of their third grade, a boy in school named Michael Tiso had a birthday party at Jimboy's, it was then one of the newest establishments in the city, it started as a bakeshop but quickly turned into a popular fast-food chain. Michael Tiso's parents were both well-known physicians, and he was an only child. The party was grand and flashy, everyone in class was invited. A hyperactive clown named Djongo hosted and he made the kids extremely restless and hyperactive themselves. Gifts were opened one by one when the party was about to end, Djongo the clown announced loudly on the microphone from whom each gift was, he opened it himself in front of Michael Tiso and announced what was in it.

Djongo picked the first gift and announced, The first one I've picked is from George Tengco, let's see, whizzy, let's see what's in it…it's, it's, a He-Man Doll! Whoowow, lucky you Mike, I'd need at least ten clown gigs to be able to afford this one!

He went on, The next gift is from Grace Assunta! It's, a Zoid T-Rex! This one is from Rene Monsod, and it's a GI Joe doll! The next one is Johan Camino and it's, oh my, a Voltron Lions set!

Some gifts were redundant, it was the era of Thundercats, Voltron Lions, He-Man and GI Joe, the birthday boy got several duplicates. Djongo then caught sight of one of the largest gifts, he himself got curious, he picked it and realized it was heavy, quite soft but compact. It was packed in brown paper, he made a few sniffs, paused, and began to laugh.

He then announced, And now, boys and girls of all ages, that includes the grandmas and the grandpas, hear ye, Djongo the herald clown hereby announces, the next mystery gift is from… Anthony Ilaya of the Kingdom of Burog! It's, it's… under this magical brown paper, it's… it's wrapped in banana leaves! Already the entire room was shaking from roars of laughter among the kids.

Djongo continued, And oh my God, Michael it's arrrrupi! Sticky, sticky as can be! More laughter followed, and Djongo went on, I'd like to hand this one to Mike, but help! Help! It's so sticky I can't get it off my hands!

Anthony was there at one corner, he felt like his soul had been slain. Parents and other kids who did not belong to the class looked around in curiosity to find out which among the guests was Anthony Ilaya. It was not so difficult to spot him, he was the child who appeared to be the least happy, he was pale out of extreme embarrassment, he was wearing khaki shorts, which was the school uniform, and an old white t-shirt with a Batman print on it, it was handed down to him by his brother Jeremy who was three years his senior. Soon, most of the kids were jeering at him.

Djongo had to tell them, Stop it! Stop it, kids! Don't take it too hard, Arupi, I mean Anthony! What matters most is that the gift came from the heart! There was brief silence among the kids, not much out of guilt but of anticipation, as no one knew the clown to be serious about anything. He had been pounding nasty humor for more than a couple of hours already, and quite expectedly, he went on saying, From the heart, boys and girls, from the heart of the coconut and cassava, put some sugar and pound it, and voila! It's like a sticky caky banana! But don't worry, Arupi, I mean, Anthony my boy, I can turn this arupi into a GI Joe, the final magic trick of the day! There was an audible Wow from his young audience. Then he went on saying, That is, if I can get it off my hand, sorry I don't have any spell for that! A mix of laughter and boos followed.

By that time, some of the parents' initial laughter had turned to concern, none of the adults were laughing, and Michael Tiso's father had to go up the stage to tell the clown to take it easy. Djongo went on with the next gift without apologizing. Anthony was numbed by this time. He recalled what he'd seen at the pet shop that summer, as they fed a little guppy to a giant red pacu in a large aquarium tank. It was a violent chase, the guppy darted across the tank like lightning, the pacu moved sluggishly and it looked like it would never get its dinner, but after some time, the guppy seemed to give up, it appeared to play dead, like intentionally making its body stiff, making it float upwards, perhaps so it would elude pain from certain death. Then with much less effort, the giant red pacu snapped the little guppy, the whole of it into its mouth. Anthony felt like that guppy, putting no contest to all the jeers, he opted not to move so as to elude the pain, he had to stay there until he was fetched, and it was like one by one the kids took turns in eating him up, piece by piece.

Except for a few girls who always played the role of champions of the oppressed, everyone in class called Anthony Arupi for the rest of the year. Teachers gave stern orders prohibiting it, but they could not be around all the time, there was always a corner somewhere in the school campus where he got called his new name. That was a party he wished he could forget, but it was not quite possible when almost everyone everyday called him Arupi.

It was the first time he got invited to a birthday party in the city, and from a well-off kid at that. In his village it was quite a common practice to give native goods wrapped in banana leaves as gifts for all kinds of events, including funerals. Necessity had not been to the city much in the past two decades, she must have been clueless about how a party there was like, or maybe she was not sensitive enough about the probable consequences of her son walking in to rich kid's birthday party bearing a gift that was more proper of a funeral, or maybe it was all she could afford. Whatever it was, Anthony thought it was his mother's big foul-up, he was mad at her, but having seen what his mother had been through for so long, he thought it was best to be silent about it and bury the grudge.

Necessity only learned about those taunts much later when one Friday afternoon she was at school to fetch her boys for the weekend. A female classmate of Anthony's told her in a very innocent, well-meaning manner, He's on his way ma'am, Arupi is coming down in a couple of minutes!

Mother and son went on talking there by the bamboo bench. Anthony said, If I got to continue at Santa Helena, they would have forgotten it when the school starts, some had begun calling me Anthony again before school closed for the summer.

Necessity could sense pain in his voice, she said, Look, I'm sorry for bringing it up, but here at the public central school everybody knows who you are, you are the grandson of Ma'am Alicia Berano, they will look up to you!

Anthony replied, Not when they learn I'm the son of Onyok Ilaya...

Necessity immediately answered, Then be like Alicia Berano with your studies and demeanor, not like Onyok Ilaya!

The afternoon had grown deeper, at the horizon of the calm Burog Bay, blue had turned to orange from their vantage point. Then Necessity said, It's dinnertime in a bit, will you help me?

Anthony replied, Of course Mama, dinnertime, you mean..?

Necessity gave a helpless sigh and said, I know it's a Saturday but no corned beef today, people were not too hungry at the bus, I only got to sell a few peanuts. But it's going to be grilled tuloy.

That's alright with me, said Anthony. It was a half-lie. He was really disappointed inside, he had been looking forward to have corned beef for the weekend, instead they were having that usual fish, it tasted good, the local sardine, but it was full of bones, too many that some were even sticking out through the belly. To him, tuloy looked like a fish that had been churned inside a bigger fish's belly and then spewed out to be fed to the poor like him.

Mother and son rose and headed towards The Blue Cottage which was just a mere ten feet away from the bench, but they had to watch out for a few porous rocks that stuck out of the already uneven ground, as it could give one a bad sprain. Necessity limped a bit, she had walked too long during the day, the town was some three miles away, she walked all the way home, she thought she could spare that money by not taking the tricycle cab.

It was early in June 1988, she was just 41, but she looked a lot older, like she'd had two lifetimes of misery. Some fishermen joked that they could see strokes of grey hair on her head a couple of nautical miles away on a clear day. She'd put on some weight, some people could not recognize the petite Necessity they knew in the 60's, and those endless waves of worries had authored deep creases of wrinkles on her forehead.

She lost her bookkeeping job at a grocer's at the central market earlier that year. The owner, a man pushing 65 years of age, caught sight of a girl, a newcomer in town who had just turned 18 and who was always wearing too short a pair of shorts, at least in the eyes of the devout Catholic elders of Burog. They said she dressed like the town was to be flooded by tropical rains everyday to the height of the average human hips, as folks usually rolled up their trousers to a level proportionate to the depth of the flood. She frequented the grocer's place, and after a couple of weeks she got Necessity's job. It was not known if she had gone to any bookkeeping course, or if she could count to ten at all, but she was offered the job, without her asking for it.

That put Necessity into deeper financial trouble. Even while having that bookkeeping job, she needed to earn a little more to make ends meet. She'd meet fishermen coming ashore at around 5 a.m., on a good day she'd have two baskets of fish to sell to stall vendors at the market before reporting to work at 8 a.m. At noon from 12 to 2 p.m. she had lunch and siesta break, she'd eat a piece of bread and rush to the bus station, hopped inside busses that made short stops and peddled all kinds of goods to passengers - peanuts, bottled sodas, biscuits, native goods like arupi and even hardboiled eggs. She had to compete with other peddlers, and business meant a maximum of five minutes per bus, and about only one or two busses passed by every hour. Peddlers like her hopped inside the bus and screamed like mad, louder and more chaotic than Wall Street brokers would, almost begging the passengers to buy anything. Without her bookkeeping job she could not afford to send her sons to Santa Helena Catholic Academy in the city anymore, even if they got some help from her brother Percivale and occasionally, from her mother Alicia who was then a retired teacher.

Percivale had a modest house in the city, and for years he had housed the boys in a little room adjacent to his garage, so school was just a mere four blocks away, and he also shouldered their pocket money. Necessity paid him in kind, which meant in the form of fish, hens, eggs, fruits, arupi and such. Now even with Percivale promising to help with about a quarter of their tuition, the resources could not suffice, so to transfer to the public schools in Burog was the lone option. Anthony was to continue in the 4th grade and Jeremy was to begin high school in the school year of 1988-1989.

They were preparing dinner in a run-down open kitchen by the west side of the cottage, there was an old clay stove which was as black as death, and a large tin plate cut out from an old container, it was just as black with soot, and that served as the griller, all these were placed snugly in an old automobile hood. Anthony watched the rice cook while Necessity grilled the poor tuloy, all six of them. Mother and son were silent, all that could be heard were the crisp crackling sound of ipil-ipil firewood and the occasional sizzling sound each time the salty juice from the tuloy dripped and came into contact with the fire.

Then Anthony suddenly spoke, Carla is having her summer holiday right now in Hong Kong!

Is that so? Necessity said, wishing she did not have to hear that.

Yes, said Anthony. She said she'd send me a postcard!

It took some time for Necessity to respond, Anthony wondered if she was interested or was listening at all, she kept

33

on flipping the fishes which were almost falling apart. She finally said, Well, that's nice, I hope it can find its way to our little village!

It never felt good for her to talk about such things, she felt like the tuloy had better fate. Her son was infatuated with someone who was having a holiday in Hong Kong while she had to borrow money for a dinner that did not impress her boys, right there at the heart of Sitio Putak.

3

$\mathcal{J}$ eremy was sitting by the old bamboo dining table, on an even older chair, also made of bamboo, looking exasperated and miserable, his right elbow was on the table and he rested his right cheek on his knuckles. He was a lean boy, but already too tall for someone in early puberty. His thick, wavy hair had tons of gel on it, it was like a towering inverted cone, and it made him look even taller. He hadn't washed his hair for four days, to save on the gel. The night had fallen two hours earlier, but he still had his shades on. His voice had not begun breaking yet, but it seemed to naturally step up an octave higher when he was upset or stressing a point in an argument. There was a mound of rice on his plate and a piece of grilled tuloy, but he was not eating, he was pulling tiny bones from the fish and tossed them to the air with his left pincers. He said sarcastically and thus in high pitch, Have you seen the final part of Bilong Buwaya?

Anthony nodded but did not say anything as it was understood, they watched the film together a month earlier at the butcher's stall where there was a television. The film

Bilong Buwaya was aired on a local channel, it was about a humongous crocodile named Bilong which escaped the farms and terrorized an entire town. It grossed well in spite of the low budget, the crocodile was obviously made of thick textile and had about seven people in it, and it was grossly unedited, as there were a couple of scenes wherein one person inside the crocodile wasn't able to coordinate with the group movement well, there was a visible bulge near the crocodile's left hind leg like it had swallowed a human being with gigantic buttocks. The film was severely chopped into pieces by commercial breaks so it took two weekends for the whole movie to be played. Jeremy went on saying, I've always wondered how that crocodile would look like, I mean his entire body after the landmine which he gobbled up exploded inside his belly...

They never got to see what happened to the crocodile in the film. After that scene of the mine exploding in Bilong's gut followed an endless stream of commercials, it was late and the butcher had to close his shop. Jeremy continued saying, Fishermen must have been inspired by Bilong Buwaya, they too must have missed the very last part and wanted to see for themselves, they must have done the same thing to this little tuloy, made it swallow tiny explosives and then blew it up!

Necessity said, Never mind how it got from the ocean to your plate, just eat it, it's getting cold!

Jeremy replied in an even higher pitch, I don't really mind how this creature got to my plate, what pisses me is why it got to my plate when I was expecting a piece of a cow from Algeria in its place!

Anthony quickly butted in saying, It's Argentina, if you were expecting corned beef!

Jeremy lowered his shades and gave his brother a threatening look, he said, You want a piece of landmine in your mouth, puny peanut head?

Necessity said calmly, Quiet boys! It's all we have for tonight, it's not a choice between tuloy or corned beef, it's a choice between tuloy or nothing at all!

I think I'd pick nothing at all, any day! Jeremy replied.

Necessity was breathing faster, clearly she was trying to control an outburst. She said, Well, had you helped at the bus terminal earlier today, who knows what might be on your plate right now!

Jeremy replied, Still tuloy, I guess! You fouled-up with your peanut peddling today, don't try to lay your failures on my shoulders!

Necessity tried to bite her lower lip, like a last recourse to avoid losing control, she trembled as she said, You have become a terrible man, Jeremy!

He rose from his seat and almost screamed as he replied, No Mama, I'm just someone who's fed up with this life! You want me to go out there peddling peanuts and eggs to people who might recognize me? It's so demeaning! I don't deserve this life, this misery, this kind of food! I graduated from elementary at Santa Helena Catholic Academy!

Barely, said Anthony.

Jeremy turned to his little brother and said, Watch your mouth you measly little putchong, or I'll grind your foul-smelling little lungs! Jeremy loved to use that derogatory word putchong, it meant uncircumcised. Even currently, boys in the country, as well as their parents, believe that retaining one's foreskin when one is old enough is the same as being a castrate, and that circumcision is the gateway to manhood. Jeremy always tried to appear like he could not recall that he and Anthony were circumcised together at the health center two summers earlier. During the procedure, Anthony cried and whined while Jeremy wailed and cursed, he screamed at the physician and swore he'd get back on him and pluck out his testicles. It did not go well for Jeremy, he believed the pain would get better if he took a dip in the cool stream and so he did, unaware that there was a herd of carabaos wading on the waters upstream. His wound got severely infected so he had to wear a skirt for a month, while Anthony, like most of the boys, had to do it for only about three days. It was how Jeremy theorized that Anthony had not been circumcised properly, he based his theory on the number of skirt days. He called his brother putchong whenever they disagreed on the tiniest issue.

Anthony was way skinnier and smaller than his brother, but he was undaunted. He fought back saying, Those shades, you could have bought an entire ranch of corned beef with that! How much did it cost you?

Jeremy replied, Absolutely none of your business! Get circumcised first!

Anthony answered back, You don't need to buy expensive shades to conceal a poorly healed circumcision wound! Or did you buy them?

Jeremy replied, Of course I did, putchong!

Anthony said, It says Ray-Ban, must have cost you a fortune, unless they're fake!

Jeremy replied, They're not fake, not like your fake circumcision! One more word and you will end up looking like grilled tuloy!

Necessity interrupted, shouting, Stop it boys or there will be no corned beef for the rest of the year!

Anthony was unfazed, he thought he'd rather eat tuloy everyday for the rest of the year than not saying what he thought he needed to say, so he went on saying, So they're not fake? Then they must cost like hundreds of dozens of canned corned beef, am I right?

Where did you get those shades, Jeremy? Necessity asked.

From where they came from, replied Jeremy as he turned his back on his mother.

Anthony was not finished, he went on taunting his brother, he said, Aren't they supposed to protect your eyes from sunlight? You're about ten hours too early!

Jeremy replied, You uncircumcised lot know nothing! This is the era of Randy, all the rules have changed! The sun never decides over Randy!

He was referring to Randy Santiago, a good-natured TV talkshow celebrity and singer who was then the latest sensation in the country, well-loved by both young and old. He had never been seen in public without sunglasses, both on and off-screen. Teens loved him the most, so a lot of them, both boys and girls but mostly boys, wore sunglasses all the time, preferably Ray-Ban which almost no parent from the lower middle class down could afford, in order to look a little bit like him, and they did so with or without sunlight, both indoors and outdoors. Teachers at Santa Helena had a hard time having them take off their sunglasses during class, and at a certain point, some teachers just gave up.

There was a problem in the city too, about five peso bills featuring the image of the Philippine Revolution hero Emilio Aguinaldo. Youngsters, using black ink, drew shades over the eyes of the hero on the bill and altered his hairdo so he'd resemble Randy Santiago. It alarmed the city government, they issued an ordinance to desist. No one was caught, no one listened, the kids just went on with it to a point that there came numerous outlawed Draw Randy on a Five competitions at schools and in the streets, and the jackpot prize was all of the five peso bill entries in the competition. A lot of teenagers, among them Jeremy, hoarded those vandalized five-peso bills, which, to their dismay later on, were declared counterfeit by the central bank.

Jeremy drew a five peso bill out of his pocket and waved it in front of Anthony. Clearly the image on the bill was turned into Randy, as untampered bills still with pristine Emilio Aguinaldo were becoming increasingly rare. He said to his little brother, Putchongs like you will never be like Randy, you look emaciated, no shades will ever look good on you, you look a lot like Isyong Buto!

Isyong Buto was a popular comedian who was extremely skinny, thus the name Buto, meaning bones. Anthony fumed and replied, Neither will you be like Randy! People like Randy's shades because he's nice and they're interested in how he looks like and he can sing! While you, you're not nice, you're obnoxious! Everyone knows how your eyes are without those shades! Your eyes stare blank all day, and when you sing, if ever you sing I pray to God to take away the hearing of those near you! It would be the ultimate Divine Providence!

Jeremy rushed in rage towards the barely on-guard Anthony who was standing behind a couch, again made of bamboo, in the tiny living room. In one swift swoop he managed to grab his younger brother by the jaw with his right hand, lifted him with almost fully stretched arm and pinned him to the wall. He yelled, I'll kill you, you useless little rat!

Let him go! Necessity yelled.

Jeremy replied, No, not yet, he's still breathing!

Necessity rushed towards her boys, she grabbed Jeremy by the right elbow and squeezed it, he grimaced then screamed in pain and lost his grip, thereby releasing Anthony who fell almost totally limp to the floor, coughing and gasping for air. Necessity was trembling in rage when she said, You hurt your brother again and I'll make sure the police will take care of you, I'll have you placed in a correctional facility where you'll straighten out your ugly soul!

Jeremy replied, Good! Maybe there's food there!

Necessity said, Yes, I heard, lugaw, salt and kamote leaves everyday! That should fit you!

Jeremy said, Or maybe all those meat and the good things, like when Papa was around!

The reply that came from Necessity was a sound slap on Jeremy's face with the back of her right hand. Her arms had grown broad and compact from years of carrying big baskets of fish from the shores into town, so the slap was a solid one, causing Jeremy to spin almost a full turn, he lost his balance and every opinion he had. He sat there on the floor trying to regain orientation, then his mother grabbed him by the collar of his shirt, looked at him straight in the eyes, her eyes went extremely red, it caused him to turn pale. She then said, Remember this, for any good thing you ate which came from your father, another human being suffered, all the things he provided us when he was alive were neither his nor ours, remember that! She released him and turned away, she walked out to get some fresh air while sobbing.

Jeremy in turn sneered, shrugged his shoulders, and went straight to his room. The room did not have a door, just a drape made from an old housedress to cover the entrance, that meant he couldn't make a classic slamming of the door after a mother and son squabble, so he just kicked the foot of his bed hard, and the bed was, like nearly all of the furniture in the house, made of bamboo so it was hard, it gave him an extreme pain on the right foot making him limp for days. Anthony recovered but opted to stay low on the floor.

A little less than ten minutes later, Jeremy appeared from his room, he looked like he was dressed up for some big event. He looked quite fine except for the large redness and swelling on his right face which resembled the map of Australia and of course, the conspicuous limping. The sunglasses were intact, unscathed from that ferocious maternal slap. They were obviously knock-off Ray Ban, he did not even buy them but snatched them from a peddler in the city. Such peddlers usually covered their bodies with cardboards full of tiny hooks on which the goods they sold hung. The cardboards made them practically immobile, or at least too slow to run after petty thieves who stole from them. Jeremy just passed by and took the sunglasses of his choice and walked away, the peddler was unsuspecting because he was quite too young and rather too fine-looking to be a thief.

Everything he had on that night was something his mother never could afford. He had on a green Lacoste sport shirt, it was not stolen, but it was not his either. He borrowed it from one of his classmates a few months earlier, he promised to return it but never intended to and never did. He also had on a straight-cut acid washed jeans which he got as a birthday gift from Percivale. He had threatened his uncle for weeks that he'd run away from home if he did not get it. And the shoes, they were high-cut black Reebok trainers, very popular among his peers that time. He got the shoes from another classmate through blackmail. He saw his classmate cheating during the final exams, and threatened to report him if he did not get the shoes. The only things he rightfully owned that night was the bruise on his face and the limp.

That was his character. He barely graduated. He was to be expelled from school for vandalism a few months before graduation. He wrote on the wall of the girls' toilet using red ink - I'm watching you! Vandals in school usually did their best not to get caught, but in his case, for reasons peculiar to him, he signed his name right under the graffiti. The only thing that earned him pardon was the pitiful look in his mother's eyes which generated some compassion among the Jesuits who ran the school.

Necessity was inside the house, she just started to pick up the dishes, she asked, Where are you going?

Jeremy replied, Some place where there's something edible! He then stormed out of the house, this time he had a wooden door to slam behind him, and he did so, it made The Blue Cottage swing to opposite poles, Anthony held on to the walls tight like everything was about to fall to the sea. Jeremy wasn't going anywhere grand or far, he just wanted to dress up like that each time he was out of the house. This time he was headed to the next village up north, Sitio Paka, and it was not at all far.

Sitio Putak and Sitio Paka were actually just separated by a cove which used to be full of mangroves but then all the mangroves were gone, so you could have a view of one village by standing at the other, and they were almost identical - shacks made of bamboo and nipa and all kinds of solid scrap both imaginable and unimaginable perched on the rocks that rose from the shallow shores.

The only difference between the two villages was their subculture. The men of Sitio Putak were mostly fishermen, with the exception of a few who were unskilled laborers in the main town, and women were homemakers and worked as small fish brokers at dawn until early morning, much like Necessity. In daytime, most adults who were not making the home were somewhere else scratching the earth for dough.

The people of Sitio Paka on the other hand, were like members of a clan, only a few worked and the rest intended to move like snails so that grace could catch up with them, or so they thought. Of the thirty or so households, only two were into fishing, some took odd labor jobs in town whenever they felt like it, and whatever they earned seemed to go around in the village. One household with the family name Boyog, had a son who got a job as a seaman overseas, and while he spent most of his days, months and years tormenting himself in that ship's engine room which was just a little cooler than hell, his mother Mrs. Boyog was making a living out of the money he sent by lending it to people in the village with 20% compounded interest, which meant almost no one could pay her back.

The gulls all flocked to Sitio Putak and very rarely to Sitio Paka, they said it was because there were still a couple of mangroves left at the former, so there were still a few small preys around, but some postulated, quite plausibly, that it was because of the incessant yelling between Mrs. Boyog and her debtors which went on everyday for many years. Even the loud gulls seemed to want peace from time to time. The poor son who mortified in uncharted seas came home about twice a year, greeted by the same news - that all of the money was gone.

There were always people in daytime at Sitio Paka, there was a steady group of mahjong and poker players and they could play all day and almost all night. Children as small as toddlers played by the rocks and tide pools, and when the pangs of hunger made them scream, the adults would be awakened from the apparent hypnosis of long hours of gambling, and then they'd realize it was time for lunch or dinner, and that they had to play some more to win money to buy their meals. When the children stopped screaming the gamblers felt some form of relief, believing that the children had either forgotten about hunger or had found some creatures to gnaw in the tide pools.

Another thing that distinguished Sitio Putak from Sitio Paka were the privies. There was only one privy in Sitio Paka, for thirty households, and it was barely used, everyone seemed to believe that the edges of the great Pacific Ocean not far from their doorsteps was one gargantuan latrine that steadily flushed.

Jeremy was headed towards Sitio Paka on that night of the big slap. He felt like he belonged more to Sitio Paka than Sitio Putak, which was precisely the case. He liked the village, with Mrs. Boyog pumping in money and everyone taking turns in winning and losing in mahjong and poker, it seemed like a financially stable little society with the world's largest latrine. But there actually was money pumping from somewhere else, an even darker source than that from an insensitive mother of a poor seaman.

Jeremy was on his way to that source, the shack of Dodong Botas, a teenage petty gang leader about five years his senior. Dodong Botas was feared by all youngsters in five villages, but not by everyone else, as his mother and five sisters took turns in hitting his head with a saucepan almost everyday. He was pure trouble and had a following of about twelve other boys from neighboring villages. Jeremy was the youngest and the newest in the gang. They engaged in hash trade and had pot sessions themselves about three times a week.

A novice like Jeremy was not allowed to have a sniff of pot until he had successfully run seven hash transactions for the group. If he made repeated fiascos in the transactions, the penalty, or at least the threat was, his corpse would be found floating on the world's largest latrine. He was to run his first test that night.

4

By the summer of 1967, Necessity was poised to be the top graduate of the commerce class of Santa Isabel College in Manila the following year. She had hoped to be an accountant, and the prospect of good paying jobs was very good. Her mother Alicia had already been pushing her to write to a few firms in New York, as one accountant in Iloilo City managed to land on a big employment in New Jersey three years earlier just by persistently writing novella-like letters to countless of companies. He was like a celebrity, he took the ferry to Manila on his way to The States and was sent off at the pier in Mulley Loney by the mouth of the Iloilo River by a throng of media men.

President Johnson signed The Immigration and Nationality Act just two years earlier, and the surge of Asian immigrant workers began, that cocky accountant was the first in the city to get direct hiring so he was like a mini-celebrity. Alicia thought her daughter was far smarter and could write better letters. One of those letters written by the local mini-celebrity accountant was published in the papers for everyone to read, Alicia thought it was wordy and murderously boring, she believed he was offered the job by the firm so that the inflow of such a dragging piece of literature would stop once and for all, after all, they were looking for applicants with a prowess in numbers, not words. But Necessity thought that the idea was still too far-fetched, graduation was a year away and after that she still had to hurdle the board exams. After graduating valedictorian in high school in Burog, she earned a full college scholarship at Santa Isabel College through the recommendations of Father Tolentino, the parish priest with many mystical connections in the country.

Alicia Berano held a rather prestigious small town post as an elementary school teacher, but that did not come with any good financial standing, the family lived modestly, sometimes sub-modestly, like many households they had to subsist on low grade corn instead of rice in the lean months of July and August. They could never have afforded sending Necessity to a private school in Iloilo City, let alone to a prestigious exclusive girls' college in Manila. But she got the scholarship, her board and lodging were all paid for, she was the best in class, the future seemed to be under her command and it seemed like it would follow whatever she wished.

Necessity was still mourning her father Armando Berano who died in the summer of 1965. He had remained a fisherman all his life and never spoke an English word except for Help and Necessity, the latter only on official occasions, for she was called more often by her nickname Neseng. She made him extremely proud. In the third grade she rehearsed her recitation of William Ernest Henley's Invictus at home during dinner and it moved him enormously, it was not clear if he understood anything but he cried out of joy and pride everyday for weeks. When asked by fellow fishermen what the matter was, that was, why he was crying, he said he was so awed by his daughter reciting something in English totally from memory, accompanied by all those hand expressions and emotions like she was fighting someone or something.

Like Jose Cañosi Baydadong, Armando Berano asked especially for Necessity to come to his side at the hour of his death. It was early in April, summer started in March and ended in June in the country, Necessity arrived home from

Manila just a week before his death. He had liver cancer, he was jaundiced and emaciated, the sight devastated his daughter, she broke down upon seeing him. When the hour had come he summoned his children, he and Necessity had a long, sad and emotional talk, it tore her piece by piece, minute after minute. When he was a few minutes from expiring, he tried his very best to speak in English, he neither asked for help nor said Necessity's name, he was trying to say something else, but could not put a word on his lips. There was a brown cat in the room which found its way to the medicine cupboard which was left open, the cat started to burrow through a large bowl full of pills. Finally, with the last of his strength, Armando Berano pointed to the cupboard and said with a tone of pride and fulfillment and in pure English, The cat…

He then expired. Cat was his last word, he had spoken three English words all his life, four if one was to count The. Necessity may not have looked up to her father in academic matters, but she invoked his memory oftentimes when she was badly in need, groping in the dark for any thought of virtue, like courage, perseverance, simplicity and hope.

She had to go on now without her grandfather and her father. She was looking forward to graduating but did not talk much about her plans, though she always had that small picture of The Empire State Building tucked in her blue Jerusalem Bible. Her mother noticed how secretive she had become about her plans, it worried her a bit, she did not talk about moving to America at all, unlike her grandfather who talked about nothing else in his last years. Necessity had become known early in school in Burog as The American Girl, that dream of her grandfather Jose Cañosi Baydadong leaked through the entire town like mercury, just as he willed it so, and the girl spoke neat English. Resentment grew among common townsfolk, they felt like Necessity was a walking signboard that said that the life they were leading was not to be desired. People talked and made no effort in withholding a tone of contempt when calling her The American Girl.

In Manila however, only people in school knew her, and they did not really care where she came from or where she was headed to or where her grandfather dreamed her desk would be someday, there she was simply known as Smart-Nes. She liked it better in the big city, there was no such small-town thinking which made the town look much smaller than it was and petty things much bigger than they were, but somehow, coming home to Burog during the summers gave her some sense of fulfillment and direction, and she felt strange about it.

Immigration to the United States eased with The Immigration and Nationality Act swinging in full force, and there were a number of accountants getting hired. So in tune with her own father's dream for her daughter, Alicia Berano decided to write the next chapter of Necessity's life - she was to become an accountant, though Necessity herself initially wanted to major in English Literature. Hers was not an unusual case, that of parents authoring their children's future, at least among those families who cared about the future. The nuns who ran the school were confident that Necessity would graduate cum laude, the commerce department hadn't had one since 1964, so she was their little pearl.

But the summer of 1967 changed lot of things. March came and it got too hot, children placed eggs on concrete sidewalks at high noon to find out if they'd really fry as the local radio stations claimed they would. They didn't. Then their mothers would chase them with broomsticks for wasting such precious household commodity, they'd run away and do it again the next day. By April the grass had turned brown, it had not rained for six weeks, the earth was scorched, whenever an automobile passed by rough country roads there'd follow a big cloud of dust which wouldn't seem to clear until the next automobile passed by about an hour later, then the dust would settle on trees, window panes, on hairs and faces of people. It made the countryside look dreary. Burog sits at the mid-bottom coast of Panay Island which sits in the belly of the Philippine Archipelago, summers could be extremely hot and humid like that of 1967, when everyone wished the summer would end barely two weeks after it started. People called that summer Sumpa, meaning, The Curse, or loosely, The Scourge.

Another scourge was yet to come to town that summer. They called the scourge Hangin, which meant The Wind. The wind would have been welcome at the height of the unforgiving heat, but it was not a wind that literally blew, it was a person. It is a kind of half-belief and half-joke in the country that when a boisterous braggart is nearby it stirs the peace and equilibrium, causing the wind to blow, sometimes to a full-blown storm.

In mid-April, a rather new purple Volkswagen Beetle came to town, along with it some big cloud of dust, stirring the peace. By the time it stopped by the town plaza it looked cream-white, because of all the dust it had gathered. It looked like the car was there in town to stay, putting the total number of privately owned cars in Burog to six.

The owner was The Scourge himself, his name was Nicanor Ilaya Jr., also known as Onyok, a local nickname of everyone who has a junior attached to his name. He stepped out of his car and walked around the plaza in strides that seemed to convey a message that he could buy anything he set his eyes upon. He looked both impressive and intimidating - french cap, aviator sunglasses, a mustache that topped his upper lip like hedges, brown collared shirt with white longitudinal stripes, leather suspenders, chino, brown loafers, a golden watch and an unfiltered cigarette. People began calling him Hangin even before they heard him speak. Then he spoke and got the tag permanently. To have him around amidst all that heat and not literally causing the wind to stir was torment. Nobody liked him.

But had he been gentle and meek and wore the same shabby clothes as they did everyday the whole summer, they still would have disliked him to a certain degree, because of his name. Most surnames in town started with B, his started with an I, which meant he was from some place far, and for the townsfolk's self-preservation, he ought to be considered hostile until proven otherwise. No proof to the contrary ever surfaced. Upon establishing the pueblos, the Spanish Conquistadores started that practice of having family names start with the same letter as that of the town, for reasons unknown, maybe to make it easier to track down dissidents. It was convenient for townsfolk too, it made it easier for them to identify outsiders or tag scapegoats, and during some periods it even simplified witch hunts.

People in Burog knew that by his family name, Onyok came from the town of Igbaras, an inland town 30 miles south of Iloilo City. Burog was roughly the same distance from the city, but to the north. People from the north were suspicious and contemptuous of those from the south, in many matters, and vice versa, the thinking had been centuries old by the 60's. Those from the north thought that southerners did not know how to fish, especially those from the hinterlands, they thought inlanders were dumb because they did not eat fish, except for the dried and salted or spoilt ones. They believed fish was the only food that made the brain grow. Those from the south also believed that northerners did not know how to fish, and those from the southern inlands like Igbaras thought that coastal northerners had a memory capacity like that of a fish, they'd take the hook which they'd gotten off a few minutes earlier. Northerners made up stories that southerners used barbwires as curtains, and in retaliation, southerners claimed that northerners used barbwires instead of toilet paper.

Onyok Ilaya was facing a formidable barrier as regards settling and blending in with the people in Burog, but he didn't mind, he never planned to blend in. Townsfolk were nearly up in arms when they thought he'd bought the white bungalow with the green roof at the foot of the hill halfway between the town and the coast. He only rented it actually, it belonged to a Dutchman who had planned to settle quite near the sea, his wife was a native of a neighboring coastal town called Ajuy, and they built the bungalow to her name. But then people began pouring to their place from three towns to borrow money almost on a daily basis, and it was almost understood, or rather expected, that they were never to pay them back, and they never did, so by the time the construction was completed, the couple had changed their minds and moved back to Eindhoven. Anyway, townsfolk thought that Onyok had bought the bungalow, and it made them hate him more.

Alicia Berano's place was not as grand, it was a two-floor house made of mahogany wood cut evenly lengthwise and piled horizontally and very neatly, it had big windows and the panes were made of capiz shells. The floor was also made of wood and was raised a few feet from the ground, as it flooded in the area during the rainy season. There was a large terrace that faced the vast rice fields, as the house was on the edge of the town nearer the farmlands. The house stood between two old acacia trees which had been there for more than a century, they provided shade and made the place cooler than anywhere else in town. In the outskirts of the yard stood numerous mango trees, the grove belonged to Jose Cañosi Baydadong's landlord, the Berano family had no official title to the house or the yard. Everything inside the house was neat and homely, it was like any modest family in town would like to have as a home.

There were hens and roosters and ducks on the yard and they were like members of the family. They had two big native mongrels named after Philippine heroes, Lapu-Lapu and Lakandula, they were supposed to be brave, so they got the names, but both were too friendly to bark even at strangers, making them unreliable in matters of home security. Lapu-Lapu looked like a half-spaniel and half-Labrador, while Lakandula looked like a half-Labrador and half-goat. They were half-brothers, their fathers couldn't be traced. The place was peaceful and very silent, but at dusk the chorus of cicadas made it impossible for people to hear each other even when they were yelling.

Necessity was almost through with her chores with the dishes one evening, it was a moonless night, it was very humid and very dark outside, she went to the terrace for some fresh air, the orchestra of cicadas had just come to a halt and there was utter silence.

Then someone from nowhere struck the guitar so loudly it startled the hens roosting upon the branches of one of the acacia trees, causing one of them to actually fall to the ground. The guitar was poorly calibrated and the one playing seemed not to have the gift for music, the dogs Lapu-Lapu and Lakandula whined in agony, it was hard to recognize what was being played, it sounded like a bag of tin cans rolling down the hill, but soon Necessity realized that they were trying to play the Everly Brothers' All I have to Do Is Dream. Then came the sound of a tambourine, it also sounded like a clanging of tin cans. Then came the voice which sounded no better than the guitar, the tambourine nor the tin cans. Then someone started singing, to add lethal insult to almost lethal injury.

What was going on was a spin-off of the Spanish serenade, known locally as the harana, and by the 60's it was almost outdated in the cities but was still being practiced in the countryside. A supposed suitor was to take with him a band of musicians and he was to do the vocals himself and try to woo an unfortunate maiden.

That particular serenade already broke the rules, as it was supposed to start when the maiden was inside the house, in her room to be precise, and if she was interested in the suitor she'd open her window and listen to more songs, and if she was more unfortunate, to poems of courtship written by the suitor himself. The suitor in that particular evening was Onyok Ilaya, the man who almost never cared about the rules.

Necessity had had several serenades at home before, though not as many as an average maiden in town would have then, as she intimidated the bachelors, they thought they had to sing only English songs and write poetry in English, and most of them could barely get past two lines.

Necessity was not impressed by the singing, the lines sounded like they were being pronounced by that of a school pupil who could not get anywhere near a passing mark in second grade English speech class, and the lyrics were defiled, the verse was unrecognizable.

The serenaders then lit their kerosene lamp in the middle of the song, and thus became visible a band of three men. The tambourine man was big and stout, almost six feet tall, he had a crew-cut hair and only his earlobes were spared from tattoos. The guitarist was a man in his thirties, leaner than his guitar, and he bore a deep, straight scar on his face that ran from his chin to his left cheek bone, Necessity thought that someone must have struck him with an ax on the face some years ago when he wouldn't stop playing his guitar. Then there was Onyok Ilaya with his mustache that drew attention, this time he was wearing a black collared shirt and a pair of locally tailored blue jeans. And there stood Necessity, petite, very slim, dark and curious eyes, beautiful eyebrows, a lean face, thin lips and skin as smooth as unripe olive.

She was already outside when they started, so the brazenfaced Onyok Ilaya took it for a positive response, as though she went outside and was therefore interested. He said, Thank you my fair maiden, for showing interest to your humble suitor, and now I'd be glad to hear your reply!

By rule, the maiden was supposed to say something, mostly about what she thought of the song, and it did not need to be flattering. She said, Well, two things - first the ducks!

Onyok was puzzled, he didn't quite get it, he asked, The ducks my lady?

Necessity replied, Yes the ducks! If you startle the ducks at night they cannot lay eggs at dawn, that means we won't be having eggs for breakfast!

Onyok instantly said, Oh, Miss, don't you worry, I'll be back tomorrow morning with a basket full of fresh eggs!

Necessity said, I never said I wanted you to come back after this!

Onyok's lips twitched and fasciculated and he could only mutter words unintelligibly.

Necessity went on, she said, And second thing, I guess you've never serenaded in the city before!

Onyok said, That's correct my lady, in fact you are the first, how did you know that?

Necessity replied, I heard there's a gun smuggling and control problem in the big cities, if you'd sung like that in the city you would have been shot dead a long time ago!

The two musicians began giggling, trying to hold themselves back from exploding into real heavy laughter. Onyok gave them a stern look and they immediately turned solemn, it was clear that they were dead afraid of him. Necessity was not to blame for her reply, the rendition of the song was completely unjust to music and art, and the two back-up musicians scared her, they looked like escaped convicts, though it was not really the case, they were actually on parole. On top of that, Onyok Ilaya could only sing on G flat and nothing else.

Necessity turned around and she could see her mother and her brothers Arthur, Lancelot and Percivale and the helper named Taray peeking through the kitchen window, all had looks of disapproval. With a suitor like that, a lady as fine as Necessity, almost on top of the world, was expected to run inside the house, bar the door at least thrice, put out all the lights and scream for help as loudly as she could. But she didn't. It was Onyok Ilaya, and to her misfortune, she did not know much more. There were hints of fascination in her eyes. He had an apparently brand new Volkswagen Beetle, he must have purchased that bungalow and he had that mustache. That mustache, it was another scourge, because it drew the attention of girls at that time, but not all who wore it were good men, especially not this one.

Come inside, she said, practically inviting trouble. The band was offered a cup of ginger tea each. None of them had any good manners. Onyok Ilaya sat on the couch and placed his feet on top of the living room table with his shoes on like he had just purchased the entire house. Upon receiving their cups of ginger tea, the guitar and tambourine men went straight to the dining area and opened the cupboard to scrounge for some sugar, without asking their hosts. The two stooges almost killed each other over the last lump of sugar left. Necessity and Onyok Ilaya chatted for an hour, and it all began.

Stay away from that man, do you hear me? Alicia Berano said to her daughter Necessity one lazy afternoon while they were sitting by their terrace plucking out each other's split ends. Necessity's eyes however, seemed fixed on as far as one could gaze at rice fields, she was half-smiling and seemed to be somewhere else, and she did not seem to hear what her mother was saying.

Alicia continued saying, That man is Godless!

Necessity just looked at her for some five seconds and smiled, then she turned her gaze far away again. Alicia went on with her motherly monologue, she said, I talked to Father Tolentino the other day, he said he met Onyok Ilaya on a baptismal banquet and asked him why he'd never seen him at church, you know what his reply was? Necessity did not reply, not even with anything non-verbal, so Alicia replied to her own question, she said, He said he was a grandson of God and that he only worshipped things that could be bartered for goods! What a horror of a human being! I don't want to catch you going out or going anywhere near that grandson of the devil himself ever again, do you understand?

Necessity of course did not understand, she did not even hear what her mother just said, she just turned to her and smiled and said, Of course, Mother! Then she set her gaze somewhere else again far beyond the dried-up rice fields.

She found herself the following day by the rocky beach near what would someday be known as Sitio Putak. It was late in April, it was very dry and trees turned yellow and orange, the scenery in the countryside was like that of a forced autumn in the peak of summer, and there isn't an autumn in the Philippines. The wind did not stir and the sea was calm, even when Onyok Ilaya was nearby. It was almost noon and the sun was harsh, Necessity covered her head, her face, and her arms with a red sarong cloth. Onyok was taking Necessity out to sea on his pump boat that had outriggers. He filled the tiny tank with crude oil and started the engine, it made an annoying sound almost similar to his serenade a couple of weeks earlier.

Where are we going? Necessity asked a bit anxiously.

Where do you think? Onyok asked back. To the mountains?

Necessity got embarrassed by that reply, she then said, I'm not a very good swimmer!

Well, I am, said Onyok, though he wasn't. He grew up in the inlands and had swum only on falls and ponds which were as deep as the level of his waist. He learned to float at sea when he was eighteen, and never swam more than twelve feet away from the boat. He went on saying, Besides, you will be onboard the best of fishing boats with the best of skippers!

Necessity stepped onboard, they sat by the rear of the boat where there was a wooden seat which was high enough to make one's knees flex comfortably while sitting. They kissed passionately for a couple of minutes, then they were interrupted by two men who joined them onboard. Onyok said, And voila! We even have the best of crew!

The first man to get onboard was named Totong, he was in his early twenties, skinny and devoid of all facial expressions, his right upper limb from the elbow down was clearly missing. The other man was Dodong, he was plump and was in his late thirties, and in contrast to Totong he could not stop smiling, most of his teeth were missing, and so was his entire left arm. It was clear that Onyok needed them both, they seemed to compensate each other, they were quick on the water like cormorants and were skillful with the boat.

Necessity was too shy and too polite to ask Onyok what happened to each of their missing arm and what they were doing there, she thought it was to be one of those romantic boat rides for two. The boat set out, the motor engine turned even noisier, and the fumes of burned crude oil made Necessity dizzy. They passed by a few small unnamed islets which were lined with white sand and crystal clear waters and in about half an hour they were at open sea at the far edges of Burog Bay. Dodong steered the boat with his right arm, and then at a certain point, he turned off the motor. There were fine waves out there and it tossed the boat lightly at the sides. Then Onyok rose and declared, Now we're going fishing! He took off his blue shirt and showed off his flat muscular abdomen, and it made Necessity blush like she had caught fresh sunburn.

Trying to divert her discomfort, Necessity asked, Fishing? Aren't we half a day late? Isn't it supposed to be done before dawn?

Onyok scoffed, You're talking about fishing in the previous century! He then cued Totong and Dodong who were each holding a whiskey bottle in their surviving hand. Each bottle seemed to contain silver powder and tiny bits of metal, and had a wicker by the mouth. They lit the wicker with cigarette lighters, and as soon as the sparks reached the mouth of the bottles, they cast them to the water, as far away from the boat as they could. The bottles quickly disappeared from the surface. One minute passed, then two minutes, then three. Nothing happened. Necessity began to wonder what that was all about, but just then the boat shook from the bottom, there was like tumult coming from the depths of the sea approaching the surface, and then from two different spots, approximately where the bottles came into contact with the sea, water spewed high up in the air, more than a dozen feet high like those from geysers or the back of a whale. It was a sight, everyone on the boat was soaked. Necessity was dazed. The waters went rocky for a few minutes, then it was calm again.

Onyok got hold of a fishing net, danced with it like a banderillero in a bull fight, giving Necessity a devilish stare from time to time. The love-struck maiden was all-smiles and her eyes never moved away away from him. He then cast the net to the sea. It was to serve no purpose, it was like for visual effects. Soon, dead fish of all kinds and sizes were floating everywhere. Totong and Dodong dived to the water, each had a large net bag hanging from their mouths. They swam like penguins and seals and disappeared from the surface for impressively long periods, and with clenched jaws at that, to hold the net bags as they had just an arm each.

Onyok jumped to the water too, but with his feet first, while squeezing his nose with his right thumb and pointing finger, and closing his eyes tightly. He swam just like himself, a little clumsier than a poodle on a pool, the best he could do to impress his girlfriend was float on his back, which every man in the entire archipelago could do.

Each time Totong and Dodong surfaced from underwater, their net bags were full of all kinds of dead fish, then they'd load the catch on the boat and disappeared underwater again. Soon they were done and had to rest on the boat. The catch was huge. They threw away the ones which were too small, those which got severely disfigured from the blast, and those which were not known to be edible.

Necessity thought for a while that something was wrong with what she'd seen, but then again, she was not thinking that much, she just hoped that Totong and Dodong would soon disappear so she and Onyok could move on to the next kiss. They headed back to shore, their catch was more than any fisherman could catch for a whole week of hard labor.

By the road near the beach, a jeepney-looking vehicle which looked like it had at least a dozen serious accidents in the past year was waiting for them. Necessity recognized the driver, it was the big, overly tattooed tambourine man. They loaded the rusty vehicle with their catch and it sped off to town to deliver the catch to the market stalls.

In the next couple of weeks, Necessity and Onyok would meet everyday at around noon at the same spot by the coast, somewhere behind the rocks. She told her mother that she was going around town to recruit children for the Flores de Mayo activities at church. Of course that wasn't the truth, and she went out at noon so that her mother wouldn't suspect that she was doing something less than decent, because something less than decent was usually done by youngsters in the dark, but indeed, something less than decent was what she and Onyok Ilaya were doing, in broad daylight. Kisses went on for hours, then the kisses moved down the neck, then the breasts, then a sudden attack of Catholic-honed conscience would strike her and she'd say, Stop! But Onyok, who was created without any conscience of any sort, seldom stopped for more than three seconds, but he did stop for minutes at times, then the girl's conscience would flicker away to limbo and they'd start again.

By the middle of May, Onyok Ilaya and his small band of convicts were into another harana stint, but this time, Necessity knew they were coming, so she carefully planned her get-up, and it took the whole day for her to fully decide which clothes to wear. She picked a knee-long blue skirt, a sleeveless white blouse, she sported a fly-away hairdo, and she buried her face in layers of make-up.

Alicia caught site of her after dinner, it infuriated the Catholic mother, she was near- fuming as she asked, What's wrong with you?

Necessity replied, Nothing, Mama, it's just the latest look!

Alicia said, The latest look? You seem to me like the Whore of Babylon herself!

Necessity said, But Mama, everyone in Manila…

Just right then, somebody at the yard struck the ailing guitar again, Alicia instinctively rushed to the kitchen to see if it was that brown cat again messing with the empty tin cans. Then a voice became audible, it did not help Alicia with her confusion about the tin cans, but to Necessity, heavens forgive her, it was the sweetest voice in the world. They sentenced the classic Cascades song The Last Leaf to death, it was one of her favorites but she did not care.

Onyok had trouble with enunciation, upon hearing him sing, Taray the house help asked Necessity, What did he say? Ducklings? To Davao? Necessity hushed her.

Alicia gnarled and said, Just as I thought, the beast himself! This time Necessity was not so lucky because Onyok Ilaya was to render a poem, the only bit of luck she had was that it was not in English but in the native Hiligaynon tongue, so Onyok could make phrases without sounding like he'd had some cognitive stunting sometime in his formative years after hitting his head on a rock, but still the poem was of no taste. The poem made poor sense and rhythm no matter how Onyok twisted his facial muscles and his torso to look like he had internalized his piece.

> If you were a rose,
>   I'd cut you down and put you in a vase
> If you were the moon
>   I'd open the windows
>   to let your light in…
> If you were a cicada,
>   I wouldn't mind your noise,
>   I'd know it's a call to make love…

Before he could finish, Alicia stormed out of the house with a frying pan in her right hand and moved to strike Onyok with it while screaming, You stay away from my daughter you bastard of Satan and the Babylon Whore! Onyok did not believe she could actually assault him so he just stood there smiling, confident as though he owned the galaxy so no physical harm could befall him. Just then, the back of the pan, all black from years of use, hit his left face. He fell to the ground, and for a while he forgot the date, the hour, the place, and why he was there. Alicia Berano, for the record, never exhibited that kind of rage before, she never assaulted anyone physically before and after that.

Necessity was devastated, and a classic mother-daughter rift ensued, that classic cause. The peace of a hundred years between those two old acacia trees was stirred, in the ensuing days and nights, there was a turbulent noise as mother and daughter screamed at each other, rendering the cicadas who had been there for ages virtually inaudible. They yelled so loudly that each could barely hear what the other was saying.

During one of their mother-daughter fights, Necessity condemned her mother as completely unfit for a teacher's post for assaulting a man. Alicia heard that one clearly, and she replied that it was an exception, because what she hit was not the face of a man but that of a brute straight out of the underworld. Necessity rushed to her room, slammed the door behind her, she cried like she was giving birth for the first time and swore she'd never talk to her mother again, a resolution that would last a little more than 24 hours.

The night when Onyok got the pan on his face, the guitar and tambourine men took their master to the central market to help him recover from the concussion. They settled at a corner where farm workers gathered in the evening to drink tubâ. They bought a pack of ice and placed it on his face, it jolted him back to full consciousness, but then they tried to comfort him with their own guitar-and tambourine version of Four Strong Winds and Five Hundred Miles, so he thought he'd rather sleep, and so he fell into a deep sleep again. They stayed there until morning.

Nothing could stop Necessity and Onyok from seeing each other, and they did it everyday, usually around noon. They talked, though Onyok did most of the talking. For every two or three phrases that Necessity spoke, Onyok injected a whole chapter of chatter.

She learned everything about him, the exaggerated version, that was, but not vice-versa, he seemed not eager to know her at all. Though she listened to him intently, she failed to notice the red flags from what she'd heard - that he dropped out of school in his freshman year in high-school and was proud of it, he got expelled for constantly making trouble. He was even bragging about the dubious sources of his wealth, explicitly saying several times that the rules of society did not bind him, that education was useless, that schooling was his biggest mistake, and that it was in fact an obstacle to his march towards creating his smuggling empire. He adored his father who was then confined in one of the most heavily guarded wards of the public mental facility in the inland town of Pototan, he praised him for hitting his mother who he thought was especially slow in many things.

Necessity heard all of these, but nothing could shake that amorous trance off her, during those weeks she completely abandoned her faculty of reason. Many who knew her wondered about that and could never reconcile the conflicting pictures - her seemingly perfect nature and her then absurd behavior, but they finally thought that it must have been that mustache, for no one could believe that she'd be shallow enough to fall for him because of the money, that car and that bungalow. No one came up with the right conclusion, she simply got caught by the snare of animal attraction.

The rains came at the end of May, the musty fragrance that came from the soil upon its first contacts with moisture filled the air everywhere, it made people move in a more relaxed pace, it was a lot cooler after two months of scorching heat.

Necessity seemed to be the only one who was tensed, she was pacing and seemed to take fast, shallow and ineffective breaths.

It was a Saturday morning and she was outside St. Anthony's Church in Barotac Nuevo, another coastal town some 10 miles south of Burog. She was there to say her confession and the line was long, many in the province believed that the Apocalypse would occur on a Saturday night so everyone had a long list to tell the priest to make sure they'd get into the salvation boat. The line was surely shorter in her hometown Burog, but the priest there knew her and her family too well, he could tell which toothbrush belonged to whom, he could even tell who didn't brush, and so she thought that the things she was about to tell ought not go through his ears, as she did not trust the tongue in-between, even though she knew he was strictly bound to The Seal of Confession.

The Barotac Nuevo town fiesta on the feast day of St. Anthony was approaching, the plaza was turning more and more festive by the day. They had placed gigantic loudspeakers the week earlier by the concrete public stage and they played music so loudly it angered the priest who claimed it drowned his sermons, and his proof was that he noticed the congregation swaying to the tune of Love is Blue in the middle of his Sunday homily which took him five days to prepare.

Necessity was fidgety, her thoughts were in complete disarray and they were somewhere far. The concrete ground outside the church was wet and she slipped from her nervous pacing almost falling to the ground, it then made her aware of her surroundings. She looked around and noticed that the sinner's line was not that long anymore and so she thought she was ready.

A Lover's Concerto by the Supremes was being played at the plaza, it was her favorite and so it made her relax a little, she'd hoped they'd play the music louder so people next in line wouldn't hear what she had to say to the priest. She fell in line, and after about an hour's wait, it was her turn. She went inside the confessional box and knelt, the priest slid the wooden cover to open the tiny window latticed with rattan which separated him from the sinners. The priest was tired, he gave a deep sigh and knocked, it was his signal to the the penitent to start.

She commenced her confession in her native Hiligaynon-Kinaray-a tongue, Bless me Father for I have sinned, my last confession was three months ago.

The priest interrupted, Too long my child, too long, that was the last time it rained!

She said, Yes Father, I'm aware and I'm sorry, please include it among the many sins I have to tell later.

The priest said, Go on, my child, what are those sins?

By this time The Crystals' Da Doo Ron Ron played very loudly, contrary to what she'd thought, it made things worse, the priest asked her to speak louder so he could hear so God could hear, it felt like she had to announce all her faults loud enough for all three towns to hear. She began with the list of her sins, starting from the petty ones, like not being polite to her mother, raising her voice at her brother, not doing her chores well, such things that wouldn't actually drag anyone to hell. She could already sense some boredom in the priest's breathing.

Then it was time for the big guilt, the reason why she was there and not in her home parish, why she was pacing around restlessly. She thought the word for her sin was too foul in her native tongue, so she said it in English - I fornicated! Then she started crying.

The priest, who was then almost asleep, made an audible gasp, sprang back to full consciousness, cleared his throat and sat up straight. He paused and thought for a while, he himself left school many years before and had forgotten a big bulk of his English, for a while he was unsure, he seemed to have mixed up the definitions of fornicated and fabricated, but Necessity's incessant crying made him quite certain, for no young girl would weep for having fabricated things. Then he thought that this one could not be one of those prostitutes who usually lined up for confession on Friday afternoons, because they preferred to use the native term for fornication which was for him, too foul for even Satan to hear, and they usually didn't sound a bit remorseful for they were sure to be confessing the same sin again after two weeks, and he could usually hear a chewing of gum instead of sobbing. But then again, no, he thought, this must be one of them whores, just a new one, just unused to the sin. He had preached about chastity for several Sundays in a row, none of his parishioners could fall for such sin if she was no whore, he thought. So he tried to be gentle, he asked her, Were you forced to do this?

Necessity replied, No Father, I consented.

The priest said, Are you sure? Then why sell your sacred body to men? You must have been compelled to do this! Was it poverty?

By this time she'd realized that the priest misunderstood, she felt the need to reply immediately to clear things out, by this time the music at the plaza had stopped, she and the priest hadn't lowered their voices, so anyone near the confessional box could hear what was being said. Necessity said, Oh no, father, it's not what you're thinking!

The priest said, Hush, my child! Not too loud, you don't need to confess to the whole town! So then, tell me what happened!

Necessity lowered her voice, she said, It's…it's a man whom I'm in love with, Father.

The priest asked, In love? Are you sure? Are you married to him?

She replied, No Father, why else would I confess it?

This irked the priest, he raised his voice a little saying, Don't sharpshoot me my child, I can give you a penance so heavy you wouldn't be able to complete it in your deathbed many years from now!

He gave her the blessing and dismissed her, she nonetheless got a hefty load of penance, seven rosaries to be prayed everyday for seven days and she was to attend seven non-Sunday masses. To her it felt like she wouldn't be able to complete them until her own grandchildren got a penance of their own many decades in the future, probably for the same sin she confessed.

She left the church on a spiritual high, she felt relieved like she was again a citizen of Kingdom Come, she was firmly resolved never to do again what she and Onyok did in an abandoned fisherman's hut by the shores of Burog Bay a week earlier. Her favorite song A Lover's Concerto was again being played loudly at the plaza as she headed for the bus stop. The song carried her away, she thought of the sin she just confessed, she thought of what actually happened, she thought of Onyok, and she was unconsciously lightly biting her lower lip.

The following Saturday, she found herself again outside another church, this time in the coastal town of Dumangas, the immediate town south of Barotac Nuevo. She was there to confess the same sin, not exactly the same sin, but the same kind, a new one, a new execution of the same sin. She was not yet thru with the penance she'd received the previous week, now she was having almost the same load, but this time she did not sound so remorseful, and she barely cried.

The week after that, she was again lining for confession at the Jaro Cathedral in Iloilo City, for the same thing. The following week she was at the church of The Immaculate Concepcion in Oton, the first town south of Iloilo City. It looked like it could go on further southwards by the week, there were still about half a dozen towns and churches south of Oton before she reached the last church at the southern tip of Panay Island, the church of San Joaquin, but she stopped at Oton. After that she no longer felt that what she and Onyok were doing was a sin.

In the last week of June she left for Manila for the school opening, Onyok drove her to Fort San Pedro in Iloilo City where the ferry docked. During the ride, Onyok tried to convince her to ditch school, he said that one did not need education to be his housewife and that it was in fact an obstacle.

She lied to her mother, she said she was taking the bus, and it looked like she did. Alicia saw her off at the bus stop by the plaza, but she got down after just a few blocks at the next stop where the purple Beetle was waiting. Before she got onboard the ferry, the couple kissed for nearly a quarter of an hour, they kissed as if the boat would later sink and she was surely not to be one of the survivors. He said that if she didn't ditch school by August he'd go to Manila and claim her himself and drag her back to Burog. She gave him a slight wink, like telling him that she'd be back long before that.

So she did. In mid- July, just about a month after she confessed in Oton, her bags were back at the doorsteps of their house in Burog, she stood just closely behind the bags, to her mother's bewilderment. She confessed to her mother, this time, that she was pregnant. Being an unwed mother at the very core of Catholic Philippines was every woman's nightmare, it was then considered worse than contracting leprosy in Biblical times.

Alicia Berano went berserk, she neither ate nor slept for two days and she almost went catatonic, she sat on her bed lifting her arms with her elbows flexed, looking like Atlas bearing the weight of the world. On the third day she began to wail like a goat being slaughtered, on the fourth day she began to eat, on the fifth day she could not stop eating so she just ate, on the sixth day she began to speak and prayed the rosary incessantly. On the seventh day she spoke to people, but her words were devoid of all emotion, and she talked about nothing but plans for a rushed wedding, and it was to be within a month, she said no mother could bear such dishonor longer than that.

She did not talk directly to Necessity, everything she needed to say to her she said it to another person, and at times when it was just the two of them in the house she'd talk to her thru the trees, the hens or the ceiling. The environment in the household became too noxious even for mosquitoes.

She used to refer to Onyok Ilaya as The Beast of the Revelation, The Bastard of Satan and The Whore of Babylon, Pontius Pilate, Judas, and even Satan himself. Now it appeared like she badly wanted him to be her son-in-law officially as soon as possible, not that she liked him badly, if he was anywhere within her reach she would have slapped the big old frying pan on his other cheek in full swing, but she'd rather have her daughter marry Pontius Pilate or the Bastard of Satan and The Babylon Whore than swallow a perceived family dishonor.

The whole town came to life. July and August were usually the dreariest and leanest months of the year, it rained mostly and it was too far away between harvests, some families literally starved, some subsisted on corn that looked like small bits of granite rock and just as hard, and tasted almost the same, they fed the chickens and the ducks with the same thing. But in July 1967, the town of Burog sprang back to life, because people had something extraordinarily huge to gloat about. Something big was about to collapse, how their eyes would love to see something colossal falling to to the ground in tiny pieces. It was The American Girl's dream, it was about to fall apart, townsfolk were being pulled together by that same passion which draws crowds to witness a gargantuan edifice being demolished.

Even people who had previously stopped talking to each other reconciled, just so they would have a bigger circle to talk to about Necessity's fate, in many ways it gave them satisfaction, it made them feel that their lives were not that miserable at all. Schadenfreude was a pastime in every small town across the country during those times, the only reason a small town would be exempt from this postulate was when no one lived there anymore.

The brothers Arthur, Lancelot and Percivale tried to wear serious, angry faces all the time. If it all happened a century earlier, society would have considered it justified if they lynched or castrated Onyok, no one would have indicted them, but then it was 1967, there were laws that stood in their way. They too, wanted The Bastard of Satan and The Babylon Whore to be their brother-in-law as soon as possible for honor's sake, they tried to appear like they could kill anybody for it.

They traveled to Onyok's hometown in Igbaras, they walked around town openly bearing rusty rifles known as paltik which had actually ceased to function more than a quarter of a century earlier, which meant before the Second World War, and none of them knew how to shoot, neither had any of them fired a gun before. It was not clear why they did it there in Igbaras when Onyok was half-hiding in his bungalow in Burog. Arthur said it was to intimidate the Ilaya clan so they too would pressure Onyok to marry Necessity, but it was rather futile because his clan did not care any bit about him, and some of them would have in fact been grateful if they lynched him or castrated him using a pickax before their eyes.

Necessity was just into the first month of her senior year in college. Just before she went home, the nuns who ran the school made a quick deliberation, the decision was completely expected and unanimous, she was summoned to the Mother Dean's office and was handed her notice of expulsion.

The grounds for expulsion was grave immorality, for committing the deadliest among The Cardinal Sins according to St. Thomas Aquinas. Her certificate of good moral character was even withheld, because the nuns thought it contradicted what was stated on the grounds for expulsion. Necessity did not mind, she offered no contest, though little did she know it would seal her scholastic fate, her future altogether, because all schools in the country required that certificate upon transfer.

She did not seem to be bothered, she still was in some sort of a trance. She was told by the dean to come back in a few years to claim the certificate, but then she'd lost all interest in academics, she was about to become the wife of a self-proclaimed deity who was about to build an empire of a vague and shady sort, and her would-be husband swore the day before their wedding that he'd shave the hair off her head if she ever attempted to go back to school.

One rainy Saturday morning in early August, there came a knock on Necessity's bedroom window. It was the house help Taray, she believed that knocking on a door inside the house like the bedroom door was bad luck for a pregnant woman who was still unmarried, so she climbed up a young duhat tree which stood outside Necessity's room to knock on her window. Someone is here looking for you, said Taray.

Necessity looked out her window and saw who was standing by the main door. Her face brightened and tears fell like monsoon rains. She ran down the stairs to the living room and then to the front door and hugged her visitor to near-suffocation.

It was Rowena Bande, they were very close friends in elementary school but parted ways later. She worked as a courier at the town hall. She was short, plump and jolly, and stammered from time to time when she talked. Her name was Rowena but she was known to everyone as Sese, she came to volunteer as The Maid of Honor for the wedding. Maids of honor were almost exclusively picked and invited by the bride, but in rushed and shotgun marriages like this one, it was considered bad luck and quite a dishonor to be picked as maid of honor, so one acquaintance usually showed up, appointing herself out of compassion for the bride, and in certain cases no one showed up.

The two ladies hugged for a long time, neither one wanting to let go, they hugged so tightly, for a while they looked like conjoined twins who didn't look anywhere nearly alike. They cried, they were so happy they could say nothing but each other's name. Necessity called her Sese, and she called her Seng.

The wedding was on August 26th, a Saturday, it was unusually sunny as the skies usually poured rain in late August like it was some rush hour before the end of the wet season. Alicia Berano thought that the pressure from the whole town was crushing her, so she opted not to have the wedding at the church in town but at a small chapel that stood on a conglomeration of rocks between the coastal villages of Barrio Buki and Barrio Banding, which would later be known as Sitio Paka and Sitio Putak, respectively.

The nosy parish priest Father Tolentino officiated, his homily was longer than the mass and the wedding ceremony combined, and he talked largely about The Seven Deadly Sins according to St. Thomas Aquinas with an emphasis on the sin called Lust. Neither the bride nor the groom looked happy.

Onyok was impatient and wanted the ceremony to end quickly. He was a professed atheist so everything that was said during the rites was to him no different from the squawking of seagulls. He was smoking cigarettes during the entire, seemingly endless homily. He had drunk two glasses of illegally distilled whiskey in the morning, it made him loud and jolly for a while but it made him very cranky by the time the wedding began in the afternoon. Their first big fight as a couple erupted just before the ceremonies began, in front of all the guests, when Onyok commented about Sese, saying, Oh, that's your maid of honor? I thought it was some hog they forgot to slaughter!

Necessity herself could not concentrate much during the ceremonies. She thought a lot about the immediate and remote future, she had the feeling that all this might be a horrendous mistake. She thought of her grandfather Jose Cañosi Baydadong, she thought, had he been there his heartbreak would have sent shockwaves that could kill the fishes swimming nearby. She also thought of her father Armando

71

Berano, had he been there he would have learned to say two new English words - Bad girl!

Alicia Berano may have thought of finding refuge from the tormenting townsfolk by having the wedding held at the shores quite far from town, but still more than two hundred guests invited themselves to the occasion. In the 60's it was still widely understood in the countryside that the whole town was invited to weddings, it was like free lunch or dinner, so two hundred was a relatively small number in small town standards, though it was big enough to bring discomfort to the already tormented mother of the bride. To make it worse, quite naturally, most of those who took the trouble going to the wedding far from town were the most curious ones, the ones who jubilated upon hearing of Necessity's misfortune, the ones who spoke badly of her.

As usual, only a tenth were present for the ceremony, the rest came just as the banquet was about to start. The reception was held at the open community hall near the chapel. The hall had a roof made of nipa leaves, it was supported by bamboo posts, there were no walls and the floor was the loamy ground itself.

Three young lechons were being roasted nearby, guests began plucking away the crispy skin of the young pigs even before the start of dinner was announced. Rice came in big buckets and were poured on long tables, so were the sotanghon noodles. There were two giant cauldrons that could fit four medium-sized adults, each cauldron was filled with native chicken adobo. There was a gigantic paella pan, large enough for an adult to have a warm bath in it, and it contained the country's sweet and sticky version of Paella Valenciana, known simply to locals as Valenciana. Guests ate like a plague of locusts in a cornfield, those who came a little less than half an hour after the banquet began were like sentenced to go to bed without dinner.

Onyok's best man was not there, he had been arrested for highway robbery the week earlier, so another convict on parole stood as proxy, his case was homicide.

Only Onyok's mother, Theresa Ilaya, five of his seven sisters and about six of his cousins were there, the rest from his side were his friends, about thirty men from ages twenty to forty, each looked like he had been arrested by the police at least twice in his life, and some of them looked and behaved like they were to be arrested right after the wedding for any crime there was on the list.

His most loyal thugs, the tambourine and the guitar man, as well as Dodong and Totong, all wore over-sized suits of colors which never matched no matter during which era in Philippine history they would have worn them, and at the reception they tried to render a song and dance, it was Sh-boom by The Crewcuts, supposedly, but it turned out to be like a woebegone hoedown act, nobody had any idea what they were trying to sing.

None of both parties' fathers were around, one was long gone and the other was in straight jacket in another town, so the mothers made the speeches. Alicia Berano made a rather short speech in the native tongue, she said she'd rather avoid saying the speech in English so Onyok would be able to understand, she said it clearly as she commenced her speech.

She talked about responsibilities of married adults and the challenges of parenthood and the like, she talked about married life, how far it was from the excitement of sneaking out of the house and doing what God Himself does not want to know what on the beaches. She ended the speech with, To the groom, I should say, whenever you feel like saying something, the best thing you can do is not to say it, just keep your mouth shut at all times!

Theresa Ilaya was called to say something too, as the mother of the groom, but something made her think that she had to say it in English, for some reasons unclear. She stood and got frozen for a long time, when she was finally half-

73

thawed from her dread she said, Theresa Ilaya, I am, Mother, Nicanor Onyok Ilaya...thank you. Then she went back to her seat, trembling.

Sese, as The Maid of Honor, was called to make a speech too, she was so eager that she bounced her way to the wooden dais. She began by greeting everyone she could see whom she knew, and it took a long time. When it was time to say the speech itself, and she was actually supposed to read it as she'd prepared and written it for days, she stammered and could not go on, she ended up crying so Necessity had to rise from her seat and go to her, she gave her a hug and led her to her seat.

The proxy best man on parole made his speech too, he looked horrible, he was having a severe case of hangover having had a drinking session with local rum the whole night. He had been released from prison on parole just three days earlier. He was wearing the original best man's barong tagalog which was twice as large his size and it was all wrinkly, he looked unkempt, he had taken off the hairband he was wearing, his hair looked like seaweeds pickled in vinegar, though children who were present called him Jesus. He could barely walk straight, he moved like every muscle ached and his right arm exhibited coarse tremors. Children asked what was wrong with Jesus and parents had to explain that he'd just had a full round with the scourging at the pillar, the Second Sorrowful Mystery of the Holy Rosary.

Then he began to speak, his voice was very coarse he sounded more like Satan, or more precisely, like a restive donkey being towed. He did not really know Onyok Ilaya, he was just the original best man's best friend, they met when the latter served time three years earlier. His speech was about himself and the original best man, he explained how he ought to have been acquitted in trial five years earlier due to technical deficiencies on the prosecutor's part, then he began screaming, I was technically innocent! I was technically innocent! Then he began cursing the politicians whom he had formerly worked for as a hitman for failing to bribe the judge to get him out. Soon he was screaming uncontrollably, Onyok rose, he ran to him and dragged him by the left arm and quite forcefully threw him back to his seat which tipped backwards making him fall to the floor, or rather, the loamy ground. Some children were crying saying, Oh no, are they going to crucify Jesus now?

The reception ended late in the afternoon, fireworks and firecrackers were expected, but there was to be none. The proxy best man on parole announced that all were requested to go near the beach to witness something more spectacular than fireworks, and so they went and stood by the rocky shores.

Then all of Onyok's convict-looking friends, most of which were really convicts, took off their shirts and trousers, jumped to the water and swam a few feet to get onboard four bamboo rafts, each of them had at least four whiskey bottles with wickers at the opening, the bottles appeared to contain silvery powder and pieces of tin foils cut in different shapes and sizes. They rowed way and stopped at some distance, then they lit the wickers and started to cast to the bottles to the sea in succession, dozens and dozens of them. Then some kind of explosion from underneath the waters could be heard, then steams spewed from everywhere several feet high to the air.

It was indeed spectacular, like all of a sudden there were dozens of geysers in one small area of the bay. It was initially met with awe, everyone was dazed, there were audible gasps and wows, but soon it turned into concern. The underwater fireworks show lasted for a quarter of an hour, and shortly after that, fishes of all kinds and sizes began to float and drift ashore, the water turned murky white because of the pulverized corals. Concern immediately turned to disgust.

The proxy best man on parole was laughing like Satan, though the children were happy because they thought Jesus was happy. Then he announced in a very coarse, brute voice, Alright, for our wedding take-home souvenirs, we'll give each and everyone of you net bags which you will fill with as many fish as you can! Isn't that lovely?

None of the guests took any of those multi-colored net bags. Almost all of them were appalled by what they saw. They were a people of the coast, the spectacle awakened in each of them varying degrees of dormant bond with the seas. They walked away one by one, and though they did not talk to each other, they seemed to agree on one thing - that what they witnessed was some form of massacre, a massacre of their own spirits which, they realized, actually dwelled in the seas.

The dynamite spectacle awakened Necessity too, to the reality about Onyok Ilaya who was actually trying to build an empire thru sinister means, one of which was blast fishing in the waters held sacred by her forefathers. At last Necessity was awake, though it was just a little too late.

5

*A*lthough he caught his fish in an unconventional and ghastly manner, Onyok Ilaya was, by some definition, a fisherman, because he caught fish for a living. It was not until much later that the government learned of the blast fishing and it took some time before law was passed to outlaw it, and it took a longer time for the law to grow enough teeth to curb it, and it would probably take an eternity before rogue fishermen abandon the practice completely. Onyok Ilaya was one of those rogue fishermen, but he fished in a conventional way too, when there were people watching, in order to look legit.

So in his little fisherman's hut in Sitio Putak he had all kinds of fishing equipment, mostly outdated, rusty and worn ones. He had three rusty iron hooks which hung from a beam made of hardwood, the hooks were used to hang- dry larger fishes like marlins and occasionally, some tuna. The hooks were rusty but the hardwood was very sturdy, it must be, for one Monday morning in October 1985, Necessity was seen hanging there for a few hours. She had gained a lot of weight then, but neither the hook nor the beam broke.

She was not dead. In fact, a wide piece of cloth was wound around her mouth to keep her from bickering or asking for help, and her hands were tightly tied with thick abaca ropes. The same type of rope was strapped around her torso like a harness, and it was tied to the hook at the end, making her look like a paratrooper whose chute got caught on a branch of a tree. She was keeping still, for the more she moved the more it hurt. Some friction sores were already forming by her armpits. It was late in October, the boys were coming home from the city for their two-week semestral break. Jeremy, who was then ten, was in his fourth grade and Anthony, who was seven, was in the first grade.

Mama! Mama! Anthony cried, he could be heard from afar, he screamed in horror with a pitch higher than that of any girl of his age, and he was wailing as he ran to towards the scene. It was an open hut, it had no walls, so he could clearly see his mother hanging like the catch of the day. Necessity moved her head sideways to give the boy some signs that she was not dead, to at least cut short or minimize his terror. Jeremy came after Anthony, he too was stunned and horrified but just walked towards the hut and did not say anything.

When he was about ten feet away from where his mother hung, he heard his father's rough, crude-sounding voice saying, If you go anywhere nearer your mother I'll blow your head to pieces! He was sitting on a rock about twenty feet from the hut, he had with him a loaded shotgun, and he was smoking a cigarette which he rolled himself.

Anthony halted but could not stop wailing. He said, Papa, take her down, please!

You keep your mouth shut and stop crying or you'll be no better than dead fish! Onyok yelled.

Upon seeing his father with the gun, Jeremy retreated and hid behind the rocks. Anthony stayed put and tried to control his crying. Please take her down, he said to his father. You can't do this!

Onyok then took off his dirty white shirt, it was so worn-out it looked like a shark chewed and spat it out at least three times over. He motioned to show Anthony something on his arm.

He did not look anywhere close to the Onyok Ilaya whom Necessity fell for eighteen years before. He was just 40 but looked a couple of decades older. His face bloated like a full moon and he had a lot of tiny scars on his cheeks from accidental dynamite blasts. He was blind in his left eye due to the same accident, it looked like someone poured a thin layer of white paint over his left pupil. He had a very large beer belly it made him rise up sluggishly, his breasts were nearly as large as those of his wife's, only the sides and the back of his head had hair, he still had that mustache but it had not been trimmed for ages, it grew long enough to cover his mouth when it was shut and the mustache seemed to have merged with his goatee that had also grown too long, almost touching his large belly when he was seated. What he wanted to show his son was the tattoo on his left arm.

Come here boy, and take take a look at this, he said.

Anthony shook his head and said, I think I've seen that before!

Onyok roared like a mad brute and exclaimed, I said come here right now!

Necessity motioned with her eyes like telling Anthony to do as his father said. Anthony took tiny steps towards his father, he tripped a couple of times over the rough stones and he was shaking.

Now, read this, Onyok said as soon as Anthony was near enough. He flexed his arm to show a worn, blue tattoo, an image of a skull with horns, and on top of it an inscription. Anthony did not speak, making Onyok raise his voice again like thunder, I said read it! Are you dumb? Don't they teach you how to read in school?

Anthony then, still shaking and crying, read out loud what was written - Apo Sang Dios.

Good! So you can read like your stupid mother! Onyok said. He had that tattoo done right after he was expelled from school, the inscription meant, Grandson of God. That was not true, he was just the grandson of Sabrino Elaya, a vegetable farmer in Igbaras. Sabrino Elaya's family name was spelled differently because the parish church's male secretary in the late Spanish era did not care much about spelling, though he took care of the then most powerful document in the land - the baptismal certificate.

No matter what was written on your birth certificate, your diploma, or no matter what you called yourself, if on your baptismal certificate it was written Rudolph Valentino, you would be officially Rudolph Valentino, no matter how you looked. That secretary held his post until shortly before the war, Sabrino Elaya had ten children, four of them got the name Elaya, five got Ilaya and one got Elaia. Onyok Ilaya was not God's grandson from his maternal side either. His maternal grandfather was a lieutenant of the Philippine Commonwealth Army who was killed in the Second World War, not by the Japanese, but in bed by a civilian husband of a woman from the nearby Negros Island.

Onyok's father was Nicanor Santiago Ilaya, Sabrino's middle child, he was known to all as Santiago. Unlike Onyok, Santiago did not speak much, he always wanted to be by himself and appeared to be thinking much, but then nobody knew if he really was thinking. People said Sabrino grew him straight out of one of his vegetable patches. Santiago only finished second grade in school, he could not really read but could write, though he could not really read what he was writing. He worked early in boyhood as an errand boy of the parish priest in Igbaras, and he was quite useful because he obeyed all orders without questioning. When he was big enough he became one of the parish priest's horse carriage drivers. He married early at the age of 18 because he got a young lady named Theresa Istas pregnant.

Theresa thought he was someone else, she sneaked out of the house one evening to meet some young man she did not know at the churchyard, it was a kind of a blind date. Santiago happened to pass by after disposing heaps of horse manure. It was dark and Theresa thought it was her date. It got her pregnant. They married, Theresa thought she did not have any choice, and so they had more children after that, seven daughters and one son in all.

Santiago joined the Filipino guerrilla forces for a while when the war broke out, but there he proved to be useless, having fired most shots but neither killing nor injuring a single Japanese, so he was discharged long before the liberation and went on to work with the parish priest. When the war ended, the priest got rid of his horses and got himself a used army jeep, Santiago was initially appointed the driver, but then he sideswiped houses, lampposts, mailboxes and souls every time he drove, so he was reassigned to the cemetery to do all kinds of work. It could not support a family of eight children so he left his post to try, like his father, to grow vegetables, but they wouldn't grow.

One busy morning in 1950 at the central market in Igbaras, the noise of vendors and market-goers was hushed by a deep, solid voice of someone preaching. It was Santiago Ilaya, claiming that he was The Son of God and that the hour had come, that he was to take the righteous with him back to his father. A very few took him seriously, but the rest just laughed, knowing who it was. He made a few people with disability line up for healing.

He took a blind man, massaged his eyes and told him to walk straight ahead without using his stick as guide. The blind man fell straight to the garbage pit. People applauded and howled mockingly. He laid his hands over an old lame garlic vendor and told him to rise and walk, and that his sins were forgiven. The man fell flat on his face, got very upset and got hold of one of his crutches and beat Santiago with it at the back of his left knee. Some people, knowing he could not really read, would show him some newspapers and asked like, for instance, Look at the headlines, when does it say rapture would come? Santiago then would reply that the paper was in English and that he could only read Hebrew.

In the next couple of months, Santiago was a fixture at the central market, preaching about The Apocalypse, trying to multiply loaves and dried fish and turning water into tubâ. Some did not mind him, some did mind him for a good laugh. That could not raise a family, the only way he could multiply loaves was to cut them to small pieces. Theresa was forced to grow vegetables by herself and put up a small fruit stand at some distance from the market where she could not hear her husband preaching, and she did laundry jobs when she could. Her mother shared a big chunk of her soldier's widow's pension with her so the family could survive.

Nobody was really bothered by a loud self-proclaimed messiah at the central market, until one day in December 1951 when Santiago abducted four small children, two of which were toddlers, and took them to the grassy hills. Villagers pursued him, they each had some kind of weapon, like bamboo spears, butcher's knives and old rifles from the war.

By dusk, Santiago found himself beleaguered at the hill, he then announced that he needed to sacrifice seven children for the Seven Angels with Trumpets coming as stated in the Book of Revelation which he just heard of and never read, and he said he was very sorry that he could only gather four. The constables, as what they called the policemen then, took him and he was placed in different public mental institutions. Having violent tendencies, he was treated like a prisoner wherever he was placed. He was to disappear from Igbaras forever, at least physically, as his children would have to bear the eternal burden of his legacy.

People mockingly called Onyok The Grandson of God. Onyok hated his townsfolk and dreaded school. Two years after his father disappeared from town, he started school in the first grade, and as expected, the entire class and some teachers did call him The Grandson of God from day one. Tired of the mockery, he decided to capitalize on such title, so he began to act like one, a grandson of God, though he behaved more like a grandson of a nether god.

On the second day of school in the second grade, he knocked down the biggest boy in class with a single punch, because he wanted the latter's seat and he wouldn't move. Soon he was respected out of fear in his class, he had a following of boys who had some violent tendencies. At break time they'd catch animals like large toads and wild ducklings, they tossed them high up to the air and let them fall limp on the ground, for all the other children to see. They did this several times until the animal was dead, then they'd laugh triumphantly. They engaged in other forms of animal torture. Onyok was sharp with the slingshot and loved to hit cats in the eyes. Almost every cat in his village had either a swollen eye or was totally blind. His favorite form of torture was putting a dark sock over the heads of ducks making them unable to see, and he made them wander aimlessly in the streets, bumping into posts and rocks or get run over by vehicles.

He also got thrilled by violence on human beings. He had an almost weekly fistfight and engaged in physically violent bullying. In the third grade he was suspended for two weeks for groping his math teacher's breasts. The teacher screamed in shock while half of the class cheered. Onyok was immediately put on detention and he questioned the principal's decision in the latter's face. He said, Why punish me? I can do whatever I want, I'm the Grandson of God!

He returned to school after two weeks and never changed, he pulled down skirts of female classmates without warning, and groped and kissed them whenever he wanted to. He was placed in the section of the academically slowest ones and he barely passed each year.

He miraculously graduated from elementary school, and early in freshman year in high school, he got expelled. He grabbed one of the girls in class, placed her on top of her desk and made actions like raping her for all of the class to see. One of the boys came to the rescue, but Onyok hit him with a sucker punch, he fell down on the floor and was unconscious for hours, everybody thought he was dead. That was the last day of school ever for Onyok Ilaya.

The week after that, he got that blue tattoo on his left arm. His mother asked him to help her with the vegetables, and in response he sabotaged the patches, watering them with seawater. He left home and moved further down south after that, to the coastal town of Miag-ao. He lived in abandoned shacks and started as a runner for blue-seal cigarette smugglers. He quickly earned the reputation among smugglers as the quick, fearless and impermeable-to-guilt little Grandson of God. He rose in the ranks quickly and worked with the more dangerous schemes, like smuggling of weapons and ammo. By the age of 18 he was already one of the smuggling lords in the south, respected out of fear by his peers.

One day, he came back to Igbaras to visit his mother. He was wearing tight leather pants, a pair of leather boots, and a leather jacket even though the earth seemed just as hot as the sun. He found her working at her vegetable garden. He took half a sack of salt with him, greeted her without a kiss or a hug, and right before her eyes he sowed the salt all over the young cabbages and tomatoes.

Theresa Ilaya was stunned and could not believe what she was seeing, but finally she yelled, Jesus, Mary and Joseph! What are you doing? You tiny fraction of an animal! You will make me and your sisters starve!

Onyok just grinned, then he pulled a big wad of money from his jacket and waved it for his mother to see. Then he said, You won't be needing these bagatelle vegetables from now on, you won't need to do anything at all to get by!

That silenced his mother. He bought the piece of lot where his family had squatted for ages and built a small concrete house for his mother and sisters. Two of his sisters who knew of his activities refused to live there. Aside from smuggling, he also partnered with other thugs in small-time illegal gambling schemes in the southern towns.

He also found blast fishing to be lucrative. Blast fishing was not yet brought to the national consciousness then, and no one knew of the deleterious effects it brought, what everyone knew was that it brought about a lot of fish to the markets, they knew something was not right about it, they just couldn't point out exactly what it was.

Onyok was quick in his rise, and also made enemies fast. Rivalry was getting rough and he was suspected of having killed a rival smuggler's runner. So he looked north, he was just 22 when he moved to Burog, far away enough from his enemies. He registered as a fisherman, just for a front, while actually maintaining his smuggling and gambling activities in the south.

Anthony was still shaking and crying, and Onyok said to him, You see now what happens to those who oppose the Grandson of God? He pointed to Necessity hanging on the hook.

Necessity was badly beaten, but she was not the kind that had resigned to the battered role passively, she usually fought back, only this time she was outmuscled. Many years before that, with a lot of village folks witnessing, she and Onyok had a terrible and violent fight. He started beating her with an iron rod, she fought back, taking hold of an unusually huge tuna by the tail, she swung it around like an athlete in a hammer throw event in the Olympics, and the gigantic head of the fish eventually hit Onyok on his right cheek, and it knocked him unconscious. The entire village cheered wildly.

What Onyok feared the most was her cured and polished stingray's tail which she used to defend herself. It was her paternal grandfather's. The stingray had been dead for ages but its tail could still sting whenever it was used, and it brought the kind of pain even the likes of Onyok Ilaya could barely stand. Necessity was very careful though, she kept it out of Onyok's reach. Onyok once got hold of it and used it to beat Jeremy and Anthony for some unclear infractions, and they weren't able to walk for days. Whenever she was outmuscled she'd fight back later on with some kind of booby traps. On several occasions, Onyok had to go to the local public clinic to have fishing hooks removed from his butt, and how he got them was never an accident.

What they fought about this time, the fight that led Necessity to hang on one of those fish hooks, was money. Onyok's little empire had fallen many years before, he had to rely on fishing, and with too many engaging in blast fishing which he himself introduced to the area, there were not too many fishes to catch. From time to time he'd get small hitman jobs from politicians and gang lords, but with his physical condition, it came less and less often.

Necessity got a job as a bookkeeper at the grocer's at the central market, pay was modest but it could barely sustain a family. Her mother Alicia and brother Percivale helped pay the boys' tuition fees at Santa Helena Catholic Academy.

What Onyok wanted was for Necessity to send some of her income to a certain Juliana Natang of the town of Miag-ao, with whom he had two illegitimate children, one of them was Renato Ilaya. Renato was about to begin high-school at San Agustin, a private university in Iloilo City. Juliana had no stable source of income, she went from door to door selling soap and and homemade potions with no known effects. Renato Ilaya however, was a math genius, he showed a lot of promise and got a high school scholarship. The natural answer from Necessity to such request was a big no, and thus the violent fight, and she ended hanging on that beam on a hook.

Onyok had several other children with three other women, he neither recognized nor gave his illegitimate children support, except those of Juliana's. His first child could have been that of Necessity's, the one that forced him to marry her and vice-versa in 1967, but she had a miscarriage shortly after the wedding, and had two more miscarriages before she had Jeremy in 1975. Renato was born in 1969, the first out of Onyok's extra-marital activities and he considered him as some kind of a flagship.

Money was not a problem in their first couple of years of marriage. The problem was the source of money, Necessity knew that the sources were from the shadows, but could not get specific details, and Onyok kept denying it to her when they were alone in the house, but boasted loudly about it when his comrades were around. The whole town knew the details however, it had spread around town even before she began dating Onyok. That alienated her further from her townsfolk, she spent most of her time at the bungalow and at the coasts, and came less and less frequently to town. Alicia did not talk to her much. Necessity stayed in the house most of the time, and Onyok, who had the inherited all of the universe's ill temper, used her as his wailing wall for his multi-colored verbal assaults each time he came home.

By the summer of 1968, she had fallen out of love. She was still psychologically recovering from the miscarriage, and the beatings had begun. She gathered all the courage to try to talk to his mother, and her response was cold. Alicia said, If you married Satan himself it would be a sin, but to divorce even Satan would be a more serious sin!

Distraught, she went to Father Tolentino for advice, and it did not bring comfort. The priest said, I understand your situation, you are badly beaten and you do not approve of his activities, but the bond of marriage should never be broken, it's a sacred doctrine! God may have a plan for all your sufferings, to make you stronger! Whenever he beats you, think of how much more Christ suffered from all those beatings and the nails on His palms and feet and the lance on His side!

87

She left the rectory in despair. She talked to other priests, again, going from town to town southwards, five priests in all until she reached the parish of Tigbauan, the next town south of Oton, and they gave more or less the same advice, like her back had to be literally broken first, ahead of any sacred doctrine.

And so she tried to endure, day after day, which turned to weeks, months, and years. In order to cope, she learned to fight back - the stingray's tail, the booby traps, the small hooks, and she was even accurate in throwing glasses and plates, it hit Onyok's forehead in nine out of ten attempts. One of their biggest fights were about her finishing her studies, to get to be a certified accountant. She won in some physical fights, but never actually won, Onyok would never support her through school even for just a year, he reiterated that school was poison to the brain.

By 1970, Onyok's smuggling empire had jaded, he lived quite far from his happy hunting ground so new lords in the south had shoved him aside. More fishermen in the northern coastal areas engaged in blast fishing, claiming it was practical and that it was in response to the government's approval of the trawls which gobbled up everything, not sparing even the seaweeds and the seabed substrate. Only those with hefty capital could afford the trawls, so blast fishing became a convenient alternative for lowly, destitute fishermen. The catch dwindled in just a couple of years.

Straightforward fishermen had a caucus in an open hut by the shores of Barrio Banding one evening, they tried to form a union to address the issue. As they moved to elect their officers, there came a big blast in the waters nearby, quite powerful that it caused the tiny hut to lean south. Then appeared Onyok Ilaya, he was with five thugs who each had firearms, they all looked scary enough, neither rifle nor blast was actually necessary to intimidate the fishermen.

Onyok declared his warning, he said, Try, just try and meddle with the way I catch my fish, you puny little putchongs, and you'll find holes in all your boats! My men will get to the holes of your daughters and wives and I won't hesitate to claim responsibility!

Onyok himself formed a loose association of blast fishermen to counter and intimidate any effort against their activities. In the next couple of years, he was considered as a mere petty, insignificant smuggler in the south. In 1972, Martial Law was declared all over the country, all the smuggling lords appeared to have been eradicated.

Onyok was arrested one night, there were millions of reasons to arrest him, but it was not clear for which particular offense he was arrested. The officer at the precinct read a few paragraphs about the grounds for the arrest but he slurred so badly and it did not matter even if he did not slur because it was in English, strangely, a quarter of a century had passed since America granted the country its independence and the laws and ordinances were still in English. The officer spoke the language in a manner which made him sound like a turkey, unintelligible to both who could and could not understand English, Onyok belonged to the latter group. Onyok was released a few days later, the officer again read a few paragraphs and slurred and articulated it even worse. Onyok went back to Burog not knowing what it was all about.

He was never an open political opponent of the regime, as he never understood real politics, so he was actually never near any danger during the Martial Law. He quickly realized that only the smuggling lords and gangs had been eradicated, the activities that built his little empire were actually still there, only reformatted, and in order to get back to his glory he had to get himself into some position, and to get close to those in power was the best position.

He started as a freelance hitman for politicians and military officials, preferably somewhere far from Burog. The job was dangerous, especially when it involved liquidating alleged rebels and political enemies who still had their private armies.

Poaching loud political activists was less dangerous but it paid less too.

Onyok became quickly well known among such employers, he was not the best man with the gun and he may have had his lapses, but he had the quality they sought the most - a complete lack of conscience and remorse. He got assignments from all over the country, sometimes disappearing for two months at a time.

Money flowed back, he was able to build a nice house which resembled that of Alicia Berano's, though it was partly concrete and bigger, just near where the bungalow stood. In 1976 he had an accident with blast fishing, the bottle with the dynamite exploded in midair just after he tossed it, and shrapnels costed him his vision in the left eye. Then he grew a huge beer belly, it made him move like a sloth, he was able to run only for some dozens of yards, after which he started panting for his life.

On assignment in the late 70's, he missed his target three times, he slacked so much on the job that his employers seriously considered liquidating him. Now the only qualification he had left as a hitman was his complete lack of conscience and remorse, but then he could not complete any job to be remorseful about. He would have been able to slay a few student activists who were easy targets because some of them were physically clumsy, but the employers would not take chances. At first he applied for torture jobs, there he had another distinct qualification - his pirate-like creepy looks would have scared even veteran pirates, but then eventually there came too many who could do that and looked like that, and it paid too little, he could earn more from fishing using a mere rod, line, hook and sinker.

Money stopped flowing, so he was back to fishing in the seas which he himself took the lead in ravishing. The catch was poor, they lost the house and moved to Purok Baka, formerly called Barrio Banding and soon to be called Sitio Putak.

They moved to a little shack which had a couple of rooms by the rocks on the shore. To console herself and the boys, Necessity suggested they painted it blue to make it prettier, but Onyok refused, warning her he'd turn her blue first before she could ever do it.

Necessity started brokering fish on a very small-time scale, peddled in bus stations, and the sight of her doing so was a delight to some of her townsfolk who had long resented her intelligence and that quixotic dream of her grandfather. Onyok, on rare occasions, would get some sort of hitman jobs, but it was more of threatening and scaring political opponents with his looks, and it could only buy them a few decent meals.

Onyok was laughing at the sight of Anthony shaking and crying, he said to his son, Have you pissed in your pants yet? Anthony did not reply. Onyok said, You want to take your mother down? Anthony nodded. Onyok, continued, You do it yourself!

Anthony was silent and looked desperate. Onyok said, You don't know how? What have they been teaching you in school? I tell you boy, stay away from school, it's poison! It's the system training you to work so you can earn them money! He then walked away, leaving Anthony on his own trying to figure out how to take his mother off that hook.

He first took a stool so she could rest her feet and the rest of her. He knew his brother was somewhere near hiding so he yelled, Jeremy help me! Jeremy came running. What do we do now? Anthony asked.

I don't know, replied Jeremy, still not having recovered from the shock. Then Necessity tried to say something, but it was all muffled with that cloth plugging her mouth.

Anthony said, I think she's trying to tell us what to do first...but I'm not so sure, I don't understand anything!

Jeremy replied, You're not sure? Then let's get that thing off her mouth first, idiot, so we may hear what she's trying to say!

Anthony said, It's too high up!

Jeremy replied, Then let's get some stick or something!

Anthony said, No, it will hurt her...wait, I think she's pointing at something! He looked at one corner, beside a box there was a big cutting knife. Then he understood that Necessity wanted them to untie her hands first. Anthony took the knife, tried to cut the rope that tied his mother's hands but it was too thick, it took some time, he and Jeremy took turns cutting it, slicing thru one fiber at a time. When her hands were finally free, Necessity was able to free herself in less than a minute. The three cuddled together, the boys at this time were wailing like newborns.

Necessity tried to comfort them, she said, Don't you worry boys, he'll get another hook on his butt!

6

*T*here were to be no more hooks on Onyok Ilaya's butt, fate would take care of him. In February 1986, there was a regime change in the country and a new order was to come. Those who used to employ Onyok Ilaya as a hitman dispersed for a while, but they were not to disappear, there was not to be much big change as regards dark practices in the land, again, just some manner of reformatting took place. The big change was the subjective feeling of more liberties.

Onyok Ilaya thought he could revive some of his old glory, so the first thing he did was to try to re-establish contact with his old gang. Most of them however, had changed significantly, some for the better, some for the worse. Most of those who abandoned the dark practices became overactive in church, some turned Born Again Christians. One of his trusted smuggling runners had moved to Manila to preach The Apocalypse in the streets. On the other hand, most of those who turned for the worse engaged in the more lucrative drug-trafficking. Smuggling was a little outdated, Onyok realized that it had to be smuggling in gargantuan scales in order to be worth the risk.

Blast fishing had already reached the national consciousness, and the coast guard had been trained and given the equipment to pursue and round-up those who engaged in the activity, the law had grown enough teeth by that time, blasts would pop up sporadically from time to time but only the most agile rogue fishermen did it. Onyok moved like a turtle that could not swim, so he had to forget about blast fishing for good.

He found himself in a rather awkward position trying to re-establish a smuggling kingdom in the new order. He was rather old and seemed to have lost command. But he was a little stubborn, he established a little imported liquor smuggling operation aiming to stretch it to a regional scale. It was to be short-lived.

In September 1986, while doing some transactions in the neighboring Negros Island, he crossed paths with James Juancho alias Boy Badlo. Badlo means phlegm, and by that name, everyone ought to fear him and keep distance, as legend said that he could spit out his phlegm to as far as five towns away, and if it hit you he would certainly find you, aided by the sinister powers of his wife who was believed to be practicing witchcraft. That was unlikely true. A more credible tale as to how he got his name was about him capable of producing copious amounts of phlegm and expectorate it just right up to his mouth and swallow it again, a warning to everyone that he could swallow just about anything and anyone. Boy Badlo's brother was a lawyer of a political lord in Luzon, Boy Badlo knew that Onyok The Grandson of God was the hitman who assassinated his brother during the Martial Law years. Boy Badlo had just been appointed commander of the private army of the same oligarch.

Onyok Ilaya's and Boy Badlo's gangs bumped into each other at a small port in the town of Escalante that fateful evening, neither group was prepared for action, everyone thought they'd leave their guns behind because they were all out for just a short walk to buy fishballs. Their eyes met, Boy Badlo immediately recognized The Grandson of God and was resolved to kill him, he only had a dagger with him and Onyok had only a much shorter butterfly knife and much shorter limbs. The other disadvantage for Onyok was that his group consisted only of Dodong and Totong who had only one arm each, while Boy Badlo had four thugs with him. It was four hands against ten.

The henchmen at first let their masters engage in a duel with their knives, Onyok had very poor vision and was much slower, and his big broad belly gave Boy Badlo more surface area to strike upon, the latter seemed to be stabbing at will unhindered. The weakening Onyok made one upward stroke with the knife, cutting Boy Badlo's chin. It was a scratch but he seemed to be bleeding profusely, and so the four henchmen, upon seeing their master wounded, drew their knives, they rushed and assaulted Onyok with as many stabs as they could. Dodong and Totong hesitated to attack, then two more thugs from Boy Badlo's group arrived, each had a handgun. Dodong and Totong fled the scene, abandoning The Grandson of God who was reduced to a mere carcass.

Necessity was widowed, though in reality it clearly was emancipation. Her face had a near-complete blank expression during Onyok Ilaya's funeral, and no one saw her cry, because in fact she never cried. Among his family, only his mother Theresa Ilaya and one sister were present. Juliana Natang and her two children did not show up, neither did anyone of the legions of women he had children with, nor did those children. There were however, a dozen of his former gang mates and henchmen, mainly the reformed ones who had become overly religious, as the non-reformed ones were either dead, in hiding, or behind bars.

Before they lowered Onyok Ilaya down his grave, the tambourine man and the guitar man played one last tune in his honor. It was the tune of The Carnival is Over. The tambourine man had a stroke many years earlier, his right facial muscles did not move, his left arm was paralyzed and he dragged his left foot when walking, and the guitar man was now as lean as the strings of his guitar, he incurred another long deep scar, this time running up his right cheek, like someone again had hit him with a pickax. Some wondered how and why, because he had reformed in the past fifteen years and started playing at church, so it must not be from those gang wars, they thought it must have been done by someone who had had enough of hearing him playing his guitar. He played a little better, to be fair, but still in the miserable level, but at least this time people knew what he was playing.

There were to be no vocals for the tune as their erstwhile lead vocalist was being lowered six feet under, but on the very last stretch of the tune, the guitar man burst into singing the last line of the song in a way only he and Onyok Ilaya could enunciate, and he erroneously, though rather appropriately, uttered Cannibal instead of Carnival.

Necessity did not wear black in the following days and weeks, contrary to custom. It was her silent message. The first thing she did after her next pay was to fix the shack in which they lived, she turned it into a cozy wooden hut and painted it blue.

*I*t was going quite well for Anthony in his new school in Burog, in spite of him going to school hungry most of the time. In mathematics, science, and the languages, he was placed at the section of the fastest learners. At Santa Helena he barely made it to the top ten in his class, while in Burog he became the biggest threat to the girl on the top spot.

One day on his way home, someone came out of the hibiscus bush by the roadside and grabbed his left elbow. It was Bryan Balbago, the biggest boy in the fourth grade, also the richest, at least he thought so himself as he always announced it, and the dumbest, of which he did not have the slightest idea. It was only in mathematics and the languages that students were placed into sections according to their pace of learning, in social studies, home economics, art and physical education, Anthony the contender for the brightest and Bryan the undisputed dumbest were classmates.

Bryan made a firm grip on Anthony's left elbow, making him grimace. Bryan said, If you don't do what I tell you I will break your arm and you wouldn't be able to write again!

Anthony, still grimacing in pain, replied, It's not possible, Bry I can't do it! It would be a lot easier for you to study and come up with the answers yourself!

Bryan sported an ominous look and in a threatening tone syllable per syllable he said, I do not need to study do you understand? My daddy can buy the entire school if he wants to, even the entire town!

Anthony was left-handed, and what Bryan wanted him to do was to start writing with his right hand. They were to have an exam in civics later that week, Bryan was seated to the left next to Anthony, and because Anthony was left-handed, his hand and arm blocked Bryan's view of his paper, and thereby, his answers. Anthony then said, Why don't you then ask your daddy to buy the seat to my right? Wouldn't that be easier?

Bryan replied, I'll tell you what's easier, I'll just break your left arm!

Then I would not be able to write any answers for you to copy, said Anthony.

Bryan said, That'll serve you right! Then we'll both fail, and I think it will hit you harder, ha-ha!

Anthony said, That will hit you hard too, I heard you will be transferring to Santa Helena next year!

Bryan released Anthony's elbow, raised his chin and motioned like dusting off his left shoulder and said, That's right, because my father can afford ten times the tuition, unlike your mother, a failed American girl who can't even afford the bus fare to the city!

Anthony had grown numb about his mother being insulted, he maintained an imperturbable poise. He just warned Bryan, he said, You know, you've got to work on your study habits to survive Santa Helena!

Says who? Bryan said deridingly. A boy who did not survive the tuition fees? Ha-ha! My Daddy can buy everything, I can survive anywhere!

Anthony replied, I'm warning you, it's the last place on earth where you can buy a passing grade!

I don't think so, replied Bryan. You just don't know how money works because you have been destitute all your life!

Bryan's family was the newest money in town. His father, Geronimo Balbago, used to be a crew member of a small local cargo ship which looked like it would sink if it collided with a jellyfish, and his mother Leonora Balbago had a stall at the Burog Central Market selling native finger food, so the family had been hard-up for a while. Geronimo Balbago however, was an industrious man, he studied further at night and on weekends and went on leave for several terms to complete schooling while his family was battling starvation, and soon he gained enough maritime credits for the highest post. He went overseas in 1985 and by 1988 he was already captain of an international oil tanker, he had enough money to raise twenty kids in Burog and he had only one.

A mansion rose in the middle of town, two chauffeured brand new cars were parked there, high walls were built around it but no matter how high it was, children in the streets managed to climb and perch at the top of the wall to have a view of the pool by the backyard, they ogled at the pool for hours with their jaws hanging low, only dispersing when one of the maids or the gardener shooed them away.

Bryan did not know how to behave with all that money. The first thing he did was to stop calling his father with the local word Tatay, and started to call him Daddy instead, and he called his mother Mommy instead of Nanay. He did not know how housemaids were to function, he treated them as objects at his beck and call, and three of them had resigned within their first month of employment because of him, despite the decent pay. He began to understand less and less why he had to go to school or make any tiny effort to achieve anything he wanted when his Daddy could afford anything ten times, or at least he thought so.

He was to transfer the following year, for the fifth grade, to Santa Helena Catholic Academy, and he liked the idea, not because he liked school, but it was a general belief in town that only the rich went there. He was to be accepted on probation for it appeared he could barely score thirty points below the passing mark on the entrance tests, and the school had the highest standards in the city. But the Jesuits wanted to give anyone who wanted to try a fair chance to prove themselves on the actual academic battlefield, thus the few admittance on probation. Those who could not live up to the standards would be shown the exit gate.

Sorrow struck again in November 1988. Alicia Berano died in her sleep, she was 68 and had retired just the year before. Necessity wept openly this time, she and her mother had somewhat drifted apart since her tragic marriage to Onyok Ilaya. Mother and daughter did not talk to each other much since that. The last time Necessity really talked to her mother was in April that year, on the former's birthday.

Alicia told her, I wish you had been happier...

Necessity answered, And I wish I had made you prouder. Deep inside though she wanted to say, I wish I had listened to you and talked to you more all these years. Necessity wanted to wear black for one whole year, but her new employment the following month would compel her to wear blue.

Even long before Onyok Ilaya died, Alicia had regularly sent part of her income, and later on, of her pension to Necessity to help the family get by. Now with Alicia dead, Necessity had to find some more means of income. She had heard that the pay for housemaids at the Balbago Mansion was rather hefty, two thousand pesos a month was more than twice a maid's salary at that time, and she would not need to sell fish in the morning nor peddle at the bus stations.

Another maid had just resigned because of Bryan, and they were looking for a replacement. The matron of the house, sticky rice vendor turned oil tanker captain's housewife Mrs. Leonora Balbago could not hide the triumph in her eyes when one morning, The American Girl showed up to apply. It felt like a satisfaction of a lifetime. Necessity got the job already in the middle of the short interview.

Leonora was kind to Necessity though. Necessity did not have cooking duties except when Leonora wanted pochero - a stew of pork, banana and pak-choi leaves. Leonora thought Necessity made the best pochero she had ever tasted.

Necessity was to receive five hundred pesos more every month if she agreed to be Bryan's English tutor. She accepted the offer though she was certain that such an assignment would end up in failure, as well as torture, that was, for the tutor.

An important condition for employment was that she had to be a stay-in maid, Leonora cited hygienic reasons, she believed the maids would bring in the hoi- polloi bacterial flora if they went home everyday. All of the four maids were from the town, so they could all go home in turns every other weekend. Another requirement was that they had to be in blue and white uniform, with skirts way below the knees, especially for the younger ones and especially when the captain was home.

Anthony begged his mother saying, Please, Mama don't take the job, Bryan has been giving me hell, I don't know how worse-than-hell would feel like, it's not just for my sake, it's for yours too, I warn you, he is not a human being!

Necessity answered, Four more months, my son, four more months and he'll transfer to Santa Helena, he'll be out of your life forever!

Not from yours! Anthony replied.

Well, he'll be away most of the time, his father will rent an apartment room for him and his aunt will be his special nanny, said Necessity.

Anthony shook his head, smiled sarcastically and said, I assure you, he wouldn't last a week at Santa Helena, he is due three years with regard to his mastery of the multiplication table, try asking him what three times five is, see if he can answer!

I will, said Necessity.

Please don't, said Anthony. His reply would not be fifteen, it would be a hard slap on your cheek!

Necessity replied, No it wouldn't happen, I'll just be his English tutor, not math...

Early in December, Necessity took the post at the mansion. She put away her black dress and vested herself with the blue-white one, though she was still mourning deeply. Jeremy and Anthony had to fend for themselves on a daily basis at home, and since Jeremy barely had the will and energy to get a glass of water for himself, Anthony had to do almost all of the chores, cooking and doing the laundry especially. He'd get a fist on his mouth, cheek, jaw and anywhere possible from his big brother if the latter did not like the food, but like his mother towards his father before, he fought back, the stingray's tail having been entrusted to him by his mother.

The day after Necessity started her maid duties, Anthony got a hard slap on his back with a hardbound book as he walked past the gate at school, so hard it would have made him throw up his breakfast. Fortunately though, as usual, he did not have any breakfast. Without needing to look, he knew who it was. Carry my books! A voice said. It was the more than familiar voice of Bryan Balbago.

Anthony asked, What's the matter? Have they gone too heavy from disuse?

Bryan replied, Well, well, what a bold remark from a son of a slave! Well, your mother scrubs my toilet seat, and last night at midnight I woke her up to make me my ham and egg sandwich, and guess what? I slapped her face with the sandwich because it tasted like sewage! Now tell me, why would her son refuse my orders today?

Anthony was already clenching his right fist and was poised to knock Bryan down with one punch, but then he recalled the story told to him by his grandmother Alicia, the incident that ended school forever for his father. He just took a deep breath and replied, Well, because it was not included in my mother's contract, that the duties she was paid for would be passed down to her sons!

Bryan yelled, It is not about contracts and salaries, you putchong! It's about class order in society! Then he boldly announced to all students passing by, Hey look everyone, I'm talking to the son of our slave, can you believe that? His mother scrubbed my toilet seat today! Then he turned to Anthony and said, And that wouldn't be all, you little slave, you'll have to buy my snacks at the canteen, I can give you a tip if you're fast, and you'll do all of my homework! Now first, my books! He slammed all of his five books on the ground in front of Anthony and walked away.

Anthony left the books where they were, it rained hard and the books got soaked, all the pages were beyond salvaging. Bryan however, almost totally forgot about the books, if he was to rank all the tangible things on earth in order of importance, books would surely be at the bottom of his list, or would not be on the list at all. Anthony refused to buy his snacks and do his homework for him. The next day when Anthony refused again, Bryan gave him an upper cut. The cut on his chin required three stitches at the local public clinic, and Leonora paid Necessity three hundred pesos to keep the peace. The incident happened outside school and eluded school authorities, such a record would have been a death blow to his chances at Santa Helena.

One Sunday in January, Leonora invited the town mayor and his wife and several of the old rich in town for lunch at her mansion. She'd longed to show them her place for some approval and acceptance to their league. Still, she was too new a money in their eyes, though they never said it. Apparently, she would need three lifetimes more with such wealth to refine her ways and be one of them. She belched during the meal, made slurping sounds with the soup, and tied the silk serviette around her neck instead of placing it on her lap. She served a few bottles of the finest Bordeaux wine which her husband had brought from abroad, but in her glass she mixed it with orange soda and ice.

The worst part was when her son Bryan showed up, he began eating at the table even before the guests were called to the dining room, and he greeted no one when they came. The sight of him made them think the family needed three lifetimes each with double the wealth to be one of them.

Necessity's pochero was among those served, and the guests agreed it was among the best. She was summoned by Leonora to the dining room so she could hear the adulation from the guests. Right after Necessity thanked them, Bryan interrupted, he said, Be watchful of your pockets, though, she is so needy she can snatch anything valuable within her reach!

As soon as the guests had gone home, Leonora dragged Bryan to the kitchen and in front of Necessity and the other maids, she gave him two big slaps, one on each cheek. Then she dragged him again to the laundry room, made him kneel and placed one thick, large Bible on his left hand, and an even thicker, larger Oxford Dictionary on his right. She ordered him to say, Sorry, Necessity I will not do it again, one thousand times. Necessity was there, right in front of him, about to begin her ironing task. She was crying. She had a hill of clothes to iron but was done even before Bryan could reach his 500th apology. He was there the whole evening but was actually never remorseful.

During breakfast the following week, he poured hot milk on Necessity's legs and claimed in the name of all the Saints and Martyrs that it was an accident. One morning a couple of weeks later, again while he was having breakfast, he threw an apple to Necessity who was seated at the opposite end of the table preparing his sandwiches for school, he aimed to hit her on the nose, but she was quick, she used to be a softball catcher in school and she was used to having all kinds of things thrown at her during her nineteen year-long marriage, and she caught most of them, about nine times out of ten, before they hit her. She caught the apple too this time, with her quick right hand. It stunned Bryan.

How Necessity wanted to throw it back, she saw Onyok Ilaya's face in Bryan, she used to throw back things thrown at her immediately after catching them, and most of the time, also about nine times out of ten, it hit Onyok Ilaya on the forehead or the nose. Then she reminded herself that Bryan was just a child, and that someday he would grow up and the woman he'd marry would certainly do the job.

March 1989 came and the plague of Bryan ended for Anthony, but Necessity had to endure one summer break more, and worse, he was home all day everyday. One day, Bryan went hysterical, he could not find the multiple-game cartridge of his Nintendo Family Computer, he stormed inside the maids' quarters where Necessity was having her siesta. Bryan yelled, Give it back! Give it back you thief!

It took a few seconds for Necessity to get oriented after being jolted from sleep. Finally realizing the situation, she opted to remain quiet. She knew the boy was impossible to deal with, let alone when screaming.

Bryan went on screaming, You wife of a thief, you thief yourself! You raised your boys feeding them stolen food!

Another maid named Teteng entered and interrupted him, What's the matter Bryan? What is it that's missing!?

Bryan answered, My new Family Computer cartridge! She stole it, I know she did!

What makes you so sure? asked Teteng.

Bryan replied, Because she's a wife of a thief! Are you dumb or what?

Teteng said, Don't accuse people without any proof, you'll get yourself into trouble!

Bryan was defiant, he said, I can accuse anyone as I please! My Daddy can buy me out of trouble ten times!

Necessity then thought it was time to speak, she said, And what would I do with that cartridge? All I have at home is a transistor radio, does it work on a transistor radio?

Bryan said, of course not! Are you dumb? Don't you know what a Family Computer is?

Teteng said, There, she surely wouldn't steal something she doesn't know anything about, and I know this woman, Bryan, she's not the kind!

Bryan said, The kind that would marry a thief! I know what she did, she sold that cartridge and used the money to buy tons of ice cream for that starving bookworm son of his, I saw him yesterday down the street eating ice cream! There! There's my proof!

Rage was gathering inside Necessity, she thought she had to walk out of the room, she did not trust herself much on what she could do to the boy if her limits were breached. She walked fast outside thru the yard, she wanted to bring the matter to Leonora who unfortunately was out somewhere in town.

Bryan pursued Necessity, he was by this time carrying a long, hard lead pipe. When he was near enough he tried to strike her, but she caught the end of the pipe with her left hand and snatched it away from him. Crying silently out of rage and hurt, she looked at him straight in the eyes and bent the pipe until it became a complete U. She showed the boy what a battered wife of a fisherman-thief could do.

He became quiet after that, and as he walked back to the house he felt something hard in the lower pocket of his walking shorts, he pulled it out, it was the cartridge. Mystery solved. Necessity thought of quitting that day, but then she took some time and sat by the lovely rose garden, and thought of her boys. She changed her mind. She was to remain in the household for the next six years.

Anthony was wrong about Bryan at Santa Helena, he survived more than a week in fifth grade there. The school had to drop him though after the first quarter term, that was, after about two and a half months. He flunked every single quiz, he could not speak a clean line of English and still wasn't able to master the multiplication table, something which was expected of a second grader. There he met a lot of richer kids, and he so was unable to find any break to brag. Whenever he tried to be mean, his classmates knew how to shut him up effectively - they talked to him in English.

Necessity was right about him, he was not to go back to the public school in Burog either. He hopped from one private school to another, staying five months the most in a school. He repeated both the fifth and the six grades and he was 15 when he started high-school, two years older than the regulars, and by then he was already on drugs.

To avoid shame, his parents sent him far away to a juvenile rehabilitation center in Mindanao in 1993, and then he very seldom came home for short visits, usually only on Christmas and Easter holidays, making life in the household more bearable for Necessity for most of the year. When he was home he was not much of a pain either, he seemed not to see people and did not talk to them. Most of the time he would stare at either the ceiling or the wall, for some reasons he avoided looking down the floor.

There was a visible crack on the wall above the back kitchen door of the mansion caused by a minor earthquake, and it became his best friend. He talked to it, sometimes they seemed to fight, sometimes they seemed to make up and talk about lighter matters. He'd talk about his concerns and hopes to the crack, naturally no one else could hear the crack talk back, apparently it just listened, like a real friend should.

8

*I*n March 1991, Anthony graduated from elementary
school as class salutatorian. He and the valedictorian
Brenda Lee Balugo had exactly the same general weighted
average, but Brenda Lee had the edge and got the top spot
because her extra-curricular activities earned her more honors
points. She was in every school play, she played the role of the
deranged Sisa in Jose Rizal's Noli Me Tangere, as The Witch
Stepmother in Snow White and again, as the witch in Hansel
and Gretel. She was also in the cheerleader squad, she actually
was to be rejected upon audition because she danced like the
Robot of 1984, but her mother came begging and crying for her
to have a spot. She sang whenever there was an occasion to
sing, even those songs composed for or by the government,
like those of the health and social welfare departments which
no one else wanted to sing, because they sounded like
government guidelines which someone placed notes on.

Anthony on the other hand, had to run more than a couple
of miles home every afternoon after school to prepare dinner
for him and Jeremy, if there was anything to cook. On
weekends he'd do the laundry. He wouldn't have managed it

in the long run if not for the angel on their shoulders - Sese, Necessity's maid of honor during her tragic wedding.

Sese had a modest income as an office errand lady at the town hall, a job she had held since graduating from high school. Her job was mostly to carry papers from one room to another when she was told to, to prepare coffee for the town council and other employees, to clean when the janitor was sick, and to dance hoe-downs during Christmas and halloween parties. For some years the town hall made her Santa Claus for the Christmas week celebrations. She went to The Blue Cottage every other weekend when Necessity wasn't home, she'd check on the boys and sometimes she'd give them a little pocket money. She loved Necessity that much.

Her real name was Rowena, and people did not start calling her Sese until the first grade. She and Necessity were seat mates, Necessity was smart and articulate while Sese had severe stammering problems, making her lose confidence in recitations because it made the entire class, except for Necessity and a few others, roar and roll in laughter. It also made her lose confidence in reading, writing and arithmetic, but Necessity knew that she was not dumb, so she helped her in every way, they'd do homework together, she read to her and assisted her in writing. Sese however, got too dependent and wouldn't go a couple of feet away from Necessity at school. Everyday on her way to school she'd make an unnecessary detour to the Berano house just to see if Necessity was going to school, because if the latter was sick or had other reasons to stay at home, she wouldn't go to school either.

The heaviest challenge for Sese was Necessity's name. She had stammering problems and her parents could not afford a speech therapist, so she'd say her best friend's name, Necesesesesesesesese, to everyone's amusement. Because of that she became known as Sese. Necessity protested and was for a time, the only one calling her Rowena.

Teachers thought that it was not getting academically healthy for Sese to be that dependent on Necessity, and her parents agreed, so in the last quarter of the school year they transferred Sese to another section. Both girls were devastated, Sese did not eat for days and was often not in school after that. She was retained in the first grade while Necessity moved on, which was not such a bad thing because with Necessity one year ahead, she could help her with her homework a couple of nights a week, while she learned to stand on her own during the day.

Years went by, Sese gained confidence and was able to fend for herself in school, she and Necessity slowly drifted apart but they thought of each other much, sending each other homemade Christmas and birthday cards and the like. After a few years it became convenient for everyone to call her Sese - her parents, teachers, Necessity, and eventually, she herself. Nobody knew a Rowena at the town hall.

Sese called Necessity Seng, with ease. It was actually Necessity's own suggestion way back in first grade because she noticed she'd stutter less with a single syllable.

On a rainy day in August 1994, Sese came running and then knocked loudly at the steel gates of The Balbago Mansion. When she saw Necessity approaching to open the gate, she called to her and began to stammer, Sesesesese-sesesesese-sesesaseng! She was too excited to say anything else, Necessity could tell. She let her in, she had been a familiar visiting face in the house and Leonora did not mind.

Sese had improved a lot with her stammering since childhood, but when she was too excited or too angry, it recurred. All she could say at that moment was either Sesesesesesng or Sasasasasa. Necessity wondered what Sasasa was all about. She knew what could calm down her friend - a warm ginger tea with a little sugar. She also had to lend her a towel because she was all soaked after running in the rain all the way from the town hall. She led her to the kitchen, they sat by the marble kitchen island to talk.

When Sese had settled down she began to speak, Seseseseng! Sasasalva Recruitment Agency! As soon as she was able to say the word Salva completely, she was able to talk with minimal stammering.

She pulled out a brochure with a big caption Salva Recruitment Agency, on the front page was a picture of women who looked like models and celebrities, all dressed in maid's uniforms looking happy, one was holding a mop, one was carrying a kid who looked like Korean, all looked very happy, smiling with their mouths open wide like saying, Whaa and at the same time showing their teeth.

Sese went on saying, A group was at the town hall today distributing this, read it, read it! It says only three years of experience as housemaid and a recommendation from an employer! Ages nineteen to fifty five! And it's thirty thousand pesos a month net pay, Seng, you'll earn more than a high school principal! They're recruiting only five thousand maids from all over the country so you have to hurry up, but with a Balbago signature on the letter of recommendation you're a shoo-in!

Necessity was going thru the three-page brochure and was half-listening to Sese. She was trying to find the information on the greatest obstacle - the fees. She sighed and said, The registration and orientation fees together is one thousand pesos. That's about half my monthly salary!

Sese immediately replied, I can lend you five hundred!

Necessity said, Thank you, but the fees in total is fifty thousand, where will I get that kind of money? That's about my salary for two years, I can raise it in two years if I don't buy a single grain of rice, and the fees are due in three months!

Sese was silent for a while, pondering. Then she said, What was that line in English you used to tell me... God will preside?

God will provide, said Necessity, correcting her friend.

Sese said, Look Seng, we'll find the money somewhere, just two months after your employment you'll be able to pay all of it! You are the best on this job, you're the only one the Balbagos have wanted to keep all these years!

Necessity smiled a bit and said, I'm not sure, I'll think about it.

Sese was excitedly beating the table with the tip of her fingers like playing the drums, she said, Take this chance Seng, this is South Korea, South Korea!!! She then paused a little and asked, Where is that near by the way?

Necessity replied, Near Japan, up north.

Sese rose and exclaimed, Yes! Near Japan!

Do you know someone in Japan? Necessity asked.

Sese replied, No, but it's near Japan, it's somewhere far, all these years they've been laughing behind your back, The American Girl who went nowhere, now it's your time to strike back, The American Girl is going near Japan!

Necessity laughed a little, and said, Why not just say South Korea?

Sese, replied, Because like me they don't know where it is!

They both laughed, Sese gave her a tight hug and said, Oh Seng, please don't forget me when you're in Korea, think of all our good times together!

Necessity this time broke into real laughter, she said, What are you talking about? I haven't even gone past the second page of the brochure!

Necessity was awake the whole night, she did not think about the money much, but about her boys. Anthony was graduating from high school, he was to end up first honorable mention this time, high school demanded more time to study and he had taken odd jobs with the butcher at the market in the evenings and on weekends he brokered and sold fish. He was alright as a teenager, he had his temper and had occasional fights with his mother but he was no big heartache to her. He was planning to take computer engineering at the Western Institute of Technology in the city, it was not as expensive as other schools but still it was a private one.

Necessity was able to save roughly ten thousand pesos in the past two years, enough for Anthony to get thru three months in college, then after that she actually really didn't know what would happen.

It was not going well for Jeremy though. He had just finished high school in March, two years behind the regulars. In his senior year in high school in 1991 there was a drug bust in the village, and he was implicated. Because he was a minor he was sent to a juvenile facility called St. George Town in the outskirts of Iloilo City, he stayed there for eighteen months. The older members of his group got harder sentences, no less than ten years, and the leader Dodong Botas got life imprisonment.

Jeremy was not at all planning to go to college, he simply did not want to, but blamed his mother whenever he could for not being able to afford it. Strangely, he was among those who referred to Necessity as The American Girl Who Went Nowhere, and even added a phrase - who could afford no college tuition for her sons.

Every 15th and end of the month he was seen outside The Balbago Mansion, because those were Necessity's paydays, and he was there for his share. He'd take odd jobs like draining private septic tanks or assisting carpenters, only when he wanted to, which was not every month. He was seen most of the time at the corner of the public market where they had Nintendo and Sega video games, some of his money went there, and he played for hours with other boys several years younger than he was. Some of his money went to small-time gambling like tumbo, wherein a coin was tossed and players would bet head or crown. Before dusk he'd join other unemployed men almost twice his age drinking cheap local rum until almost midnight. He would then walk home drunk, in most instances he was not able to find The Blue Cottage.

Every single day, Necessity thought about what would happen to Anthony after three months in college, now it seemed she had the answer, and it came at the right time, she thought Sese might have actually been right, God actually did preside. Now she was about to see if He would provide.

She called the number of Salva Recruitment Agency the next day, the man who answered sounded very friendly and eager to help. She was relieved and encouraged upon hearing that they would accept payment in installment within six months, as long as half was paid by October, a month after the applicant had received a notice that she'd been picked.

Necessity talked to Leonora about this and the matron of the mansion cried. For the first time in six years she asked for the recipe of her pochero, so she could train someone to cook it in Necessity's place. Necessity for her part laughed a little, saying nothing was yet certain. Leonora reluctantly agreed to let her go if she was picked, but she understood her situation, especially with Anthony going to college.

The following week, Necessity took the bus to the city. She was to go to a certain room at the Iloilo City Public Market where the recruitment orientation was to be held. It took time to find the place, she had to go thru a labyrinth of vegetable, meat and fish stalls thru damp, muddy floors and the place was so loud, people there had gotten used to screaming at each other when talking even when not necessary.

No one could help her find her way, she had to look for that room number 62 and she could see no room, just stalls. She decided it was best to follow stall numbers then, and she was right. She came to stall number 62, it looked like one of the stalls but it had been recently emptied, and blue, decaying wooden chairs and green plastic ones were in place. The chairs resembled those in nearby stalls which served street food and batchoy, it did not look impressive. There were big posters on the crumbling carton walls of that so called room, they were identical to the front page of the brochure, so Necessity was certain she was in the right place.

The room was almost full, the session was to start in about twenty minutes. There were still a few women lining up to register. A man was seated by a small rusty iron bar table, there was a sign that read Register Here. She was given a registration form, she paid a thousand pesos and took one of the remaining seats. There were nearly fifty of them seated when the session started, about a dozen more came later and had to stand.

The speaker was a lean lady in her thirties, she was not so pleasant, it appeared like the heat was weighing her down, and she smoked cigarettes. From time to time she'd turn her back on the audience to spit on the floor. The room was like a furnace, there were two fans which blowed even hotter air. They had a microphone connected to an old karaoke stereo, still it was barely enough to drown the noise of the market.

The talk started, the lady introduced herself as Anette, formerly a domestic helper herself in Seoul, and now works in the recruiting agency. She talked mostly about South Korea, where it was, how it looked like, where to go on your free time. She talked about how pleasant the households were there, and how nicely the domestic helpers were treated.

In the middle of her speech, the man who was at the registration table started to distribute snacks, it was something that resembled a hamburger, as was the thought actually. It was miserable, the buns were crumbly and the patty was almost round and hard as cooled volcanic rock, the inner bottom of the bun had a few strokes of banana ketchup and mayonnaise. All were starving though, and did their best to eat it up. Now the speaker had to compete with the noise of the market and the sound from her audience eating the hamburger-looking snack, which was like that of volcanic stones being crushed by a nutcracker. Lemon-lime soda was served, the contents were poured in small transparent plastic freezer bags and they had to drink it with a plastic straw.

Two ladies who introduced themselves as current domestic helpers on their annual vacation also talked for about ten minutes each, they gave testimony about the wonderful work conditions and the efficiency of the recruiting agency. Then it

115

was time for questions and Annete said she'd only entertain three.

The first lady who asked wasted the question slot by asking how it felt like inside a Boeing 747. Annette seemed to like the question and answered thoroughly, sharing a lot of known pilot and flight attendant jokes.

The next applicant asked about the payment which was already stated on the brochure. The third and the last question slot was again wasted by another lady who asked if it snowed in South Korea.

What Necessity wanted to know was the selection process. They were to pick only five thousand among the countless applicants all over the land. In Iloilo alone there were about over sixty applicants in one orientation session alone and there were to be twenty such sessions. She wondered what the criteria were, as the registration forms only asked for name, address, telephone, signature and experience. There were to be no interviews. There was also a small space to describe oneself.

Must be the recommendation letter, she thought, she hoped that Leonora's description of her being loyal, able to speak good English and cook her favorite stew was enough. She did her best to describe herself on that little space provided, she hoped that the other applicants would boost her chances by writing mainly about their excitement in boarding a Boeing 747 and playing in the snow.

Before they were dismissed, Annette announced something that may have answered Necessity's question partly. She said that when they received notice that they had been picked, they should forward the money in cash as soon as possible, because they took into consideration those who could pay in full, and might give the slots to those who may be put on the waiting list but could pay duly. Then she said they had to pay fifty pesos for that volcanic rock burger and the drinks in the plastic freezer bags.

Everyone went silent in disbelief, everybody thought the same, it couldn't cost more than five pesos at that time for the drinks, and one ought to be paid to eat that pseudo-burger. Then Annette said that if they could not pay for the snacks it would be added to their fees later, but she warned, If you cannot pay for a snack we might not be able to trust you to pay the fee which is a thousand times bigger!

There were about ten who could really not pay. Necessity took a look inside her wallet, if she paid she wouldn't be able to pay the fare back to Burog that day, but then she thought if she did not pay she would not be going anywhere. So she paid, and walked about half a mile to the house of her brother Percivale to borrow money for the bus fare.

Her contemporaries in town who knew her sprang back to life again and talked. The American Girl who was to have her desk at the Empire State Building was going to scrub South Korean toilet seats, promoted from The Balbago Mansion.

Jeremy seemed to have changed overnight. He usually refused to talk to his mother and was embarrassed of her in public. This time he was very nice, he volunteered to cook dinner when she was home the following weekend. It was chicken adobo, he had never cooked his entire life, not even a hard boiled egg so the adobo was far away from being edible. Necessity appreciated the thought though, and loved the way he kissed her forehead. How it touched her, he'd never kissed her since he was 10. Anthony was at the other end of the table, rolling his eyeballs, still nauseated from the chicken adobo, he knew why Jeremy apparently reformed overnight. Necessity gave him a wink, like telling him to let his brother be.

In the third week of September, she received a call at the Balbago mansion that she had been selected. She cried tears of joy. She had gathered enough funds, she had ten thousand pesos from her savings supposedly for Anthony the following year, Leonora lent her another ten thousand, and she borrowed five thousand from a local lender in town with ten percent monthly interest. That was half the fee, she was to pay the rest as soon as she got her salary in South Korea. She went to Iloilo City again after three days to that same place at the central market and paid in cash, and she got a receipt. The fees would cover plane fares and she was to retrieve the tickets on the third of November, she was to fly to Manila on the fifteenth and then to Seoul on the sixteenth.

She was given a little notice of employment, and two copies of a five-page employment contract which she signed, she kept one of the copies. She was to work at a certain Jong Woo household, to take care of two toddlers and do household work. They took her picture too, they said they would process her passport and that it would be ready by the time she claimed her tickets.

Sese was hysterical, in a jubilant way. She was so happy she went stammering for days. She volunteered to have the farewell party at her home two days before Necessity was scheduled to leave. She had a modest wooden house near Burog Central School which belonged to her maternal grandparents. Her husband was a regular employee at the health department so they had enough dough to keep the place. Leonora agreed to keep Necessity until a week before her scheduled departure, so she could earn a little more for pocket money.

Necessity started packing. She started her tours to a few old friends' houses to say goodbye. She visited her brother Percivale in the city and had dinner with his family. She called her brother Arthur who was in then in Pasig, part of Metro Manila, she was to stay at his place overnight before flying to Seoul. Lancelot was a scout ranger in Mindanao and could not be reached, so she wrote him a letter.

On her free time she'd walk around the town plaza, she thought of the bond she had with her town and how painful it was to part. She thought of what might have happened if Onyok Ilaya did not come to town on that hot summer day of 1967, how different her relationship with her town would have been. She wasn't sure which was it that would fuel their contempt towards her grandfather's dreams - her failure or her success. She had a feeling of deep attachment to her townsfolk, no matter what, and that was why she never left even during those lowest and most shameful years. Now she thought of her boys, a hometown ought not too difficult to drop for their sake, nothing ought too difficult to drop for them.

The boys reacted differently. Jeremy became overly sweet while Anthony talked less and less to his mother. This bothered Necessity and in late October, she confronted him at home while they were eating supper. She said, Tell me, what is it? Now don't tell me it's nothing because I know it's not nothing!

Anthony stopped chewing his food, his eyes swelled with tears, he appeared to force to swallow what he'd partly chewed, drank a little water, and finally spoke, You know, I can support myself thru college, I can work and wait a year or two, you don't have to go!

Necessity tried to talk without any emotion, the best she could. She said, Tell me then how are you going to support yourself, tell me in details...

He replied, Well, McDonald's is opening in the city, I can work there while I study. Jimmy Batong studies maritime and works at Dunkin Donuts, I can do it!

Necessity said, His aunt pays for his tuition, I heard. His aunt is a doctor. Who's going to pay for yours? Your mother is a housemaid. Tell me more please.

Anthony was silent, he thought hard then said as he started to cry, I don't know, I can't give the details, but you know me, Mama, I always find a way!

Necessity put her right hand over his and said, I have found a way, and I can give you details on how I can put you thru college, and even Jeremy. As soon as you can stand on your own after college I'll be home for good. It's four or five years, it will go fast!

Anthony was, by this time, crying loudly, he said, I can stand on my own, so don't go!

Necessity also cried a little, she said, Think of this, you'll have comfort, it won't be much luxury but comfort, something you didn't have your whole childhood, something I failed to give you, just give me this chance...

Anthony replied, I'm not comfortable with comfort, perhaps I was born not to seek it because it won't make me into anything! Look at Jeremy, he seeks it too much, it has destroyed him! If you send him money and make him comfortable he will just be the next Onyok Ilaya!

Necessity said, Don't speak of your brother that way, he is just a scarred boy! She paused, sighed, and continued, Oh then, so are you, but you know, we all get wounded and we react so differently, we choose different paths in finding our way out of pain!

Just then Jeremy came home, his breath smelled of alcohol, but he did not appear too drunk. He was half-dancing, he was holding a portable CD player and had head headphones over his ears, it was pitch dark outside but he had aviator sunglasses on. He greeted his mother with a kiss on the forehead and gave his brother a pat on the shoulder. Anthony shrugged. Jeremy said in a rather unnatural festive mood, Good evening, so what's for dinner?

Anthony replied dryly, I think you can see what's on the table!

Oh, tuloy, Mama, it's my favorite! said Jeremy, quite exaggerating as he feigned delight.

Anthony said in a clearly inimical tone, You hated it all your life!

Jeremy replied, As much as I hate you, but I love it now, who knows, I might love you tomorrow too, so don't despair, little prince!

Where did you get that thing? Necessity asked, pointing at his CD player.

It was Anthony who replied, It's a Sony portable CD player, Mama, it's new, it must cost at least three thousand pesos!

Jeremy shifted to a serious, annoyed tone, he said, I borrowed it from a friend, I'll return it next week!

Anthony asked, Which friend? I thought all your friends were out of jobs and could not pay for a daily bottle of rum?

Why, do you want a list of all my friends little prince? Jeremy asked, clearly getting more defensive.

Anthony looked down under the table and said, And wow, look, brand new Nike Air shoes! Are you friends with some PBA player and you talked him to lending you a pair of those?

Jeremy was silent for a few seconds, then he said angrily, You know, I've always longed to have a good pair of shoes to wear when I kick your mouth, I think the time has come!

Necessity interrupted, she said, Quiet! Tell me, Jeremy, where did you get them? Don't tell me you stole...

Jeremy raised his voice, Of course not Mama! I borrowed them! What's wrong with you both? Can I not have something nice for myself? He headed for the door, before he walked out he said, That's the problem with us having been destitute all our lives, we don't think we deserve nice things!

Necessity visited her parents' grave on November the 1st and bade them a long emotional farewell. November the 3rd came, it was rainy, Necessity travelled to Iloilo City to the Central Market to retrieve her tickets, she had with her a big synthetic leather bag to keep the tickets and the documents from getting soaked. She arrived before lunch as she was told to.

The market was even noisier than usual but in a different manner. People were curiously staring at one corner to listen to a commotion, there was a sizable crowd. Necessity thought there was a brawl going on, as there were policemen on the scene. As she was getting near stall number 62, she could hear more and more hysterical voices, then quite familiar faces, there were too many people so she couldn't get thru. There were a couple of men in white long sleeve shirts and ties who looked like politicians, and they were being interviewed by some members of the press. She pushed her way thru the crowd, until stall number 62 was in sight. It had turned into a dried fish store. Then she could clearly hear what the men in white shirt were talking about, they appealed for calm, some of the women who were going hysterical were difficult to console, they had to be restrained.

Necessity then understood what was going on and almost went hysterical herself. The Salva Recruitment Agency was a scam, it appeared that all who applied were given notice that they had been selected, and were made to pay in cash. They operated in Bacolod too and now they were at large and the authorities promised to pursue them, but could not promise money-back.

It was in the news, the entire region knew about it by nightfall. Necessity was still in shock and could not fathom how it could happen. The news reached town, needless to say, the townsfolk talked, especially her detractors. There were two other women from Burog among the victims, but Necessity was a special case, she was The American Girl and they had been following her story in the last four decades.

She slept at The Balbago Mansion that night, or at least tried to sleep. It then came to her, no wonder why the process was too short, there were no medical check-ups, no interviews, and the vague criteria for selection, and why they did not have a decent venue for the orientation and that volcanic rock burger that costed more than two decent meals. Many things. She felt so stupid.

She could not function the next day so Leonora gave her a three-day leave. They were to discuss later on how she could pay back the money she owed. She went home to The Blue Cottage the following morning, Sese came to visit her, again stuttering and getting hysterical, this time out of embarrassment and guilt. She said sorry almost every minute and explained how authentic the recruitment firm looked. Necessity never blamed her at all.

Anthony stayed home from school to comfort his mother, and also to avoid being mocked. Necessity was sitting at the bamboo couch, she looked clearly ruined, Sese was sitting beside her, wrapping her arms around her from time to time, saying sorry every minute, this time without stammering.

Jeremy came home, it was just 10 a.m. but he smelled of alcohol and was clearly drunk. He was in Iloilo City the day earlier to watch Forrest Gump, he slept over at his uncle Percivale's and heard the news there. He too, went hysterical, drank cheap whiskey on the bus on his way home.

Jeremy stormed inside the house and yelled at his mother, You stupid, stupid woman! You are the epitome of failure! How could you be so gullible huh? What am I supposed to do now?

Necessity was calm, she replied, Do as you are supposed to do, find work, or work your way thru college!

Jeremy became more furious, and yelled louder, That's your job as a mother! You're supposed to work and send us to school! Now look at us!

Sese felt sick in her gut from what she was seeing and hearing, so she had to interfere, firmly and without stammering she said to Jeremy, Don't talk to your mother like that boy, she had been thru no other woman could endure, she doesn't deserve this disrespect!

Jeremy replied, You stay out of this you warthog! It's your fault too, you gullible moron, you'll have to pay for your mistakes!

Anthony came out of his room and tried to say something, You... But then Jeremy took off his right shoe and threw it at him, it hit his mouth and he wasn't able to say anything more. Jeremy knew more or less what Anthony was about to say and surely did not like it. Anthony went down on his knees in pain, his mouth and his nose were bleeding.

Necessity rose and screamed, Don't you hurt your brother again you criminal!

Jeremy yelled back, Alright, defend your little prince, you mother of all failures! Failure! Failure!

Sese by this time turned very red and very upset, she tried to say, Demon but started stammering, Dedededededede....

While she was stuck in stammering, Jeremy jeered at her, saying, Yes, Miss Warthog? You want to say something? Are you partying now? How much did you get in kickbacks from that agency huh, Miss Piggy?

Words could not come out of Sese, so she put it into action, she charged towards Jeremy, he was standing right by the door so she had some distance to gain momentum, she was round, plump but had big muscles and could produce a lot of power, she gave Jeremy a head-butt on the chest and he flew outside like a bowling pin. He landed on his back upon the rocks and luckily did not hit his head. Necessity and Sese rushed outside to see if he was alright. He lay there crying and repeatedly said, What am I going to do now?

They did not know what he meant by that. It turned out, he borrowed around seven thousand pesos from a private lender in town to buy his CD player and his new shoes and because it was known in town that his mother was going abroad, he did not find it difficult to get the loan. On top of that, he told his creditor that he was using the money to start a little fishing business. It was understandable that he kept asking what he was to do next, for there were not much options.

Necessity agreed to work for the Balbagos for six months with negligible pay in order to pay a small part of what she owed. It meant near-hell for Anthony, he had to work on free time to survive, but Sese was there to see to it that he did not starve and his uncle Percivale sent a little amount every month. Jeremy was being pursued by his creditor and was facing jail for small-time swindling. He disappeared and went south for a while to live with relatives in Igbaras.

Anthony and Necessity were sitting on a bench at the plaza eating siopao buns and they had a bottle of Coca-Cola each to celebrate his high school graduation. The bronze medal for the honorable mention was still dangling from Anthony's neck. Necessity handed him his graduation present - a bar each of Butterfinger and Mars, his own little idea of happiness. It was a hot day in March 1995. They were talking about the future, the very near future, on how they were going to survive in the coming months, and they were discussing details. Necessity had two months more with the Balbagos and then she was to quit. Because of the fiasco with the fake agency she found it more and more difficult working as a housemaid. She thought of going back to selling fish and gave some thought on putting up a little food stall at the bus station.

Anthony also laid out his plans. He was not to start college as Necessity just blew her savings, and it did not matter much anyway because those savings could sustain him for only three months in college, he would have to quit after that anyway. He planned to get work at fast-food chains like Jollibee and McDonald's in Iloilo City. Then he said, I cannot lay down the details after that, Mama, but we'll get by, as we always have, I'll get back to you on the details.

9

*I*t was a big bunch of bananas Necessity was trying to deal with, the long stalk was studded with fruits so tightly that no insect larger than an average human thumb could get in between them. When she knelt on the floor the whole bunch was way over her head. There had been no major typhoons around Panay Island since 1995, so the conditions for good harvests were more than favorable, most of the banana shrubs were broken not by the wrath of nature, as usually was the case, but by the weight of their fruits.

The summer of 2000 was not so harshly hot either, which was quite unusual, it rained already in early May, all kinds of fruits were abundant and so Necessity had no trouble finding the sab-a variety of bananas she needed for her pochero stew. She had put up a little food stall at the bus terminal, she named it Seng's Carinderia.

Burog is midway between the city and the last town at the tip of the island, the town of Carles, and so it is the most perfect area for a food stop. Hungry bus drivers and passengers would swarm the stalls, food had to be ready when they arrived because they stopped for no more than ten minutes and competition was stiff. Food stall owners screamed like agitated ducks to attract the attention of customers, but regular travelers, which comprised more than half of the passengers, knew where and what to eat. They came and went like locusts plaguing a rice field, and one would know by the serving platters and trays which were left untouched and those wiped clean which food and which stalls appealed to their tastes.

Necessity put up her stall in early 1997 and the first months were harsh, as was the case for newcomers. With just ten minutes at their disposal, regular passengers did not have the luxury of time to explore something new, they were there to fill their bellies and then go their way. It took about half a year before Necessity's big cauldron of pochero stew began to go almost empty by the time the last bus had left at around 8pm. The others in her menu - pinakbet, sinigang, chicken and pork adobo, ginataan, pancit guisado, dinuguan and other usual housewife's dishes were left for the flies to feast upon.

Her little business became like a one-dish wonder, and by 1998 she became known to bus and jeepney drivers as Seng Pocherera. She never changed the name of her stall, but regulars could never recall what it was really called, despite the big sign sponsored by Tanduay Rum that said Seng's Carinderia, they all referred to it as The Pocherera. It made things easier for her, she started to serve almost exclusively pochero, all she had to procure was a steady supply of pork, pak-choi leaves and the sab-a variety of banana, and of course, the rice, as nobody ever ate pochero without rice.

Her stall was isolated from the main food stalls, her spot was at the northern corner flanked by a machine shop on one side and a tailor's shop on the other, but quite a number of passengers disembarking from busses and jeepneys were always seen streaming towards that corner, for the pochero. She earned enough to pay the rent for the stall, to pay off her debts in installments, to keep The Blue Cottage shiny blue, and to send Anthony at least one school term a year to college. The boy was struggling to finish, and after five years on and off in college, he was just barely halfway to getting his computer science college degree.

Necessity thought of him a lot that day as she knelt on the wooden floor of The Blue Cottage trying to figure out how to pluck the bananas from the stalk without breaching the peels. Computer science was fast developing, and so was the curriculum, if Anthony did not finish by 2002, all the units he'd earned would have to be forfeited and he had to start all over again.

With what she was earning from her pochero and with what he was earning from his contractual jobs in the city, it would take him about four years more to finish. She could not figure out anything at that moment, about how Anthony could get his baccalaureate and how she could pluck those bananas out of the unusually tight bunch. She had a headache and was a bit distraught, she made a deep sigh, rose and looked at the window to find some comfort from the sight of the bright blue bay, but what she found instead was another form of headache approaching The Blue Cottage.

It was a short, stout lady wearing a bright, scarlet dress which was way too small but way too long for her, she had a badly matched purple sun hat, she was holding a blue-gray handbag on her right hand and on her left a large multicolored fan. She was fanning herself excessively like a hummingbird flapping its wings even though it was a cool and quite blustery day in July. She was working her way through the rocky foot path and was tripping forward from time to time as she kept on treading on the tip of her dress.

Necessity prayed that it was just an apparition brought about by hunger because despite her failing eyesight, she could recognize who it was. It was the last person she wanted to meet, and she was working her way yard by yard towards The Blue Cottage. She was still quite far when she began yelling, Neseng! Neseng! Neseng! It was Belinda Legaspi, formerly Belinda Belanda, a classmate in grade school.

Necessity recalled when they were already in the second grade in school, how Belinda still wasn't able to read and write, not even her own name. Her first and family names sounded and were spelled a little alike and so she was confused as to which was which, to complicate matters. At school she wanted to sit beside Necessity, and during written tests she'd loudly call on her to help her with the answers, the teacher reprimanded her every time but she never understood how and why it was wrong. The teacher made it sure that Necessity sat at one end of the room and Belinda at the exact opposite end.

Then came the first spelling test, after about the third item was read, Belinda could not help it, she rose and walked across the room, undaunted by the teacher's warnings. She stood behind Necessity, looked over her clever classmate's shoulders and probed on what she'd written on her quiz pad. The teacher then realized it was not necessary to stop Belinda, as she was not able to write down what she was trying to copy anyway.

Belinda was retained in the second grade for two more years and was once suspended for two weeks for slapping a male classmate with a hardbound book after a heated argument on which letter of the alphabet came first, K or M, and Belinda was cocksure it was M. Necessity's mother Alicia Berano was among the most respected teachers in school and it was she who took up with Belinda's parents the need for a work-up for possible dyslexia.

Belinda's parents had a decent status in town, her father was a clerk at the public high school, her mother was a bookkeeper at the town hall, and both taught catechesis in Sunday school. The Belanda couple was sorely offended by Mrs. Berano's suggestion, they thought it was an arrogant proposition from someone sitting on an enviable teacher's chair. They maintained that their daughter only panicked each time she saw letters, and that she would outgrow it if the teachers were fair enough.

On her second year in the second grade, she barely made progress. She could write her name, but with an inverted B. Her parents started to blame old Rosa Balio of sorcery, they claimed she had cast a spell on their daughter, making her unable to read and write. Rosa Balio was a widow in their neighborhood who had developed severe agoraphobia after her husband died, she rarely went out of her hut and had to subsist on wild vegetables which she gathered from the thickets and fruits that grew near her place, and sometimes she'd catch frogs and stray chickens for meat.

The Belanda couple petitioned the town mayor to banish Rosa Balio from town, they sent dozens of letters to him, each letter contained at least ten pages. The mayor got fed up and finally convened his council about the matter, but no one among them could find any law to support the move.

A couple of months later, Rosa Balio died after accidentally ingesting a poisonous green frog. Months passed, and Belinda made little progress. She could apparently read words if these were used to label pictures, simple words like apple, flower, and the like. Her parents still claimed it was progress, and the spell of Rosa Balio would soon fade away. Then after some time they were summoned at the principal's office, Belinda got into trouble again, she got into a fight with another girl in class over a flash card, it had an image of a rooster on it and it was clearly labeled rooster, but Belinda insisted it read chicken. She stayed for another year in the second grade.

Having no one left to blame, the Belandas harbored resentment towards Alicia Berano, they believed it was her arrogance that ruined it all for Belinda. The poor girl was many years post puberty when she finished grade school, and that was the farthest she could go in academics. Her parents however, told her almost everyday the same line, almost like a mantra, that someday she'd fare better in life than Necessity. It became like their life mission.

One could safely say that it was the Belandas who led the town's resentment on the talk about Necessity going to

America someday. They did not start it though, as the resentment had been there even before Necessity started schooling, but the Belandas were among those who perpetuated it. They never hid jubilation as soon as misfortune befell Necessity. They were there at her wedding reception, they invited themselves because for them, her unfortunate marriage to Onyok Ilaya was a significant triumph, and they did not want to miss a single minute of it.

Belinda married a man from Manila named Miguelito Legaspi, in contrast to Onyok Ilaya, this man had no criminal records. The Belandas went around town and told almost everyone that their daughter was marrying someone without a criminal record, as if she was the first in town to do so. But he had no school records either. He stared at the skies most of the time until a significant stimulus like a loud sound or a bright light made him do something else, or at least made him change bodily position. He found work at an automobile repair shop doing errands for repairmen, like preparing their coffee and handing them whichever tools they needed, he did all kinds of work that had nothing to do directly with repairing automobiles.

To highlight Miguelito as a good man, and to emphasize that he was going to heaven while Necessity's husband was already booked in hell, the Belandas saw to it that he was assigned to play as one of The Twelve Apostles in church ceremonies during Holy Week year after year. It is still a practice in every parish in the country. Twelve men are picked every year, dressed in multicolored silk-like togas which nobody wore in ancient Judea. All these Apostles have to do is walk behind the priest who is understood to be Jesus during lenten processions, get their feet ceremonially washed during the Holy Thursday mass, and eat dinner with the priest during the reenactment of The Last Supper.

That Last Supper reenactment is still being held every Holy Thursday at town plazas for everyone to see, and they are neither eating unleavened bread nor drinking wine, they eat like it is a real feast and soda is usually served. The audience is not served food, and in Burog at that time, most of them were really hungry, so watching The Last Supper was for them a tortuous spectacle, like a penance that could cleanse even the gravest of their sins and the sins of their descendants down to the twelfth generation. Children would stare and swallow their own saliva at the sight of each Apostle pushing a large piece of chicken breast down his throat.

Nobody among the Apostles ate more voraciously than Miguelito Legaspi, no matter which role he played - Peter, Mathew, James The Lesser or The Great, or Judas. A chance meeting with Necessity and Alicia at church in 1969 made Belinda haughtily introduce her husband to them as Miguel Legaspi from Manila, though his name was Miguelito, and she emphasized that Manila was a city closer to America, and that he had no criminal record. It was the Holy Week and he was playing the role of Judas that year, so he ignored them because he was not in the mood, not because he got the traitor's role, but because it meant he was going to leave the dining scene early, before dessert, as he was to betray his Master, and he was also going to miss the Easter Lunch, as the character he was portraying would be dead by then.

With five children, Belinda and Miguelito lived below poverty line, but as soon as she heard that Necessity had started working as a maid at The Balbago Mansion, Belinda borrowed a brown and green office uniform from a friend who worked at the Land Transportation Office in the city, the skirt was too small for her, it barely covered half her thighs but she didn't mind, she only needed it for a few days. She wore that outfit and strolled in front of The Balbago Mansion for hours everyday, she didn't stop until after the eighth day when Necessity finally spotted her and vice versa, they waved, and she made a most triumphant smile. She was in that office uniform while Necessity was in a maid's uniform.

The truth was, Belinda had been out of work for years by the time Necessity started to work for the Balbagos. She had a memory of a milkfish and could not follow even non-complicated instructions so she could not stay employed for more than a week. She opened a variety-kiosk near the bus terminal in the early 80's, but she made poor accounting of her sales and gave away goods for free to those who flattered her with words and to those who spoke ill of Necessity. Freeloading was thus easily decoded. Less than three months after putting up the kiosk, she was out of business.

Finally, in 1990, she herself applied as a housemaid at The Balbago Mansion, vowing to her aging mother that she would outshine Necessity so she could eventually ease her out of the household. Leonora Balbago always had a lot of requests everyday that one had to write them down, and Belinda still could barely write, and she had a memory of a milkfish which had grown many years older. The employment lasted three days.

Belinda made sure that her five children had Anglo-American names - Anne, Dorothy, Archibald, Peter and Mercy, though she could spell only Anne's name, and on rare instances that she got to talk to Necessity or Alicia, she did not refer to them collectively as The Children, but enumerated them one by one by their western names, and she did not allow anyone to call them by local nicknames.

In 1997, something occurred that made Belinda think she could claim ultimate victory. Her youngest child Mercy who was then 19 years old, started to work as a waitress at a bar in Boracay Island. After about a month on the job she started dating a customer, a widower named Tom from Wisconsin who was there on a holiday to celebrate his 75th birthday. A week after they met, he proposed. Belinda learned of it a week later thru a letter, she was overjoyed and extremely pleased with her daughter who simply did what she was always told. Two weeks later, Belinda's mother passed away, smiling, and her father followed just about half a year later, also smiling. Mercy and the widower married in the summer of 1997, and before the end of 1998 she'd moved with him to Wisconsin.

Packages of all things American were shipped to the little Legaspi house almost every month - oversized dresses, signature bags of doubtful origins, soaps and shampoos, ibuprofen tablets of various brands, chocolates, sun hats, knock- off signature bags, make-ups and perfumes. Belinda could barely understand the labels and she went out everyday for months wearing perfume which was clearly labeled pour hommes, and she more than once had a heated argument with her son Peter because she insisted on adding a couple of teaspoons of milk lotion to her coffee, as she could only read the milk part.

She thought her utmost joy would be to meet Necessity in the streets, she wanted her to see her all pimped with her American stuff, so she made sure she wore those things, everyday, from stockings to make-ups. It annoyed her terribly that Necessity was seldom seen in town, she had to call Mercy to send more make-ups because they were running out fast. She went to the bus terminal a few times, and got more annoyed because Necessity was either too busy to notice her, or too unaffected with what she was seeing whenever they met up close.

Finally, on that day in August 2000, she decided to go to Necessity's house to show her how she had conquered America and to extract that bitter look out of her face. It would be to her like a march of triumph for the Belanda family over the Beranos.

Neseng! Yelled Belinda. She finally got to the foot of the small, short wooden stairs leading to doorstep of The Blue Cottage, but still she was yelling like she was far away. Neseng!

Necessity appeared, but she stopped just by the doorstep and with her face devoid of emotions, she said, Belinda, good morning, what a pleasant surprise! Of course she lied, the visitor's presence was not anywhere near pleasant for her.

Belinda said, still not lowering her voice, Neseng! It's so hot, what are you doing there inside? Do you have air conditioning there? She was fanning herself intensively with that large reed fan, then she took off her purple sun hat as the wind threatened to blow it away.

Necessity replied, No... I think it's a relatively cool day!

Belinda scoffed and said, Oh, that's nothing compared to West Consin! In West Consin you have a t-shirt, then another t-shirt, then another t-shirt, then a sweater made of lamb's wool, then a sweater made of animal fur, then a big thick jacket, because it's very cold in West Consin!

Necessity, the smartest in class, knew that she meant Wisconsin, but did not want to provoke her with any kind of correction, she'd seen her having tantrums more than once, so she just thought of getting along and said, Wow, is it winter right now in West...

Belinda interrupted, West Consin! West Consin, if you remember your history it's in the west, so it's very cold! I can hardly stand the cold!

Necessity smiled a bit and asked, So when did you come back?

Come back from where? Belinda asked back.

Necessity said, From America, from West...

The question annoyed Belinda some, she said, I haven't been there yet, I didn't say I've been there, did I? It was Mercy who told me that it was very cold!

Sorry I misunderstood, said Necessity.

Belinda immediately replied, But soon I'll go there! Soon! In a few years! That's why I'm trying not to get used to the heat anymore, oh it's so hot here in your place, Mercy and Tom are footing the bill to renovate my house, it will not be finished until December but they have already installed AC's in three rooms! I can't stand the heat outside the house!

There was an uncomfortably long pause, then Belinda asked, So, aren't you going to let me in your house?

Well, I don't have any AC, replied Necessity.

Belinda clucked with her tongue and said, Of course, I understand you can't afford one, but I need to sit down, I walked all the way from the crossing, Mercy and Tom promised to buy me a Land Cruiser soon, so I can get anywhere all over Panay Island regardless of the terrain!

Necessity was rather enjoying what she was seeing, but she did not show it, she knew Belinda would never leave until she had seen a hint of bitterness on her host's face. She politely said, Ok, please do come in and have a seat!

Belinda mumbled as she ascended the wooden steps, Goodness, ipil-ipil stairs! It's so pre-American! Then as soon as she got inside she fanned herself vigorously and said, Oh, I'm about to faint, it's so hot, I envy you, how you manage to survive in this kind of environment! It's never like this in West Consin!

Have a seat then, said Necessity, more amused than annoyed.

Belinda slumped her entire weight on the bamboo couch, then grimaced and squeaked, Aww! That hurts! My thigh, aw, this couch is so hard, don't you have any cushion?

Obviously not, replied Necessity.

Belinda said, Mercy bought us a sofa from the city, it's too soft it feels like you're sitting on the clouds, problem is, you'll find it hard to get up again, it pulls you down... aww, my thigh!

There was a moment of silence. It was a kind of conversation that one would find hard to sustain, Necessity thought she had not much to say, but finally said anyway, So how are the children?

Belinda replied, The children? You mean, Anne, Dorothy, Archibald, Peter and Mercy? Oh they are doing fine! Anne is in the city, she has five kids, Dorothy is here you, know she has three kids, Archibald is not married, Peter has two kids, and you know Mercy, she has a daughter named Ashley, she's so cute, she's one year old and she talks da-da-da to me, not the

Filipino way but the American way, they call me every week, and she says da-da-da like an American girl!

Do they sound differently? Necessity asked.

Belinda rolled her eyeballs and said, Goodness Neseng, it's so self-explanatory! In America it's cold and they have money while here it's so hot and people don't have money, so naturally, they'd be saying da-da-da differently! Of course it's hard for you to tell, never having had an American grandchild! I have one, mind you, and more to come, so you ought to believe me!

I'm sure she's a sweet girl, said Necessity.

Belinda said, Oh I should have brought the pictures with me! She's pretty and she will be like the Slice Girls when she grows up, you know, the ones who sang Tenyente-Wachuwan-Wachuwan! And Mercy says she'll send all of my grandchildren to school, especially my darling Charlatan, he will be a fine lawyer someday at the American courts, Mercy said she'll take all my grandchildren to America, all ten of them and she should, they are not used to the local life anymore, my grandchildren you know, they cannot eat local chocolates, I don't want them to, I think they're allergic, so they only eat the American ones! I have some for you by the way!

She dug her bag for the chocolates while babbling about whatever little she knew about America. Charlatan is the family's flagship among her grandchildren, but he was just seven years old then, Belinda had heard of the word charlatan from a B-grade action film and thought that it was the name of the dashing villain, as the movie's heroes kept calling and referring to him as charlatan in almost every scene. Charlatan might not have been in the vocabulary of the local priest, or he just wanted to spare his energy and chose not to argue with the Belandas, as they all stood there during baptism with chins up high, very proud of the name Charlatan. The name was approved all the way to the chancery, which had become quite progressive recently. Necessity knew what Charlatan meant, and wondered what would happen to him if he eventually moved to America as Belinda claimed he would.

Belinda finally found several half-molten Butterfinger and Mars bars and handed it to Necessity and said, There you go, as soon as you take a bite you'll never want to eat the local chocolates again, believe me! Belinda never knew that those brands of chocolates had been available at the supermarkets in the city since the late 80's, but Necessity received her gifts politely.

Oh, thank you very much, these are exactly Anthony's favorites! Necessity said, quite delighted.

Belinda replied, Oh don't pull my leg! Anthony has never been to America, especially to West Consin, he could never have eaten these before!

There was a brief moment of silence, Belinda raised her chin triumphantly, forgetting to fan, forgetting to pretend she found it hot inside. Then she thought she could drive another dagger to Necessity's chest, she asked, And how are your two boys?

She knew what was going on with them, she just wanted to see Necessity suffer while she retold it.

Necessity knew that Belinda would only claim more victory if she replied showing any negative affect, and so she said as dryly as she could, Jeremy's trial is pending, maybe in six months, as an accomplice he might be spared the capital punishment but may spend his entire life in prison.

Oh that's horrible, said Belinda, pretending she did not know and pretending she was affected. She asked, But why drugs? Of all…

Necessity interrupted her, saying in a firmer tone, And Anthony is struggling, he's been going on and off at the Computer College, he has to pause and work and save…

Belinda interrupted her too, she said, Poor boy, working at three fast food stores while studying, I suppose? My Mercy is thru with her maternity leave, she works at a restaurant, but mind you, it's American, it's called Windy's, here in Iloilo City they use hamburger buns from local bakeries, there at Windy's, they buy from American bakeries, I mean, bread from America, it's not the same!

Necessity asked, And what does Tom do?

Tom was almost 77, Necessity forgot about that, and so he was retired, he used to be in the navy and then worked as a typewriter salesman. The most widely used term for a retired person in the Philippines used to be the Spanish term pensionado or pensionada, but it was later supplanted by the English term as it is - retired. But Belinda had her own peculiar glossary, so in response to Necessity's question she said, Oh Tom? He's got a lot of money, he's retired-ed!

Necessity said, Oh I'm sorry, was he like that since birth?

Belinda laughed scornfully and said, Oh Neseng, you are so naive and ignorant in matters about America! You can't be retired-ed from birth! You have to work many years before you become retired-ed! Tom became retired-ed when he turned 65! He he's got a lot of money and he sends me a whole bunch of it, as you can see, I am like a retired-ed woman too!

Necessity could not hold it, she laughed heartily, but it caused no one injury, as Belinda took it as though her host was impressed.

Anthony entered the house, he looked tired and worn and was clearly not pleased upon seeing their visitor. Good morning Ma, he said as he threw a bag of laundry at the left corner of the little living room. He just nodded at Belinda.

Belinda was pleased, she thought she was like hitting two birds with one stone. She began fanning herself, raised her chin and said, Anthony, hijo, you look tired, have you been working all night?

We close at midnight and I had a late shift, he replied without looking at her.

Belinda was reveling at the sight of Anthony getting annoyed, she continued, Oh, hard work huh? You know, my Mercy works at Windy's and soon she is going to be a millionaire, if the peso continues to devaluate, I hope so! She laughed, and she laughed alone.

Anthony replied, Oh Wendy's! That's great! There are a lot of Wendy's in Manila right now, I wonder when they are going to open shop in Iloilo, everyone in the city awaits, dreaming and drooling!

Belinda chuckled and said, I'm not talking about Manila, boy, I'm talking about West Consin, West Consin in America! It's cold there and when you live and work there you become very rich! You have to come by my house as soon as we finish renovating!

Anthony began to get amused, You mean Wisconsin?

Belinda replied, You talk funny English, Anthony, it's West Consin, your mother was the smartest in English class, she ought to have taught you! My Mercy lives and works there, in West Consin!

Anthony asked, And her husband, what was his name? Thomas?

Tom! Belinda replied. She never knew that his real name was Thomas.

Anthony said, Oh yes, Tom, sorry...how's he doing?

Belinda again proudly replied, Oh I just told your Mama, he's retired-ed!

Anthony, in all sincerity said, Oh, I'm sorry to hear that...

Belinda scoffed and said, Oh don't be sorry, boy! He has more money than you can ever earn your whole life!

Nobody found anything to say for a long, uncomfortable moment. Then Anthony asked Belinda in a mildly exasperated tone, So what brings you here?

Belinda cleared her throat, and said, I have come to extend Mercy's warm regards to your mother, we all know your mother is still planning to go to America someday, I just thought I'd give her some tips on how to live like an American, I gave her some chocolates, and here are a few more things!

She took out of her bag a couple of soap bars, a small tube of facial cream, and a Wisconsin souvenir key chain. Necessity received them and nodded as if to say thank you.

Belinda by then had realized the growing discomfort among the humble hosts, she felt she had humbled them enough, she rose and said, I have to go now, I'm having a terrible headache because of the heat and I forgot my medications!

Necessity obligingly said, I have some paracetamol here!

Belinda replied, Oh not that, please, they won't do me any good, I'm allergic to local brands, they give me rashes! You see, in America they use borborpain, it's for headache and fever and it's the only one that works for me, it works in seconds! She took out a small empty box and showed it to both mother and son.

Oh yes, Ibuprofen, said Anthony. It's Ibuprofen! We have several brands here too. That's good!

Belinda was not amused upon sensing that Anthony was again trying to correct her, but she tried to laugh and said, Ha ha, you talk funny English, Anthony! And there's no borborpain in the Philippines! Wait until you get to talk to Mercy, she'll teach you how things are said in America! Have a good day, and hope it rains soon so you won't suffer much further from this heat! I'll see you again some time, as soon as I get some more ideas on how to live in America! Then she walked out of The Blue Cottage grumbling loudly, Oh so hot, so hot! How can people live here?

Anthony and Necessity watched her leave until she was out of sight, then they looked at each other and shook their heads. Necessity went on with the plucking of the bananas. Anthony resisted the urge to gobble up those chocolate bars which happened to be his favorite, he just placed them, along with the other things which Belinda gave them, in a small plastic bag. He looked at his mother in the eyes, then threw the plastic bag in the garbage bin. Necessity did not protest.

Without saying a word, they agreed. They refused to be defeated that day, or ever.

10

$\mathcal{J}$eremy's trial came sooner than Necessity expected, it was a complex case and it was sensationalized in the media, it was delegated to the Regional Trial Court. Already in early October 2000, Jeremy and three others from their group were handed the life sentences for their roles in the drug trafficking case, they were used as runners by the drug ring. The head of the met-amphetamine ring - the Desentro brothers, two young men aged 30 and 28, were sentenced to line up to the gallows. Unluckily for them, capital punishment had been signed back into law several years earlier. The Desentros had been shouldering the legal expenses along the way, they were going to appeal the verdict, but only to save the heads of their sons. Jeremy and the three others were to swallow what was handed them, and were to be shipped to the Bilibid Prison in Manila within a couple of months.

Necessity appeared calm at the court as the verdict was being passed, Jeremy refused to talk or even just to look at her, she just watched as the officers in blue uniforms took him away, she was almost never blinking though her eyes and cheeks were soaked with tears. She and Anthony stayed in her brother Percivale's house for the night, his entire family was there to give her support, but no one did talk much.

They spent the night virtually staring at each other while consuming several bottles of Coca-Cola, they barely stirred, no one could finish more than a couple of sentences in a row, it was too painful to talk. Necessity was distraught, she was awake the whole night. She dozed off in late morning and was wide awake again by noon.

In the afternoon she complained of an intense pain on her nape and the back of her head, she vomited a couple of times. Anthony insisted they went to the hospital, but the idea nauseated her more, as the two nearest hospitals were private ones, she feared her single visit might put her in debt for years.

Then Percivale's neighbor Jocelyn who was then a student nurse, dropped by and suggested they went to San Bernardino Hospital which was just at the next district, she said the emergency room was brand new as the State University was about to annex it as their training hospital by the end of the year, and it functioned like a hybrid hospital taking in both well-off private patients and poorer ones as charity cases.

Charity meant they wouldn't pay as much, but they still had to pay for a lot of things, like medicines and needles and gloves as needed, and the emergency room fee that would cost them like their lunch. As charity patients they would have to agree to be examined almost entirely by junior medical interns in their final year in medical school, supervised by the more experienced residents on training. It could mean interns on their first day at the clinics, according to Jocelyn, but it was October, and most of the interns had already been exposed to the clinics earlier in April. It would be alright, Jocelyn assured them.

It was not that bad. When they arrived at the emergency room they were received by a triage nurse who was supposed to ask them questions, but didn't, she left the job to the interns because there were not too many patients at that time, it was just past 7pm. Anthony was asked to pay at the cashier and procure an ER chart, Necessity was given one of those wheeled stretchers as she was too dizzy to sit or stand.

Half an hour later, Anthony submitted the ER chart to the nurse, a female junior medical intern approached, she introduced herself as Yolanda. There were a few things to thank for, Necessity thought, at least it was not Yolanda's first day at the clinics, it was her third. She went on leave for half a year before starting with her clinical rotations so she was new, but at least, it was not her first day. She was left-handed and was shaking a bit as she held the pen and the chart, she had been working for about twelve hours and she had twelve hours more, plus another eight hours of oral reports and paperwork. She had just come back from what was supposed to be her lunch, a very late lunch at 6:30 pm, as it was very busy in the afternoon. If she was lucky she would be having dinner by midnight. Her face projected pure dread but she was polite and friendly, at least initially, and she was very pretty, like a china doll with a silky black hair dangling way below her shoulders. Anthony could not help go blushing each time their eyes met, but it was a lopsided feeling, Yolanda thought of nothing but the near-impossibility of seeing the light of the next day with her wits intact.

Yolanda began asking how their house was like. Mother and son were stunned by her opening question, had she not introduced herself as a medical intern they would have thought she was one of those provincial housing surveyors. But she was green to clinic work so she asked questions by the book as they were taught in medical school. Necessity never answered that, and it took half a minute for Anthony to finally mumble and describe how The Blue Cottage was like. She scribbled down a few lines, she then asked what Necessity did for a living. Necessity answered politely and tried to elaborate on her pochero stall, but Yolanda interrupted and went on asking if there was any hereditary disease in the family.

Necessity thought for a while, she wondered if they bore any weight. Her father died of liver cancer, her mother died in her sleep and it was never known which disease took her soul, and her maternal grandfather, aside from having the pathologic urge to talk too much, had tuberculosis, but that was almost half a century ago. She wondered what these things had to do with her headache, so she finally said a faint and uneasy No. After about ten minutes of interview which touched on lifestyle like smoking, alcohol, exercise, if she had pets, and other private things like how many children she had, if her parents were alive, if her neighbors were nice, Yolanda finally asked why they were at the emergency room.

Necessity told her of the headache, then a series of questions about the headache followed - how it was like, and she said it was like The End, how the dizziness was like, and she also said it was like The End, and how the vomiting was like, and predictably, she said it felt like it was The End. Then Yolanda asked about weight loss, Necessity could not answer that, the last time she was on a weighing scale was in 1978 before she delivered Anthony. There was a stretch of silence, then Yolanda tried to rephrase her question and asked, If you were like ten pesos before, how much are you now in terms of weight?

The impatient Anthony answered, She was like ten pesos in the sixties, now she's like ninety-nine pesos and fifty cents.

Mother and son looked at each other and burst into laughter. Yolanda had neither the time nor the mood to join them laughing, in fact she tried her best to show she was not amused. She scribbled down a short phrase - Significant weight gain in 40 years. Then she rose and drew her elegant lilac-colored Littman stethoscope, unbuttoned Necessity's night dress from the chest down to the navel, and began auscultating while looking at her watch. After about fifteen seconds, she said, Hmm, about a hundred and four per minute, four beats too fast, do you have chest pains?

Necessity shook her head, she felt something in her chest but she couldn't say it was pain, so she used the local word pin-ot which was more of a feeling of a gentle squeeze inside the chest. Yolanda jotted it down, then drew a small lab-request sheet and scribbled ECG on it, then handed it over to Anthony and said, Here, you go and pay at the bursar's, then come back with the receipt and we'll take the ECG. Anthony thought the ECG might cost him like a night's duty at McDonald's, but then a rush of a feeling of well-being took over, he'd gladly do it for his mother.

As he turned to head to the bursar's, Yolanda said, Oh wait a minute, I'll take her blood pressure. She was still clumsy with the sphygmomanometer, so it took a while. Then she announced the results, Hmm, it's one hundred ninety over one hundred, that explains it, go buy this at the pharmacy instead, we'll do the ECG later. She handed Anthony a prescription pad, it was a prescription for Catapres to be taken now, then twice daily.

Anthony headed to the pharmacy across the street, and was back within half an hour. He handed the pills to the nurses who were to give the dose to Necessity. Yolanda was nearby, she checked the pills, looked a little disappointed and said to Anthony raising her voice a bit, Hey I said Catapres! It's Clonidine!

Anthony replied, But the pharmacist said it's the same thing, it's just the generic!

Yolanda displayed a sigh of disgust, like telling Anthony she ought to see the imaginary steam coming out of her nostrils. One of the nurses confirmed that indeed it was the same thing. The young intern blushed out of embarrassment, then she said to the nurses, Alright...OK, give it to her! It looked like she shrank, then she turned around and walked to the other end of the room to attend to another patient.

Necessity felt more and more relaxed, she did not know if it was the Clonidine or that burst of laughter during the interview that did the work, but she became more and more composed and soon that stiffness on her nape was gone. The headache persisted though.

She felt underdressed, the new emergency room was impressive, there was still the smell of fresh paint, the tiles were new and sparkled in spite of the scattered traces of blood and slime, the stretchers smelled of fresh synthetic leather and they made squeaking sounds like they hadn't been used before. The entire emergency room complex was an open one, there were no walls nor rooms dividing the departments, which meant internal medicine, pediatrics, psychiatry, obstetrics and surgery patients had full view of each other, plastic drapes were occasionally drawn when needed, rows of stretchers were smartly arranged.

For poor charity patients like Necessity, the place was like luxury, they were used to the idea thru experience that public emergency rooms in the country were not much better than the butcher's station at the wet markets, they were over-crowded and patients lay in cartons and newspapers if they were lucky not to be placed in stretchers that were almost completely made of rust. What was more impressive about the San Bernardino Hospital's new emergency room was that the relatively well-off and the way much well-off private patients lay side by side with the charity patients. It ought to look like an egalitarian utopia with the standards of services to the indigent being raised, though it was more ideal than real.

Private patients did some efforts to distinguish themselves. Apart from being better clad, one could tell they were private patients by the way they behaved. A number of them refused to be interviewed or examined by interns. Anthony saw in just two hours two patients ignoring Yolanda and her fellow male junior intern, and they requested the nurses to summon the resident physician to call their attending private deck physicians who in turn appeared promptly within an hour, making grand entrances which only patients in coma would not notice.

Parents of private pediatrics patients would make junior interns do private errands for them as though they were members of their household staff, like fetching diapers from the car, and they'd drop names of medical school professors in pediatrics if the interns appeared to be hesitant to oblige. It was obvious how differently the emergency room personnel, though not totally consciously, reacted to calls from private patients in comparison to those from charity patients. They stiffened and listened as Pavlov's dog would drool when it heard a bell, even at the height of chaos.

Both private and charity patients bleated a lot, but there was a difference in their tone, one could tell the tone of those who whined and knew something would happen, from those who knew they were airing their complaints to the walls. Private patients name-dropped feared and established physicians, while charity patients name-dropped news reporters of local radio news stations and politicians whom they never got to meet.

Two hours had passed since Necessity swallowed that Clonidine pill, still Yolanda had not come back, she was busy with four other patients and was called to the surgery area to help resuscitate a patient who went on cardiac arrest. The emergency room complex was getting more and more crowded and very noisy.

Just before 11 pm, Necessity got a new neighbor to her right, it was a jolly, plump lady in her early 60's, she was wearing a bright light flowery housedress, she had a little black transistor radio with her as she was listening to late evening adult drama-comedy program called Whispers in the Night, and she was smiling and laughing incessantly. One could tell she was not healthy though, her right big toe was gone and there was an active, oozing wound on the stump, her feet and calfs were swollen, she was laughing and smiling all the time, but only with her left face, the right side did not join the fun.

How are you doing? The lady asked as she lowered the volume of her transistor radio, assuming the friendly-looking Necessity would answer. The woman was slurring a bit.

Necessity replied, I'm alright, I think I might be able to go home now, if that intern releases me.

The lady burst into laughter, then introduced herself, My name is Diosdada, the old terror math teacher of Janiuay, haha! She reached out her right hand for a handshake.

Necessity amiably shook hands with her and introduced herself, she said, Neseng, pocherera of Burog Bus Terminal!

Diosdada laughed out loud and asked, So what brought you here?

Necessity replied, Oh just a headache, I must have been stressed out, but it's gone now and I ought to go home, to give my place to others.

Diosdada, still laughing, said, Oh maybe you ought to, you converse ten minutes with me and I guarantee you your headache will be back!

Necessity couldn't help but laugh a bit, then she asked, And you Diosdada, what brought you here?

Diosdada replied, Oh it's nothing, I was cracking jokes during dinner when my crazy husband claimed that I was laughing only on the left side of my face, he tried to drag me here so I tried to slap him with my left hand but my left arm wouldn't move, then I fell to the floor so he won the battle! She paused for a couple of seconds then again burst into laughter.

Necessity began to look concerned and said, You must have had a stroke, don't you think?

Diosdada replied as she began to appear a little more serious, Yes i know, I've had this before, it went away after a few hours, I've actually gotten better since a couple of hours ago when no one could understand what I was saying! You wait and see right after midnight how I kick my husband's butt and we'll be out of here! Then she laughed again so loudly she drew the attention of everyone in the emergency room. Then she said, Here he comes now, the old cowboy of Janiuay!

Her husband appeared with the ER chart, he looked fidgety, he had an ashen face and he was clearly shuddering. When he got to Diosdada's side he said, I hope they attend to you promptly, you seem better than you were a few hours ago, but it may recur!

Diosdada replied, With the way I laugh no one will take me seriously!

Her husband said, Then maybe you should stop laughing like that!

Diosdada said, What? How then would they know I'm lagging on my right face if I kept my mouth shut? She was a little teary eyed but she kept laughing.

Then a nurse approached, she did a quick glance on Diosdada and called on Yolanda, Hey Intern De la Paz, I think it's a priority here!

Yolanda at that moment was trying to palpate the abdomen of an elderly woman who had diarrhea, she rose from the examiner's low stool and grudgingly and listlessly walked towards Diosdada.

Diosdada watched Yolanda approach, and she said to Necessity, Look at that poor intern coming towards me, she's overworked, she'll be dead in the morning! She then went on laughing.

Yolanda was dragging her tongue to say any word, she greeted them neither good evening nor hello, she did not introduce herself, she just went straight to the interview in the same manner she did to Necessity, beginning with how their house looked like.

Diosdada, still in a jolly mood, replied, Oh the house? It's an old shack in the middle of the farm which we rent! But don't you worry, we won't be staying there long, we were unable to pay the rent this year so we are up for eviction! She burst into laughter while her husband shook his head and turned his back on them.

Yolanda then asked what she did for a living.

Diosdada replied, Nothing, I just wake up everyday finding out I'm still alive! But seriously, I was a math teacher, but diabetes took my right toe and the vision in my right eye and my failing kidneys took my energy away, so I could not run and catch pupils by their ears anymore so I had to stop working! She again burst into laughter.

Yolanda appeared exasperated, and asked in a haughty tone, So you have diabetes, do you take any medication?

Diosdada replied, We barely have money for food so I make my own medicine, I boil guava and guyabano leaves and drink the juice everyday, or would you classify it as tea? Ingenious huh?

After about fifteen minutes of interview Yolanda finally asked the single most important question, on what brought Diosdada to the emergency room. Diosdada told her her face was lagging on the right and she had difficulty moving her left limbs and she couldn't utter a word two hours earlier, then she blurted out loudly, They thought I was possessed by a stray spirit! She went on laughing.

Yolanda then looked up and saw that the right face was indeed lagging, something she just noticed. Immediately the young intern rose and did a textbook neurologic examination, step by step from head to left toe, it dragged on for about half an hour.

Anthony in the meantime got engrossed with what he was seeing in the emergency room. It was almost midnight and it got too crowded, the room was very noisy, everyone who had to say anything almost needed to scream. There was pandemonium as a middle aged man who smelled of alcohol was rushed inside on a stretcher, there was a dagger stabbed on his left chest straight to his heart, his eyes were open but he was already dead. He was taken to the surgery area where another patient, a man in his thirties, had been waiting for a chest tube as the resident surgeon was to instruct his eager intern how to do it. The man also had a dagger wound on his left chest but it was nearer his shoulder, and he was alright, he was talking on his mobile phone and and had in fact been laughing and joking though he was gasping for air a little. But he turned pale as he saw the dead man being wheeled in, he wondered if the same thing would happen to him anytime soon, he went berserk and went screaming at the resident surgeon urging him to insert the chest tube himself ASAP.

At the pediatrics area there were three children having severe diarrhea, the interns and the pediatrics residents were busy calculating fluids and inserting IV's thru the delicate babies' veins. One baby had bouts of diarrhea every ten minutes or so, and the mother wailed each time, apparently losing just as much fluids thru her tears. Another mother was very loud, she was harassing the intern who tried and failed four times to insert an IV needle on her baby, threatening to be right at the stage to block his graduation come summer and to call the radio stations to announce to the whole province that the government wasted a big deal of money for his medical education. The intern appeared numbed and accustomed to such maternal tantrums, and succeeded on his sixth try.

By midnight, Yolanda was done with her thorough neurologic examination on Diosdada, and concluded that she lagged on her right face and had difficulty moving her left limbs, just as Diosdada herself said, and just as anyone would notice by just looking at her. Then the intern took her blood pressure, and feebly announced the result, One hundred eighty over ninety!

Necessity said to Diosdada in a low voice, That's lower than mine.

Diosdada laughed loudly and said, See? I told you, after about midnight I'll be kicking my cowboy's butt!

Yolanda scribbled down an order to the charts, this time she wrote generic Clonidine, she gave Diosdada's husband the prescription, and he headed to the pharmacy across the street and disappeared for a while. A nurse soon approached

Yolanda and asked in front of every soul present, Intern De La Paz, Clonidine for this patient? Are you sure?

The obviously offended Yolanda replied, Of course I'm sure, I know what a hundred eighty over ninety blood pressure is!

The nurse disappeared for a few minutes, then came back with the resident internal medicine physician Dr. Ronald Dapog. His hair was in a disarray and there was a fresh red mark on his forehead, he had been resting his head for a short while on his desk just several steps away from the emergency room. He was quite upset and called his intern, he said, Yolanda, she had been here for almost two hours, why was I not alerted?

Yolanda panicked and could not answer. It was Diosdada who made a remark, saying, Oh had it been two hours? Time flies when your doctor is amusing! By this time she was clearly slurring and appeared more drowsy.

Dr. Dapog did a quick check on the patient, checked her pupils and began giving her commands, Frown, smile, whistle, show me your tongue, raise your arms, nose to finger like this, raise your legs. In thirty seconds he was done, he began cursing, Jesus, Mary and what was his name? Yes, Joseph! Ma'am do you have any folks with you?

Diosdada replied, slowly and slurring, My husband is out to buy some magic pill!

Dr. Dapog said, Oh no, you're not going to take that pill! You need a CT scan immediately! He then looked at the chart and said to the nurse, Please call me as soon as her husband arrives, and you, Yolanda, follow me please. He walked out of the emergency room, Yolanda anxiously followed.

Diosdada turned to Necessity and said, Did you hear that? A CT scan? We have been borrowing money for food in the past month, and he talks about a CT scan? She chuckled and closed her eyes to rest, at least her left eye, as her right eyelid wouldn't move.

It was almost 1 am, they had been there for six hours now, Necessity fell asleep, Anthony headed to the toilet. Right outside he could hear a female voice sobbing, and a male voice that was surely of Dr. Dapog reprimanding somebody, and no doubt it was Yolanda. Dr. Dapog said, How could you waste your time extracting and writing information on the chart like this? That their roof is made of old zinc, that they have a cow which they pawned, and that there are three cats that wander their lawn but one does not belong to them, and all of her three sons are alcoholic? Yolanda this is the clinics, and the emergency room at that, this is not a freshman medical school getting- to- know- you session! And Clonidine? Do you know what's going to happen if it's an ischemic stroke?

Anthony walked away as soon as he was done at the toilet, he could not stand what he was hearing and he panicked a bit, his mother swallowed that Clonidine pill as ordered by the same intern. What would happen to her? He rushed to Necessity and woke her up.

What? she asked, annoyed and a bit disoriented.

Anthony replied, Nothing, I just wanted to see if you're okay!

Necessity replied, I'm alright. Shall we go home?

Anthony answered, I think it's best we wait until Dr. Dapog has read your charts and reviewed what they'd given you.

Necessity said, Review what they'd given me? It was just one pill!

Anthony said, Exactly, that one pill!

Diosdada's husband soon arrived with a little plastic bag with two tablets of Clonidine. Dr. Dapog was back on the scene, and Yolanda, whose eyes and face were still soaked with tears, trailed him closely. Dr. Dapog took the husband to one corner and they talked. Diosdada woke up, this time she was slower and more drowsy. Dr. Dapog could be heard asking her husband, So can you think of anyone you can call?

155

Diosdada's husband nodded, he was led to the nurse station as he asked to borrow the phone. Diosdada turned to Necessity, exerted an effort to laugh and said, He's going to call, whom? Santa Claus in North Pole? We have three daughters in Janiuay and they have just enough to eat, we have three sons in the city but none of them is sober tonight and they must have borrowed enough money for their booze! I have a brother here in the city, and he's selling balut, I don't know if my husband can reach him because he's been unable to pay his phone bills for months, he has no money for that, let alone a CT scan...

Necessity's eyes swelled with tears, she reached out to touch the back of Diosdada's left hand and said, I wish there was something I could do for you...

Diosdada smiled faintly with the left side of her face and said, Yes there is, Neseng. Smile, I like people who are smiling! She then again closed her eyes, her left eye at least, to rest.

Anthony could not stand what he was seeing, he asked to be excused for a while, he moved to the entrance of the emergency room where he still could see the scenes at least partly. At the surgery area a father was threatening the surgery residents that he'd leak their names to the local radio station, he wanted his twelve year old son to have an emergency circumcision that night because he was being bullied at school for being putchong and he had not been going to school for weeks because of that.

The man who had that dagger wound on the left chest and who was alive was wailing loudly, he said he was going to die though he already had a chest tube and his injury was minimal. The thing that was troubling him was the sight of the other man who also had a dagger thru his left chest and who was stone dead but was still lying on a stretcher beside him, they were waiting for the police to arrive before they could move the body, and it drove him out of his wits. Surgery resident physicians were discussing with the psychiatry resident physician on duty if the man with the chest tube was a case for them and she said no.

The psychiatry resident had a problem of her own too. All over the emergency room could be heard a loud, stinging voice of a woman singing her own version of Evergreen, with altered lyrics, she was not singing about love but about the annoying voices of what she claimed dead ex-boyfriends she was hearing. That kept the psychiatry department busy.

There was also a commotion at the obstetrics area, there was a loud, violent screaming. A young woman was in labor, but she was calm and composed, it was her husband who was screaming at the residents and interns, she was a private patient and her obstetrician's mobile phone mysteriously went out of reach, the husband was going berserk.

Radio news reporters were swarming outside waiting for a story to inflate to the airs. They were barred from entering the emergency room though they were regarded by many charity patients as heroes and icons of hope. If the doctors could not cure their ills, both real and imagined, at least these news reporters could destroy their doctors on air.

3 am, Diosdada's husband was crying as Dr. Dapog appraised him on his wife's condition and chances. They did not even have money for her fluids so the CT scan was out of the question. Diosdada became less responsive, she only opened her eyes, or her left eye as her right eye didn't close, when enough painful pressure was applied on her chest. Dr. Dapog asked for assistance for another IV line. Yolanda was not anymore functional, she could not tear a plaster for the IV as she was trembling badly, so Dr. Dapog called out loud, Somebody, anybody, please help me with this thing! Before any nurse could arrive, Anthony stepped in and helped tear those pieces of plaster, it appeared like a task anybody could do. Dr. Dapog thanked him. Then the doctor went to the Diosdada's husband who was asked to sign a waiver stating that the hospital was not liable for whatever the outcome was for Diosdada, because they did not have any dough to save

her. He agreed, and he signed, and it included a no-CPR waiver. Shortly after that she was transferred to the wards, she was not to be alive by sunrise.

Necessity's neighbor to the left was also going to sign a waiver. He had been at the ER since early morning and was moved beside her only after midnight. She had not been talking to him much because he had been spewing stench. He had high fever and bloody diarrhea and was a suspect typhoid fever case. He was a man in his early thirties, he had eight small children and worked as an unskilled laborer. He was ironically excited to sign the waiver and go home. He could not afford the tests to confirm if it was indeed typhoid fever, he did not even have money for IV fluids and antibiotics. He had to sign a waiver that stated that he would settle with empirical but likely suboptimal oral antibiotic treatment, and that he was refusing confinement.

After signing the waiver, he gave Anthony a wink and said, If I went home and take that worthless antibiotic I might live, I might die, but if I stayed here, that single dose of IV antibiotics would surely sentence my family, and that includes me, to death thru starvation! He rose and walked out of the emergency room with his wife, his brown pants all soaked with literally bloody diarrhea.

It was almost daybreak, a white Audi car stopped just at the main entrance. A woman in elegant blue house dress and with a hairdo like a twirl that was reaching to the ceiling alighted, she walked and moved like she was seriously ill, and two maids followed her, one carried her handbag, the other one carried a bigger travel bag. Yolanda approached her but Dr. Dapog stopped her and said, I'll take this!

It was a private patient of one of the big physicians. She had a sore throat and Dr. Dapog had been notified of her case, he was to write the admitting notes and she was to go straight to her suite on the fourth floor for a work-up on possible bacterial tonsillitis.

There were only a few patients left. A young, petite lady had been there for almost 24 hours and she was never placed on a stretcher, so she remained sitting on a chair the whole time. She insisted she had to be examined immediately because she had an infected pimple on her left cheek. By daybreak she was finally seen by Yolanda's male colleague whose pimples were about twenty times worse, it made the patient understand that she was not going to die after all.

Then it was Necessity's turn, finally. Before Dr. Dapog could say anything, Necessity said, It's quite a relief when you are among the last to be seen, it means you've got nothing serious...

Dr. Dapog just gave a weary smile and said, So how are you…is this your name, Necessity?

Necessity replied, Uhm, strange huh?

Dr. Dapog stammered as he said, No, ah, I mean, I mean…

Necessity said, You mean it's quite a strange name, I understand.

Dr. Dapog just shook his head as if telling her to forget his reaction as he had no time to explain himself, he just went thru her ER chart, the lab tests and the ECG and said, Your BP is now down to a hundred thirty over eighty, that's alright, you got Catapres and… and, Yolanda, where's your neurologic status?

Yolanda just went teary-eyed again and just shook her head.

Dr. Dapog then carelessly said, The same mistake as of Diosdada, Yolanda, same mistake! Always rule out ischemic stroke before pressing down your blood pressure!

Necessity got alarmed and rose from the stretcher, Doctor, am I going to have the same fate as Diosdada!?

Dr. Dapog immediately assured her, No ma'am, no, I'm sorry, you'll be alright, it's more of a textbook lecture here!

Anthony, who earlier knew what it was all about, helped his mother calm down, he said, No Mama, it's alright, you're okay!

Necessity asked Dr. Dapog, Am I okay, doctor?

You're okay ma'am, you're okay, said Dr. Dapog. He then did a quick neurologic examination on her that lasted over a minute. Then he assured her saying, You're in good form, ma'am, can you tell me what happened?

Necessity, now much relieved, replied, It was a terrible pain on my nape, and a headache, but any mother who had been thru this would have felt the same, or worse! Tears began rolling down her cheeks.

What happened? asked the curious Dr. Dapog.

Necessity replied, If you have been listening to the news about the Desentro case, one of those boys who were handed the life sentence is my son.

Oh I'm sorry to hear that, said Dr. Dapog who did not have time to listen to the news, and thus did not know anything about the case. He asked, So do you wish to talk to our psychiatrists ma'am?

Necessity replied, No! Of course not! It was not I who kept singing Evergreen the whole night!

Everyone laughed. Then Dr. Dapog said, Alright, you may go home, but be sure to have your blood pressure checked, you may come to our out-patient clinic here after a couple of weeks or you may do it at your local health center in Burog, whichever is convenient.

Necessity replied, I'll think about that.

Dr. Dapog said, But promise me you'll go on a follow-up okay?

Necessity playfully said, Shall I sign too? A promise that I'll book a check-up somewhere and that you are not liable for anything in case I break that promise?

That would not be necessary, said Dr. Dapog. They shook hands.

As they were leaving, Anthony asked his mother, Is your headache gone?

Necessity replied, Every bit of it!

Anthony said, Whew! So intern Yolanda was right about the Clonidine after all!

Necessity replied, Honestly, I took a couple of ibuprofen and paracetamol when no one was looking!

Anthony chaffed, he said, What? The borborpain Belinda Legaspi gave you? You weasel! You bowed to our archenemies the Belandas?

Necessity replied, Well, apparently, it was all I needed! And of course, poor Diosdada's laughter!

Anthony then said, I was kidding, Mama. Let's give Belinda the credit, just this one time! Anything to make you feel alright!

They walked out of the hospital and proceeded to the cafeteria nearby. They had some money left, enough for a cup of coffee and a bun for each of them. They had seen too much in just one night, it was like the state of the nation in a single room, both could barely say a word.

Anthony finally broke silence, he said, What a night huh? I've never seen anything like that!

Necessity said wearily, Me neither.

Anthony said, Can you imagine? A brand new emergency room, the desperately poor and the filthy rich side by side? Unbelievable!

Necessity was silent, she pondered for a while and then said, Though I'd rather have the rich and poor segregated, I mean the rich were there side by side with us but they were not really there, it made me feel poorer an awful lot! Tears rolled down her cheeks.

Anthony held her by the right hand and said, I wouldn't put it that way, but you were the patient last night, so you have the word!

Necessity was crying but she was at the same time pensive, she said, That fine matron with the sore throat, and Diosdada whose husband had to sign away her life, I just… I just don't understand how they can be in the same country…

Anthony appeared puzzled but he somehow had a grasp of what she was trying to arrive at. Yet he said, I don't really know what you mean…

Necessity held her son's hands firmly, gave him an unyielding look and said, Oh yes you do, you know what I mean. Get out of this country, don't raise your family here!

Anthony did not take her seriously at first, he laughed a bit and said, Out of the country? But Mama, that…

Necessity interrupted him saying, Yes, I know, that dream, that horror, that monster of a dream, that dream that ruined things between me and my hometown! But it's a new dream, it's for you now, it's your dream now! You may not admit it but I know, you've had that for a while! Promise me you'll get out of here!

Anthony could only shake his head, and thought it was a wonder how his mother could read his inner desires so precisely. He said, I don't know how to promise you, even if I could swim across the Pacific I still wouldn't have enough papers to my name to get me a job to feed me when I'm that far away from home!

Necessity, who now had stopped crying and begun to sound ecstatic, said to him, Oh the way you tore those plasters last night, you were a natural! Why not become a nurse?

Anthony burst in laughter, snorting coffee out of his nostrils, he coughed and felt like choking, it took some time before he could say, Oh Mama, that was a task anyone could execute! Packer boys at the warehouses can do better!

Necessity said, Oh yes, but those were medical plasters, I know a natural on the job when I see one!

Anthony said, Sure, and you get inside a hospital like once every three decades, how can you tell what a natural is? Just as he said that, something from the left field of his vision caught his attention, three pages of white bond paper posted at the cork board near the cashier. He had very good vision and he could read from afar, it was an announcement for the entrance examination for the nursing school of the State University for

162

the next school year. Necessity easily noticed that something caught Anthony's eye, so she turned around to take a look, by that time, Anthony had risen to take a closer look. She followed him.

Necessity said, There you go, auspicious huh? The dream is just a couple of minutes old and the road is already being paved!

Anthony replied, Mama, this is the top nursing school in the country, the absolute top, among the hundreds! This is no joke!

Necessity said, Neither are you a joke! It's three weeks away, the last day of registration is next week. We can get all your papers ready in a few days!

Anthony felt dizzy, quite all of a sudden his life was making a sharp turn. He said, I know it's a state university, it won't be that expensive, but still it's a nursing school, there would be a great deal of expenses and…

Necessity interrupted him, she said, You hurdle the test first and then we'll tackle your concerns later, in detail!

11

*I*t was raining hard, Anthony was sitting on his bed which, again like almost every furniture in the house, was made of bamboo. He was staring out the window, he watched the skies pour infinite amounts of water on earth, that ruthless October rain. His mind was wandering somewhere far, in places he hadn't actually been to. Necessity came in without knocking, and it jolted him and brought him right back to his room, from wherever his mind had wandered.

What have you been thinking? Necessity asked.

Not much, replied Anthony.

The test is two days away, said Necessity.

I know that, said Anthony.

Necessity said, I know you know, that's why I know that you have been thinking much.

Anthony said, Alright, I've been thinking much, I've been thinking about all the other examinees.

What about them? asked Necessity.

Anthony replied, Well I mean, most, if not all of them, are six years younger than I am, I feel old, awkward and outdated!

Necessity said, Well, the test is about aptitude in nursing, it's not about how young, cocky and trendy you are!

Anthony said, Maybe you're right. But six years, it feels like a gap of an entire generation, maybe two!

Necessity patted him on the head and said, Just think of yourself as six years wiser!

The day of the examination came, Anthony thought he was right about the other examinees. Their concerns, their choice of music, the way they dressed, and how they banally reacted to trivial occurrences like a spill of coffee on the floor, he felt like he belonged to another century, not that the previous century was just a year before as the year was 2000, but a whole century, he really felt like he was at least four generations ahead of them.

Necessity was right though about the examination, aside from determining the level of intelligence it was also an aptitude test which gave the old and wise an edge in testmanship. A thousand hopefuls took the exams, and three hundred were to make it, Anthony battled hard item after item, he never ceased thinking all the while that the nursing school was the country's absolute top, and it was the cheapest option, but still, he did not know how to pay his way through those four long years. It was the State University or bust for the three week old dream, he had to clinch the 300th spot. It would not end there. There was to be an interview in March the following year, three months before the school year opened, and they were to admit only a hundred and fifty.

It looked like he overdid it, test results came two weeks later and he ranked second among all examinees. Necessity was overjoyed. That weekend she had a little celebration, she bought two roast chickens, Coca-Cola, a bar each of Butterfinger and Mars. She invited Sese over.

Necessity said to her son, Nine hundred ninety-eight young, cocky and trendy examinees are under you, how do you feel?

Anthony replied, Well, I still feel old, awkward and outdated!

Sese said, No you're not, they can still turn you into a fine nurse! You hurry to America, boy, it will make Belinda gnash her teeth and overdose on what was that? Borofain-fain?

Borborpain! Anthony butted in.

They laughed and made a toast with Coca-Cola in former Nescafe glass containers, for a dream that was just over a month old. The interview in March was to be the next hurdle, it felt too far away, Anthony thought he would be basking a long time in glory over that feat in the examination, fantasizing about a spectacular career in health care, like jumping out of a chopper in air ambulance uniform saving an injured policeman by putting his gut back altogether right there by the roadside, or doing CPR on an old man at a casino, eventually succeeding in reviving him and there was that big audience of amazed pensionaries dropping their canes and crutches to give him a thunderous applause, or delivering twins in the middle of the sea on an outrigger pump boat amidst the woman-in-labor's deafening scream which caused considerable ripples on the water surface. He daydreamed while flapping burgers at McDonald's, serving noodles at Chow King and peeling bananas for his mother's pochero.

It went fast. March 2001 came like it was the next day. He found himself one hot and humid March morning at the corridors of that black and orange College of Nursing building, lining up for interview with three hundred other hopefuls, most of which were way long his juniors and way too hopeful, confident they were to be the next Florence Nightingale though they were fully aware that only half of them were to make it. Anthony worried about how he was to reply when confronted by a question on how he was to finance his way thru nursing school, while the two girls right in front of him were concerned about how to get the latest Nokia phone before school opened, and the the three boys behind him were flaunting their new Nokias and were trying to figure out how to talk to those two girls.

The most difficult thing about the interview was that they were not being interviewed alone, unlike that when catholics say their confessions in a dark box. They were interviewed in groups of eight by a panel of nine professors, including the dean, in a spacious, well-lit room and so the entire panel and the entire group of eight would be able to hear whatever one had to reply to whatever was asked. They never missed out on asking about family finances. Though it was a state university, there were a lot of miscellaneous expenses during the entire four-year course, not to mention student board and lodging in the university district, especially if one lived as far away as Burog, and drop-outs due to financial constraints were not uncommon. They all heard it, the panel and his fellow applicants, they all heard about Necessity and her pochero stall at the bus terminal and Anthony hopping everyday between three fast food stores, not to eat, but to earn the dough.

And how do you map out your way financially thru the entire course, Mr. Anthony Ilaya? One of the professors asked.

With a staggering tone of optimism, Anthony replied, Well, I, I suppose I'm resourceful and I can work on my free time and…

The dean herself had to interrupt him, she said, You can do that maybe if you are taking a literature course, Mr. Ilaya, but not nursing! I don't think you've had a full grasp of what this course is all about.

Anthony thought that it was a fatal blow. He blushed, got very warm, got sweaty, then got very cold. He was silent, he had nothing to say. Then something reminded him that he ranked second in the entrance test, that was his best shot, and anyway, if all was lost, there ought to be no harm in speaking out whatever came to his mind at the moment. And so he spoke out, Alright, I might not be able to map out in detail how I can pay my way, but how about giving me a chance to find out, one or two terms and if I find out I'll knock on your office doors one by one and tell you how I figured things out. It would be some kind of a learning process, for other underprivileged pupils to follow, don't you think?

The dean took off her eyeglasses, looked at him with a wry smile and said, Very inspiring, Mr. Ilaya, but every slot is being shouldered by taxpayers, it's not up to be gambled!

Anthony's face sank to the floor. He thought that that was it. An underprivileged applicant like him was not uncommon in state universities but tragically, he was the only one in the group that day. Upon hearing how they grilled Anthony on finances, the other hopefuls geared up on revealing and exaggerating their parents' financial assets, whether or not they were being directly asked about it.

A flamboyant and overly confident girl in the group said to the panel, I'm actually quite nervous today because we just came back from a tour in Australia and the Southeast, but my daddy bought me an MP3 device with all the relaxing music, and he said I'm going to get a brand new car as soon as I get started in the freshman year!

One male professor in the panel said, Yes I understand that, Miss Notelio, it seems like your father can afford to pay someone to listen to you talk all day everyday for forty years, but still you haven't answered my question - How aware are you of the discrepancy between healthcare in theory and actual practice in the field?

She was just one example. The other applicants talked in a more or less similar manner. Anthony was not paying much attention to what was being asked of others. He thought about having his entire life spent working at fast food chains, and how he would die alone, half paralyzed with multiple bed sores at The Blue Cottage by the sea.

The interview was over just before lunchtime, Anthony was on his way out of that black and orange building, he felt like his shoulders were below his toes, he thought of taking a vacant pass that evening at Dunkin Donuts and then plan the rest of his life from there. There was a big, thick, young palm bush in a clay pot by the main door, it was twice as tall as the average height of any person in the country, he could see a familiar blue dress lurking behind the plant as he approached, then he recognized the familiar figure, then the very familiar face. It was the dean. Anthony gave her a low, quick nod, then he went on with his eyes on the floor, and headed for the exit.

Mr. Ilaya, a word please, said the dean. He turned around and looked up, she was looking at him over her eyeglasses which hung low over the bridge of her nose. Then she said, Will you follow me please? Then she walked down the hall and up the stairs without looking back, assuming Anthony had no choice but follow. He did follow. She led him to her office, she left the door open, and as he got by the door he took a peek inside the room and saw the entire panel of professors that interviewed him half an hour before, all nine of them, they were all looking at him tenderly this time, they looked like they were not going to ask any more questions, at least not about anything that had to do with his family's finances, at least he hoped so.

Come inside, said the dean, who now was sitting regally by her big desk.

Have a seat, said one male professor who was the associate dean. He asked, Mr. Ilaya, you are well aware that we are trying to keep our place as the finest nursing school in the country, and that every year we strive to get top spots at the national licensure exams? Anthony shook his head slowly, pretending not to know. The professor continued, Oh you ought to know!

A female professor said, We have been working in this college for a long time now, we know a potential topnotcher when we see one!

The dean said, Needless to say, you have been admitted to the college and we expect you to shine and help us keep the college on its comfortable spot at the top, if you understand what I mean...

Anthony thought it was best he did not speak, or else he'd run the risk of saying anything that might change their minds, so he sat there, silent, looking down on the floor.

The dean asked him, Have you heard of Bobby Hong?

Anthony thought hard, he thought it might be a local male Florence Nightingale that he missed to read about, then he recalled the name, it was familiar, then he recalled that restaurant, he applied for a job there some years ago, he got accepted but opted for the offers at the fast food chains instead. He replied, Isn't he the owner of Spring Manor House Restaurant?

Exactly! At least four of the professors simultaneously replied.

Bobby Hong was quite known in the city, but only a few had ever seen him. He directed his business from the kitchen and very rarely went out to meet guests. Some said he was a giant standing almost seven feet tall, some said he was obese like a sumo wrestler.

In reality he was a skinny man with a flat belly and an unmistakably Chinese face with a goatee like those depicted on classic Lao Tzu images, and he stood no more than 5 feet and eight inches. He had been wearing a plain white t-shirt, black trousers and rubber flip-flops all his life, so if anyone claimed to have seen him wearing something else, then it was most certainly not he.

He came from a very poor village in Guizhou, China. His father was a sentry in the Chinese Nationalist Army and his mother was a cook for a relatively well-off household in the neighboring village. He was seven years old at the peak of conflict in 1947, his father was captured and executed by the Communist Army that year. A few weeks after that, communist soldiers came for his family. His mother had asked him to go to the herbalist outside the village to get a balm for his sister who had fever. When he got back he found out that his mother and seven siblings had been massacred. To survive, he stood by one of the public wells in the village all day everyday for many weeks, he drew water from the well for people for food. Some would give him a piece of bread or a cup of rice, some had nothing to eat themselves and thus had nothing to give him but a tender pat on the head.

He was sitting by the well one rainy afternoon, shivering and starving. He had stolen a couple of cabbages from a garden three days earlier and it was all that he'd eaten since then. He was staring blank at a puddle trying to count the raindrops that fell on it when on the ground appeared two pairs of military boots, and simultaneously a small pan filled with rice and smoked fish was placed before him. He did not look up to see who it was that gave him food, he just grabbed the pan and ate up the rice and fish in less than a couple of minutes. He then looked up to see who it was. To his horror he saw two middle-aged ladies in Communist Army uniforms. In anger he threw the pan at one of them, hitting her hard on the face. Both did not move much, they grabbed him by the arm, he struggled but they were too strong and he was too scrawny and too feeble.

They took him to a small tent by a grove of bamboos outside the village. When he found out that they had ample supply of rice and canned goods, he thought he might as well stay there as their prisoner forever. The patch on the left arm of their uniforms and on their caps indicated that they were army nurses. They introduced themselves as Li Na and Zhang Min.

Bobby, whose name then was Wang Yong, did not introduce himself, he refused to talk to them, he was just resigned to be their captive for good, to have access to food. They never chained or restrained him in any way, he had all the food he could eat and did not think of running away. They seemed kind too, they took care of him like their own child. Everyday he could hear that they were planning to desert the Maoist army, flee to the nearest shore, take a boat and drift to wherever the winds and the current would take them, and day after day the plan was getting clearer. Hearing this, he realized they were no communists to the core, so he began to talk to them when he needed to, and they did not talk much either, so he needed not talk more than a few short lines a day.

After a few weeks, he began calling them both Mama, though they didn't ask him to, though he didn't really want to. He got to know how every tiny pinch of hunger felt and any woman who could take away hunger deserved to be called Mama, he thought.

Li Na and Zhang Min first planned to volunteer to assist the army near Macau where the conflict was harsher for the communists. They were to take Bobby with them and introduce him to their comrades as their errand boy, hard-line communist since the day he was conceived. Bobby didn't mind, as long as they gave him food, as long as they went on with their plans on dumping the communists.

They left one morning for Macau on a captured Nationalist Army truck, Bobby sat by the rear, he looked back as they drove away, he saw his village disappear from him in the thick mist forever. They arrived at their assignment, and quickly the ladies dropped their uniforms, slipped into Macau, to a cove near Pozaiwan and boarded a small refugee schooner which set sail eastwards on Christmas Eve of 1947, loaded over its capacity. There were two phenomena that stood out on the boat - hunger and dysentery. Dysentery came first, it contaminated and spoiled the food supply, and thus followed hunger and dysentery again like a vicious circle. Almost a dozen died on the journey and the bodies had to be thrown to the sea.

They were headed for Taiwan, but the boat skipper was a sailing novice who failed sailing tests twice, once landing in Okinawa when he was tasked to take a small fishing boat from Xiaodong Bay to the nearby Xiewan Bay in Macau. So in mid-January 1948, the schooner ran aground the shallow shores of Antique on the western side of Panay Island in the Philippines, a little more than a hundred refugees waded their way thru the shores of Barbasa, they were met by friendly villagers. It was largely a fishing and farming village, people were hospitable and offered their fishing huts for shelter, fishermen shared their catch and farmers offered fruits and rice.

The refugees and the hosts did not understand a word of each other's language, but then there was that language of amiability and hospitality that did not need much words. All went well, for a few weeks, at least.

In less than a month, the visitors began to grow resourceful. They lumped most of the fish and the fruits which the villagers gave them and sold them to nearby villages for profit, Bobby was one of their fastest and most efficient runners. This angered the villagers of Barbasa, and the language of suspicion and hostility quickly took over.

By March, even before the authorities could figure out where to place them, all of the refugees had moved out of Barbasa. Li Na, Zhang Min and Bobby found themselves in Iloilo City which was then feverishly trying to rise from the rubbles of World War II. There was already a considerably big Chinese community in the city when they arrived. Some families had been there for decades and were rich and established, some just arrived a few days earlier, miserable and destitute.

Li Na and Zhang Min introduced themselves as nurses from the mainland, and it did not take more than three days for everyone in the community to learn about it. The news secured them a place to stay - a damp, moldy apartment on the top floor of an old building from the Spanish era near Plazoleta Gay. The roofs of the building had been blown away by American incendiary bombs during the Liberation of 1945 and had been replaced by loose amakan grass leaves which actually did not stop the rain from falling to the floor.

In a couple of weeks, Li Na and Zhang Min found themselves in want and need of sleep, not just because of their damp beds, but also because the Chinese community had placed them on eternal on-call to respond to illness, both real and imaginary, from colds to cancer. Wang Yong was renamed Roberto Hong, everyone called him Bobby, and he became part of the nursing team, he was introduced as the begotten grandson of a mystic herbalist from Guizhou, though not a bit of that was true, he didn't mind, for his sole task was to deliver balms and ointments to wherever they were needed.

Li Na died of typhoid fever in June. A few months later, in February 1949, Zhang Min died of tuberculosis. Bobby was just a little over eight years old, and he found his family wiped out for the second time. A couple of families wanted to adopt him but he refused, he ceased to believe in families, or at least he stopped believing that they would last. He worked as an errand boy in a small dimsum restaurant for a few cents, for food, and a place to sleep, which was in the kitchen itself.

Bobby was not a stranger to the kitchen, he began helping his mother when he was five and he knew what it took to make a perfect dumpling, and a dumpling had to be perfect or else it would have to be rendered inedible, there was no middle ground. He was just fifteen when he put up a little stall, and he sold only two things - siomai dumplings and siopao buns, all to go. He made sure they were perfect, that was, by his mother's standards, and soon enough he had to deal with long lines of customers. There was rarely a day when his dumplings didn't get sold out, and it only occurred during typhoons, extreme floods or transport strikes.

When he turned 18 he became eligible to own a licensed establishment, he opened a five- table restaurant near Plazoleta Gay, it put a lot of customers on standing room, some had to stand lining for hours, so within a year he was compelled to expand it to thirty tables, but still the lines were long. The Spring Manor Restaurant was a landmark in the city by the mid-60's.

In 1970, Bobby Hong expanded his business further to three floors and renamed it Spring Manor House Restaurant, the word House was added for unknown reasons, people just assumed he had to make the establishment's name longer as it expanded. In 1975 he built a four-star, five-storey hotel beside his restaurant, he called it Spring Manor House Hotel. It sounded a little awkward, Spring was the only thing clear, the rest of the phrase was confusing. He himself later realized this, so in 1977 he renamed it Spring Manor Hotel. By 1978 he was the second highest taxpayer in the city.

Anthony still did not know about Bobby Hong's story and what the dumplings magnate had to do with him becoming a nurse. The associate dean had to enlighten him, she said, Since 1989, after his only child finished college, Bobby Hong has been picking two nursing student scholars every four years, one from this college and one from St. Paul College, deserving students whose families cannot afford to send them to college, two scholars from 1997 just graduated this month, it's time to pick a new pair, and he leaves the selection process entirely to us. You're lucky you applied just this year, Mr. Ilaya!

Anthony was still in disbelief, he felt like someone was figuring a way thru life's treacherous maze for him. He asked, What do I do to get selected?

The dean dropped her glasses low down her nose again, and looked at Anthony over the rim, she said, Usually the selection process is long, we need to gather documents about parents' income, but this time we know clearly it's you. We know about your mother, how she makes a living, there were two lines written about her in the papers when your brother got convicted last year.

Anthony's eyes were all of a sudden on the ground again, just right after having bouts and bouts of elation, he said, Oh, that…

The dean said, Don't worry, we know you are not your brother!

The associate dean said, It's a hefty package, Mr. Ilaya, all of your school fees and books and uniforms are paid for, you'll have student allowance and your lodging on a reasonably priced boarding house will also be paid for. Which means, if you don't get to be a licensed nurse by 2005, you'll only have yourself to blame!

Anthony gave them a weak, embarrassed smile, he asked, How do I get to meet Bobby Hong, just to thank him?

The dean replied, Don't bother, I've never even met him myself, all these years!

Then a young lady clinical instructor from one of the panel of interviewers said, You'll get to meet him on Chinese New Year at the Spring Manor House Restaurant, he hosts a dinner for his scholars, past and present, every year.

The dean introduced the clinical instructor to Anthony, she said, Miss Gargan here is one of his 1993 scholars, she graduated in 1997.

Miss Gargan said, And I'm proud of it! See you at the next Kung Hei Fat Choi dinner!

One of the male professors said banteringly, Or if you really want to see him, go to the Tanza Cemetery on All Saints' Day, right at the middle, you'll see a Chinese looking guy in plain white t-shirt and black trousers and flip-flops!

Everyone in the room laughed, except for Anthony, who was still in shock. Li Na and Zhang Min were interred in Tanza cemetery at the very bottom of a wall of stacked tombs. However, with no one to pay for their spot, their remains were removed and thrown away a couple of years after their burial. Since then, countless others had been interred and removed from the tomb site, but Bobby Hong had been visiting the very spot every year on All Saints' Day, lighting two candles, oftentimes puzzling family members of those interred there. It was one of the rare times he was being seen in public, not often enough to debunk the myth of his height and size.

He wore a plain white t-shirt and black trousers when he arrived in Antique aboard that refugee schooner in 1948, and had been wearing the same kind ever since, except during his wedding, when the parents of his bride threatened to cancel the wedding if he did not show up in coat and tie. He did show up in coat and tie, and rubber flip-flops. His would be in-laws were dismayed but the bride insisted the flip-flops were not mentioned in the deal and so the wedding ought to go on. Rubber flip-flops were actually the only wardrobe upgrade he'd made since arriving as a barefooted refugee.

He hosted a banquet for his scholars at his restaurant every year on Chinese New Year, but he did not join them, he hid in the kitchen as usual, and before the dinner ended he'd show up briefly to acknowledge them by making a toast with service jasmine tea, without saying a single word, except in 1999 when he accidentally spilled a few drops of tea on the shoulder of one of his scholars, after which he said, Oh, sorry! That was the only time he ever spoke to them. By the Chinese New Year of 2001, only Miss Gargan among his former scholars was left in the country, she was joined at dinner by the two on-going scholars who were to graduate in March. Hiring abroad would reach its peak in 2002, within a year those two would leave the country too.

The associate dean said to Anthony, You'll get to know all about Bobby Hong in due time, it's an hour past lunchtime, we have to adjourn!

Anthony thanked them, he could not recall what happened next, he just found himself at the nearby St. Clement's Church, praying. The first person to receive the good news had to be his mother! He had earlier borrowed from a co-worker at Chow-King an unknown brand of mobile phone which squeaked whenever one touched it, from which he could send text messages, but then he recalled that his mother did not have any mobile phone, so he just wished he could shout loud enough so she could hear him 30 miles away. He headed for the bus terminal to get to Burog, to The Blue Cottage before nightfall. Usually when Necessity saw someone running towards the cottage it was bad news getting delivered, it was to change this time, this one would be a first.

12

The Gunter Kalman Choir and Ray Coniff Christmas songs were already playing several times a day on every radio station, Happy Holiday, Good King Wenceslas, Jolly Old St. Nicholas, and it was just mid-September in 2007, very typical in the country where Christmas season begins on the 1st of September. It's coping, it's hope, and the earlier you start playing those songs the longer you bask in the period of hope.

Things had not been going too well since the turn of the millennium, the country saw a vast number of those it had educated leaving, seeking a new life abroad, from the neighboring Southeast Asia to Australia, to Europe, Canada, and of course, the former mother country, the United States. Most of those who'd been leaving were registered nurses who were hired abroad, and many who had been doing something else previously and wanted to leave the country tried to become nurses. They were established doctors, engineers, teachers, lawyers, businessmen, and they thought of abandoning their trade because the nurse working somewhere else on the globe got a much better pay.

Nursing schools flourished like training camps would for soldiers during a great war. The mood was upbeat, many were marching to the tune of eagerness and hope of finding a better life abroad, like soldiers would in what they believe would be a just war, but ironically, the parade seemed to pass by on a backdrop of despair and gloom. For medical students, knowing that the respected professor lecturing in front of them would later in the evening go to school for another career was quite demoralizing, the same thing went for students of law, engineering and other professions, even for regular nursing students themselves who were to wade their way thru nursing school for four years, seeing those already with other baccalaureate degrees do it in less than two years.

Then came 2006, there was a significant slump in direct hiring of nurses from abroad. Slowly, medical, engineering and law professors were returning to their posts, only this time with nursing degrees. Some nursing graduates still managed to find a way out of the country through some other grounds for migration and sought employment themselves, but slowly the country was getting swamped by registered nurses, all fully skilled and qualified but were finding employment in boutiques, in fast food restaurants, in amusement parks. Some formed rock bands.

By September 2007, Necessity's entire life had become like an endless symphony of hope and despair, it seemed like she had earned the right to play Christmas songs all-year round. She was at her food stall, slowly pouring broth from one cauldron to another. Just over her head on a weak beam of her stall was the sign Seng's Pochero, this time printed under the sponsorship of a local laundry soap. Oh Come All Ye Faithful was playing and she was singing along. The stall was small but it looked smart and pretty, too smart and pretty for the bus terminal, it could fit just about three persons her size, customers bought their pochero there and sat and ate by long wooden tables at the terminal which was open to the public.

On the wall behind were she stood to serve customers hung a Tanduay Rum calendar with models in skimpy bikinis, a smaller framed image of The Sacred Heart of Jesus, and an even smaller clipping from a 2005 newspaper that read, 13,108 Out of 24,287 Passed the December 2005 Nursing Licensure Exams. Then underneath it was a tinier clipping, the texts were very small, you'd almost need to poke your nose on it to see that it was a part of the list of successful examinees whose surnames began with the letter I, and there, highlighted with neon yellow marker was the name Ilaya, Anthony Berano.

Anthony never made it to the top ten examinees but he passed, and the State University retained its spot on the top, it was all that mattered. He was Necessity's pride, a registered nurse who was, almost two years on, a lead guitar player of the local band who called themselves The Quitters. He had learned to strum when he was little as his uncle Percivale had a guitar at home, and after high school in between his passes at the fast food stores he'd drop by to practice. He was a natural with the instrument.

He played with the band about three evenings every week and got paid about 300 pesos per gig, and that was about forty songs in one evening. In daytime he worked at a little shop at the Robinson's Mall that printed custom-made buttons, keychains and t-shirts. It was enough to pay the tiny room which he rented and shared with the band's drummer. He was practically back to his old state just before he took up nursing, and every night he lay and pondered and felt very bad about it.

The only progress he'd made at that point was that he was able to buy deodorant without his mother's help. He thought about the morning his mother awakened him to the dream of leaving the country as a nurse, and he he would have made life easier for her by now, retired to a fine home, she could go to the bus terminal to serve pochero just for the love of it, not for survival, and how the people in town would at last respect and look up to her from deep in the most silent of their thoughts, he could be taking her to a tour in Singapore and Japan, and who knows, to The States, finally on top of the Empire State Building? He would have given her her life's trophy by now, finally fulfilling that dream of her grandfather. But it did not look good, he felt like he was doused in hope for years only to wake up to where he began.

On Chinese New Year in 2006, a couple of months after he passed the licensure exams, he had dinner with a few of his fellow Bobby Hong scholars at the Spring Manor. How he shuddered with joy and pride as Bobby Hong appeared on the scene to greet them and made a toast with the service tea, he even gave him a little nod like saying congratulations, and disappeared again without saying a word. In 2007 Anthony asked to be excused from the band to be at that same annual dinner, this time he was going reluctantly, this time his head hung low and he wished Bobby Hong would not appear, he didn't feel he had something to be proud of. But Bobby Hong did appear as he did every year, greeted them, made a toast, and then broke from tradition, to everyone's surprise and to Anthony's horror, he placed his hand on Anthony's right shoulder and asked, So what are you doing now?

It couldn't be worse, Anthony thought. By this time he was sporting a shoulder-length hair, had piercings on the earlobes and was unshaven. It was not good to lie to the person who put you thru nursing school, and he thought Bobby Hong knew everything that was going on so, after some hesitation, he finally replied, I play the lead guitar in a band, it's called The Quitters. Bobby Hong just gave him a pat on the shoulder and left.

It was a Saturday in mid-September so Necessity was expecting Anthony to alight from one of the busses anytime. She'd been running the stall for a decade, the endless routine had begun to feel painful to the spirit, although she got a little lift when Belinda Legaspi stopped hanging out by her stall three years earlier. She frequented the place before that, at least three times a week she'd be there staying for hours for a chit-chat, mostly on how Necessity's stall was the hottest place on earth and how the high life in America was waiting for her, and she'd flaunt everything she got from the package her daughter Mercy sent, from ibuprofen tablets to baseball caps to winter jackets, some of which she wore, while complaining loudly about the heat.

In 2003, her aging American son-in law, more than a decade her senior, had a major stroke and was put in a home. The only career progress Mercy had in The States was getting a full-time job at a local diner, from previously part-time jobs at various fast-food stores. They lived off Tom's modest pension which was quite enough for the family but Mercy had to work in order to finance her mother's boisterous narrative back in Burog.

When Tom became incapacitated she was forced to quit work to take care of their two children, a post previously held by Tom. Tom had a stroke which was quite severe it erased his recent memories, and that included Mercy, he could not recognize her and had no memory of getting re-married, although he still flirted with her each time she made a visit. He hadn't written his will yet. His children from his first marriage were already laying grounds for a legal battle against Mercy as regards his assets in case he passed away.

They did not like Belinda especially, and understandably. Apart from her absolute and perpetual crassness, they thought she was ungrateful, they didn't like what they heard from Tom's friends who visited the Philippines that she'd been spreading word around town that their father was retarded.

December 22, 2004 was the last time Belinda Legaspi was seen at Necessity's pochero stall at the bus terminal. It was Christmastime but she got no package from The States, all she had to show were some pieces of lipstick which she'd shown-off a few months earlier, a scarf which she actually bought in Iloilo City, and a few ibuprofen tablets which she gave away, something which was also given away for free at the government health centers. It was in fairness, some good deed as she helped people with their headaches, but it was doubtful if she gained any merit as she was the cause of their headaches in the first place. She refused to believe the fact that there was ibuprofen in the Philippines and all over the world, though there was not one borborpain anywhere. Then she kept telling people how wonderful life in America was, she'd never been there, but would get there someday. She bragged about Mercy not needing money to get food, she said Mercy had special treatment in West Consin, she only needed to show stamps at the grocery store and she'd get what she wanted.

The following year, Belinda moved with her husband to an inland town in the western part of the province, the town of Janiuay. They were to move into a small and dilapidated rented wooden house. They actually didn't know anyone there, but she thought she had to leave town before people got wise about Mercy's situation. She was in denial, she told people that they were moving to Johnny Way, an anglicized manner of pronouncing Janiuay. Miguelito became a staple Judas at church in Burog during Holy Week every year until 2001, then they retired him. Belinda said that he became a retired-ed Apostle because his bouts of gout attacks rendered him unable to join the processions and eat what was served during The Last Supper. Belinda was never to visit The States. Life at the terminal became more bearable for Necessity.

A bus bound for Carles stopped at the terminal, most of the passengers alighted for lunch. Anthony was among them, Necessity saw him, they waved at each other, though both were aware that it would take a while before they could talk as customers were pouring in, she had to make a living first. Half an hour passed, the last customer from that rush was being served her stew, Anthony approached, he did not look at all excited, but Necessity knew he had something to tell her.

He said, Do you remember Anders Bjorge?

She replied, Barely, but he sounds familiar!

He said, Oh you ought to remember him, the Norwegian exchange student in my senior year in nursing!

Necessity's eyes opened wide and she began to laugh, Oh, the Norwegian guy who dropped that newborn baby but caught her in midair?

Exactly!

Of course, how can I forget him?

Yes, he was here for a weekend and ate only pochero! He's sending his regards!

Oh, you talked to him?

Well, I joined Facebook a couple of months ago and he found me.

What's Facebook?

It's like where you meet friends on the internet, like Friendster which I talked about before, of course, you wouldn't remember. Anyway, he said there was a way I could get a residence permit in Norway and possibly get employed as a nurse!

How?

I can apply as a student learning the Norwegian language, at the same time try to find part-time jobs until I complete the requirements for foreign nurses and get employment!

Necessity was silent, it sounded like a riddle of impossibilities which one could somehow solve, if one thought hard enough.

Anthony said, I know it doesn't sound so convincing, it sounds like one has to spend a fortune in trying to survive until one gets employment, and fortune is one thing we just don't have. Anyway, it's nice to have something new to tell you on a weekend!

Necessity remained silent for a while, then said, And I think it's the most expensive country in the world, if I'm not mistaken...

You're right, said Anthony. Then they looked at each other, smiled and shrugged their shoulders, both quietly agreeing that if they pursued this one, it might be another dud, like the rest of their dreams, only this one would come at a greater price, if it was to be a dud it would drive them to the streets begging for the rest of their lives. Anthony gave his mother 200 pesos as a kind of token from a couple of weeks' labor, and she gave him 50 pesos as some kind of token, for lunch, which meant he'd buy his lunch somewhere else in the bus terminal, something other than pochero.

He stayed overnight at The Blue Cottage and not once did they talk about Norway. The Quitters had an engagement the next day at an alumni homecoming in a catholic school in the city, Anthony was up early, the clanging of the church bells at Burog Parish Church calling for the second mass at 8 a.m. could be heard as he was putting on his street clothes.

I'm going now! He said, knowing Necessity was still in her room, he could hear her counting coins. He was just a few steps away from The Blue Cottage when Necessity appeared by the door to see him off.

Think about it! She said.

Anthony asked, Think about what?

She replied with a hopeful smile, Norway!

Anthony just tittered and walked away. But he did think about it. First he thought a lot about Anders Bjorge. Anders was not exactly an exchange student, as no one from Anthony's class actually took his seat in Norway, he was a more of a visiting student trying to get voluntary clinical exposure for three months in his second to the last term, joining Anthony's class in their clinical rotations in maternal and childcare nursing.

Anders was very tall, he stood out in class, literally. Juanito Can, the tallest guy in class who stood five feet and ten inches was an inch below Anders' chin, when the latter slouched. Anders was bespectacled, but removed his glasses each time he gazed on something or when he read, and he had this habit of picking his nose while reading, drilling almost half of his finger into it. Those were favorite moments for the class to witness and laugh at. Everyone was curious about him but

185

only a very few ever talked to him because he spoke in English which made many in class uncomfortable. Although the medium of instruction in school was English, many were jeering at anyone who spoke any English phrase outside classroom lectures, mimicking their lines in ridicule. Anthony was among those few who talked to him, and many of those who would like to say something important to Anders made Anthony their medium.

Anthony had fond memories of Anders and he tried his best not to laugh all by himself during the bus ride to the city. Anders' duty partner was a boy from the hills of Maasin named Gregorio Magpilas who was very bright in the clinics but always nearly failed in every required English course, he refused to speak in English if it was not an English speech oral exam, and he even had to repeat his oral exams at least once to pass. Having Anders as a duty partner distressed Gregorio, he lost a lot of weight and it gave him intense neck pains. They went on duty together for weeks, Anders talked to him in lengths of sagas like he was more than a duty partner, but he never said a word in return, he just either nodded or shook his head, and they got by.

In their final week, almost the entire class was at the hospital cafeteria for a quick lunch and a pep talk from one of the clinical instructors, Anders was approaching his seat having fetched his lunch from the counter, but he left his chocolate cake by the cashier, the lady was calling his attention in Hiligaynon, he must have heard but did not understand what it was all about. Obligingly, Gregorio Magpilas rose from his seat and said in English, Anders, your cake! You left! Chocolate! Everyone was all of a sudden on their feet, roaring in cheers so loudly it awakened the bats hanging at the ceilings of the hospital chapel. Anders gave Gregorio a little hug, took him by the right wrist and raised his arm, it generated cheers thrice as loud. Gregorio's neck pains disappeared from that moment on.

Anthony was vigilant in trying to protect Anders from pranks. Some of the boys taught him swear words, fooling him about their definitions. One morning, he went around the maternal wards saying to everyone, Lente kamo tanan! His classmates told him it meant, How are you all doing? It actually meant, Damn you all!

He moved very clumsily, and mischievous boys in class loved to see him in panic because then he would run to and fro with his arms swinging and wiggling frantically in all directions, as one of the staff nurses put it - like a marionette whose puppeteer was having seizures. So they loved to scream in prank, DDR! DDR! Which meant Direct to Delivery Room, that is, a woman in labor was on the brink of spewing out her young, it could happen any minute, everyone had to drop whatever they were doing and go straight to the delivery room. Anders would then go frantic and run around the hall in that peculiar manner and everyone would go to the scene to witness it and have a good laugh.

Being the class vice president and way more mature than the rest of the class, Anthony took the lead in trying to stop the pranks, he was very vocal about it during class officer meetings and threatened to report and recommend disciplinary measures to the clinical instructors if the pranks did not cease. For a while he got the nickname Killjoy Ilaya.

There were instances however, when Anders was beyond Anthony's protection. Women in labor were usually told to rub their nipples lightly to release natural oxytocin which would help induce uterine contractions. The instruction in Hiligaynon was, Missis, i ba-id ang imo suso. Anders diligently practiced the phrase day and night, however he could not get quite close to sounding intelligibly. A female obstetrics intern went in panic one afternoon, she thought that one of the women in labor had seizures because she seemed to be grinding her teeth sideways. The intern called for the emergency code and in a few minutes, all obstetrics, internal medicine, anesthesia and pediatrics physicians swamped the labor room. The woman seemed alright and was herself puzzled why everyone was dead worried about her. The intern was being grilled by angry colleagues for calling the emergency code so she had to act out what she saw so her colleagues could have a clinical picture.

The woman in labor was herself embarrassed and she said, The Kano nursing student told me to rub my teeth!

Ngipon is Hiligaynon for teeth, Anders forgot the Hiligaynon term for nipple, which was suso, so he said the exact word nipple, and the woman took it for ngipon. Almost every patient Anders met referred to him as The Kano Nursing Student. Kano is the street term for American. Every caucasian is considered by many among the masses in the Philippines as American, even after having been proven otherwise.

In another incident, Anders' group was at the delivery room watching their clinical instructor assist the resident obstetrician. The baby had just been delivered, the woman was bleeding quite profusely, the obstetrician was so stressed out, she needed small ampules of oxytocin, and by local jargon it was referred to as mere oxy. Anders naturally stood out because of his appearance, and literally because of his height, so he was likely to be asked to do it. The obstetrician said, You, Kano student, get me some oxy, now! He nodded and promptly left the room. He was expected to be back in less than fifteen seconds, but a minute passed, two minutes, three minutes, no sign of him coming. The obstetrician was getting hysterical, she yelled, We're bleeding here! Kano, where are you!? Where's my oxy!? Then came a rumbling sound, like that of a heavy tin drum rolling on the floor, everyone froze, staring at the door, it took about half a minute, then appeared Anders, and with him was a huge, loaded oxygen tank which he was trying to roll by its base. There was intense laughter, even from the patient herself. The obstetrician relaxed and realized it was what she really needed - laughter. It became the most unforgettable hospital anecdote.

As Anthony thought of those moments, he buried his face in a newspaper so people on the bus wouldn't see him laughing by himself. He still thought he did rather little to help Anders during his three-month stint in Iloilo for the latter to be kind enough to assist him in getting a job in Norway. Then he remembered one more incident, and maybe he thought that was it that made Anders not forget him ever. Anders was assigned to a patient who developed postpartum psychosis. The woman just all of a sudden began screaming, demanding she'd be released from what she thought was a death camp. She was at the maternity wards. The psychiatric team was summoned and they were on their way. Then she directed her aggression towards Anders who did not understand a single word from what she was saying, except maybe Kano. She repeatedly screamed in Hiligaynon, You Kano, get out of my country you tyrant! Release me from this prison! I'm Darna and I can fly!

Darna is the Philippine version of Wonder Woman. The hospital guards arrived, as soon as the woman caught sight of them, she fled. She was stocky and strong, she knocked down everyone in her path. She went thru the fire exit, the maternity wards were on the ground floor, so it was easy. The guards ran after her, so did Anders. The clinical instructor called on Anders to leave it, but he seemed not able to hear anything. Right outside the wards was a concrete wall more than twelve feet high and leaning on it was a dying talisay tree, it appeared to the woman that she had been cornered and had nowhere to go. But then, before the eyes of everyone who pursued her, she climbed the talisay tree effortlessly like a squirrel, and she screamed, Darna!!! She then jumped to the other side of the wall, landing on a lump of sand by the sidewalk, and ran southwards to the National Highway.

The guards tried to climb the talisay tree but they couldn't get more than five feet from the ground. Anders found a way, he saw someone opening the red gate some fifty yards away, it was the gate where they transported corpses out of the hospital from the morgue. He ran frantically and inefficiently, indeed like a marionette whose puppeteer was having seizures. When he got out of the gate, the woman was nowhere to be seen, but people by the roadside were pointing to which direction she ran, some were screaming, There! There! Some were pointing silently. A pedicab approached, Anders waved a bundle of hundred peso bills to flag the pedicab and he made sure it stopped. He told the driver he'd pay a hefty sum if he agreed to pursue the woman. The pedicab driver naturally agreed, he understood only four words from what Anders said - woman, run, after, and pay, and he saw the big wad of hundred peso bills. He drove to the direction which the people in the streets were pointing to, not knowing that the woman was running three times faster than his pedicab which was powered by no other than his arthritis-worn knees, and he had no idea which woman they were after, he just pedaled the best he could, smiling because his usual whole month's earnings were guaranteed that day.

The clinical instructor tried to run after the pedicab, she called on Anders to come back, but she herself was running thrice as slow as the pedicab. Just a few seconds after she was out of the gate, the pedicab had turned to a corner and disappeared. Anthony came to the scene, the clinical instructor asked him to run after Anders, she was more concerned of the foreign visiting student now than the patient who, not having been assessed yet by psychiatrists, could still be juridically considered a patient fleeing against medical advice.

Students were not allowed to use their mobile phones while on duty, so Anders' phone was sitting snugly somewhere inside his locker, safe and useless. Anthony thought hard, then he remembered that one of the hospital guards stationed at the main gate had a bicycle. It was a long way to run to the main gate, and he had to plea with the guard who initially wouldn't lend that piece of rusty tubes with two wheels, the bicycle was so old and rusty it looked like it had been salvaged from the wreck of the Titanic.

He surprisingly got the guard's nod, he pedaled, but every hundred yards or so the the bicycle chain loosened and got detached, and so he had to stop and repair it. By the time he was out of that red gate, most of the people who witnessed probably the year's main event for the alley had dispersed, there was practically no one reliable enough to tell him which direction the woman and Anders went. Two people pointed to one direction, two others pointed to just the opposite. He just had to make a guess, he tried to recall to which direction the clinical instructor was looking while calling on Anders. He guessed the right direction.

Soon he was by the National Highway just across the SM City Mall, he felt lost in a very familiar city, he did not know which way Anders went, it had been nearly an hour since he took the pedicab. The sidewalk was full of squatting food vendors, all busy with their customers. In desperation he cried out loud, Has anyone seen a Kano on a pedicab? All of a sudden the vendors and most of their customers stiffened in attention, their necks were stretched out like alerted meerkats, and they all, in almost perfect synchrony pointed to one direction - west. Anthony thanked them and pedaled westwards, but after about a hundred yards, the bicycle ceased to be a bicycle, it broke so badly it was beyond repair and recognition, so now he had to run after Anders while pushing a heavy piece of junk as baggage, though it was not anymore that difficult to find out where he went, almost everyone in every corner remembered seeing a Kano on a pedicab and the direction he took.

After about two hours of walking, the fastest one could while pushing a piece of junk, Anthony saw Anders, he was walking back towards him, then they finally met face to face, just outside Christ the King cemetery. The pedicab driver stopped when they reached the town of Pavia, they did not catch the fleeing woman, he took all of Anders' money and refused to drive him back, claiming it was not part of the deal, and the driver's knees got all swollen he was pondering about retiring that day. Anders was shaken and silently sobbing, Anthony did his best to comfort him. His back was aching, he was too tall to be sitting in that pedicab sidecar. Outside his mother's womb, that was the longest time he ever crouched. Anthony had just enough money for a jeepney fare for two back to San Bernardino Hospital, and it took them two rides to get back. They did not talk much, both were still in a state of shock after all that ordeal.

Anthony returned the bicycle to the hospital guard, he wondered if he could ever pay the damages but the guard did not seem to be bothered, he took a look at the what was once a bicycle, now a mere conglomeration of rust with rubber wheels. Then the guard said, Just place it there, I'll take care of it! He sounded like it looked worse when he purchased it.

Before they entered the maternity wards, Anders gave Anthony a pat on the right shoulder and said, You are a good man Anthony, you are going to go far!

Anthony chaffed, he replied, You're even the better man, you went much farther! Both were too tired to laugh. They both learned later that the police had caught the woman barely an hour after she fled, under a small bridge by a narrow creek roughly a block from the hospital, and they took her to the wrong hospital some five miles away.

If there was something that made Anders never forget him, it must have been it, Anthony thought while on the bus ride to the city. He could never forget Anders either, and there were a lot more from the class and from the hospital other than him who would never forget Anders. When Anders left for Norway, Anthony sent him off at the airport. Anthony thought that Anders would be filed in one of his fondest memory shelves for keeps, and that it would be the last time he'd see him. But the age of social media came too soon, Anders was back almost at the center of his life and it drove him laughing all by himself on the bus. Anders was a lousy augur though, he thought, having prophesied that he'd go far in life, and there he was, a lead guitarist in a band that earned just enough so they'd need not ask their parents to pay for their deodorant sticks.

He thought of Anders, and day after day he laughed less and less about those comical memories of him, and thought more and more seriously about the prospects of success in Norway.

13

*N*ecessity was once again wrestling a big bunch of bananas
one evening, it was a long one, high up to her waist, and
she was carefully plucking them one by one, if she
pulled too hard they'd ripen fast and rot unduly. Then she
came upon a pair of bananas right in the middle of the bunch,
they were liked conjoined twins, two bananas inside one peel.
She paused and thought, and then smiled briefly and shook
her head. It is believed that if a woman ate twin bananas she'd
give birth to twins, but if she's past childbearing age, it means
good luck among her children. What made her shake her head
was the thought that she only had two children, one was
serving life sentence at the Bilibid Prison, and the other was in
the metropolitan jungle of Manila for the first time, fighting his
way to the Norwegian Embassy. It could only get better, she
thought, whatever would happen to them, it could only be
good luck.

Anthony managed to get return economy ferry tickets to
Manila. It was not one of those regular ferries, it was a smaller
one which took occasional trips when the larger ferries were
full, and the fares were much cheaper. The trip took a little
more than sixteen hours, it was much slower than the regular
ones. The steerage area was jam-packed, passengers slept in

double-deck beds in an open hall, if one looked solely at that area, it would appear to be like a refugee ship, or a cargo ship for cattle. It was in mid-March of 2008, the hottest, driest period of the year had begun and the sea breeze could only do little to help.

The trip was miserable, children were screaming from heat and want, enough number of passengers did not follow no-smoking rules making the ship look like a floating thurible, wives were yelling at their husbands and vice versa, a group of young male adults got drunk and were loud and for a while, they were overly friendly to everybody, and when the alcohol left their blood they turned overly hostile.

Anthony saw this sight of a young mother sitting on one of the steel beds with rubber mattresses, she was flanked by six small children, the youngest was a few months old and the eldest was too small and gaunt to be six but he ought to be at least six. They all looked hungry and were scrounging pulverized bits of hopia pie from a transparent plastic bag, and the mother had been looking, staring blank at a corner of the bed for a long time, her face was almost a complete summary of hopelessness.

Anthony turned to his right and he saw this old man past his seventies smoking a rolled cigar, he had been staring at him for a while without any hints of emotional expression, and he kept blowing smoke right to the face of his wife who was just as old and just as devoid of affect, and who had also been staring at Anthony for a while. The sea was calm like a pool, and that was the only consolation, still the trip was all in all a misery, Anthony thought for a while that if the captain ordered to abandon ship it would have been a welcome relief.

A young man named Greg Buswang whose father also had a stall at the bus terminal in Burog had agreed to host Anthony during his three-day stay in Manila. Greg fetched Anthony at the harbor and it took four jeepney rides to get to his place. His place was actually a rented little room in a shanty in the slums of Pasig. Uncle Arthur used to live in Pasig, but by that time he had moved with his family further north in Tarlac where he worked as an office clerk.

After alighting from the jeepney in the main street, Anthony and his host had to go on foot, crisscrossing a labyrinth of muddy footpaths amidst shacks made of all kinds of materials on earth that nobody wanted, like bits from old billboards, cartons, rice sacks and metals from vehicular wrecks, and old tires were used as weights on roofs so they wouldn't fly away with the morning breeze. To get to Greg's shanty, they needed to cross dozens of makeshift bamboo planks and bridges that connected the shacks, as the entire slum rose from a swamp which was unofficially a large common toilet. The water from the swamp looked like rich dark chocolate, but it was not that thick, as people could still fish mud perch from it.

It was Anthony's first time in Manila, and what a sight! Greg's place stood on a mound in the middle of the slum jungle, the walls were partly made of used plywood, partly carton, the roofs were of rice sacks tightly bound together, but still his place was considered by slum dwellers to be relatively well-off, because he had dry soil for his floor. And he had a rather new television with cable, a pair of very loud speakers, a small fridge and several boxes full of all kinds of mobile phones. There were two bedrooms, Greg rented one of them, each bedroom could fit two people lying side by side, and the area which they called living room was about twice as spacious, or rather, twice less cramped. Greg showed Anthony to his bed, it was a pile of cartons, and his pillow was a rice sack stuffed with crumpled rice sacks.

Anthony dared interrogate Greg about what he did for a living. He asked, So what do you do?

Without any ounce of shame, Greg replied, Well, I am a petty criminal, I snatch cellular phones and sell them, I belong to a ring called Esnut Sirs, we are the fastest and most cunning in Pasig area! He giggled delightfully in pride.

Anthony did not know what to say next, he just shook his head a little and instinctively looked at his very old and very rusty mobile phone which had been in his possession for so long not even he could remember, and it was the only one he'd ever had.

As a skilled pickpocket, Greg was keen as to people's actuations, so when he saw Anthony looking at his old mobile he laughed hard and said, Oh don't you worry about your phone, I'd never touch that, it's sacred, because God created that before the dinosaurs! My father told me not to sell anything sacred, it's Simony! He laughed for a while, and then continued, Besides, I'm a criminal, stealing that would not be a crime, it would be an act of mercy!

The next morning, Greg accompanied Anthony to the Norwegian Embassy. The interview was to be at 11 a.m. but they had to start at 5 a.m. due to near world-record traffic. It took two jeepney rides and a ride at the metro rail, and they were at the embassy before 10. Greg had to go, he had to earn a living, but it appeared like he was already making a living while he was escorting his guest. Before they parted, he flaunted before Anthony two mobile phones which he snatched along the way, one was a very old gigantic gizmo-looking device which he casually threw away at a nearby garbage bin, and the other was a new HTC which he slid into his pocket as he walked away. He was to fetch Anthony at the same spot at 3 pm.

Anthony went inside the embassy thru the big glass door. Having slept in a shanty the night before and in a shabby hut almost his entire life, the well-polished offices of the Norwegian Embassy did not feel so welcoming to him, despite the friendly, helpful faces and the signs of Velkommen everywhere. Norway was vying to have the world's highest living standards, while he felt comfortable enough literally hitting the rice sack the night before.

He felt a rumbling in his stomach, then the urge to rush to the toilet, he still had a little less than an hour. He had diarrhea and realized it did not have the smell of mere nervousness, he thought it had the odor of microbes that could probably wipe out civilization and take over the stewardship of the planet from mankind. He remembered drinking water from a bottle which Greg took out of his fridge, it wasn't crystal clear, it looked like a much lighter version of the water from Pasig River, and he recalled the taste, it tasted like he'd rather be thirsty. He rushed to the toilet three times before his name was called for the interview. He forgot about nervousness and the probable questions which he might not be able to answer, or might answer wrongly, he did not think about Norway nor the future, he thought only of the toilet seat.

He did fine, he answered as briefly and as correctly as he could, he thought longer sentences seemed to trigger bowel movements. Anders paid for the application fee which was roughly four thousand pesos, and he agreed to stand as guarantor for Anthony's initial survival as a student in Oslo, which meant, he was to stay at Anders' and Anders had to show proof he had the means.

Anthony was to study the Norwegian language and later on, a completion course in nursing, and if he could find an employer there he could get a residence permit. Despite the study permit, he was still to be considered a foreign visiting student which meant he was not entitled to free education like those with residence permits and the citizens, so Anders had to show proof too, that he could pay for at least one term's tuition. That was what they officially told the Norwegian Directorate of Migration.

In reality, Anders was still reeling financially, he just moved to Oslo from Trondheim after breaking up with a female nurse aid whom he'd moved in with a couple of years earlier. He just got a job as a nurse at an elderly home, he'd be stable in half a year, but at the moment, he even needed to borrow money from Signe, his sister who was relatively well-off, only to show the Utlendningsdirektoratet that his bank account was fat enough for a foreign student's upkeep and tuition.

The actual agreement between the two which they kept from the directorate of immigration was that, Anders would pay for the application and stand as guarantor, but Anthony would find other sources to help pay part of his upkeep and tuition, and that he would pay Anders later on when he'd found a job. As soon as he arrived he'd need to find an employer for any sort of work, to get residence and work permits so he could get to avail of a subsidized completion course in nursing.

Anders had prepped him and sent him loads of information about his little short life so the embassy would be convinced that they were that close as friends. Anthony got to know all about both the important and minute details of Anders' life, like how his father left them when he was little to join a meditative hippie group in the Himalayas, how as a child he was placed under observation at the hospital after swallowing a live garden snail, how he dislocated his left shoulder while trying to cushion his big music teacher as she slipped and fell to the floor. None of those were brought up during the interview however, but Anthony knew more than enough. Then he rushed to the toilet twice more before leaving the embassy.

The next day, he was on board the ferry again back to Iloilo, this time, he was standing close to the toilets as he still had diarrhea. He was not too hopeful, aside from thinking mostly of toilet seats, he also thought about what he'd do with a visa without a plane ticket, or with a visa with a plane ticket with no guarantee of survival or a job, in a few months he might be desperate again to get a ticket back home.

He and Anders agreed it was a high-stake gamble. The fact was, Anders went into a major depression after breaking up with his girlfriend, he had been placed on observation for suicidal ideations, but the thought of his time in the Philippines and having someone from that blissful warm era somewhere near him brought him back to life. It appeared as simple as that, the thought of moving to Oslo and to move a part of the Philippines near him, it made him decide to go on living. He was willing to gamble, but Anthony was quite hesitant after witnessing and going thru a lot of fiascos in his life. He did not think much during the ferry trip back home, for as of that moment, the toilet was the only place where he'd rather be.

In late May 2008, the rains began to fall and the soil began to breathe out that scent which smelled of the earth trying to accustom itself to the ways of heaven. A small envelope with the logo of the Norwegian Embassy was delivered at The Blue Cottage in Sitio Putak, Burog, Iloilo. Anthony gave all the powers to Necessity to open his mail if the sender had such logo. It said they were happy to inform him that his application for student visa had been granted, he was either to send his passport thru mail, or he could drop by in person at the embassy before he left the country so they could attach the visa. Necessity asked Sese to inform Anthony about the letter thru a text message, he received the message, and he came home that night.

The mood was mixed, mother and son could not really tell what was in each other's minds, but both believed that showing some signs of celebration might trigger the winds of Burog Bay to unleash another fiasco, so both tried to appear subdued, both tried to hide every bit of jubilant emotion. There was a humongous financial obstacle between Sitio Putak and Oslo but they forgot about that for a while. They took turns in getting inside their respective bedrooms to let a few tears roll down.

There was a small internet station near the public market in Burog, Anthony went there the next day to have a video chat with Anders, and it was without audio, they had to type whatever they had to say. Anders was going wild in celebration, it was still early morning in Oslo but he had already opened a bottle of Prosecco. He was wearing a red shirt which was a little too small for him, and on it the print,

Norwegian Playboy. Then after a while, they went back to the details of the plan, and reality quickly stepped in.

The last day of filing applications for spring term which would start in January would be in late August, and Anthony had to be there physically by then, if not, he would have to wait to apply in May 2009 for the fall term in September, and by then his visa would have expired. Anders just received his first paycheck in a while, and it was clear that he was not likely to be the source of the plane fare, but he might possibly step up if nothing happened by the end of July. Sometime in the middle of the celebrations, the fun would have to be spoiled in order to put into substance what one was celebrating about. Anthony walked back home, a little desperate, a little defeated, a little hopeful.

Four weeks later in late June, he found himself playing at a concert for a cause in Mellow Town, an area along the National Highway in Iloilo City where a lot of bars, restaurants and cafes had been established. It was where the younger generation flocked in the evenings and on weekends, it was also where journalists flocked when they had nothing else to report, for sooner or later there would be petty incidences like girls pulling each other's hairs over love triangle issues, or boys threatening to shoot each other with virtually unloaded guns, or a young lady going wild in the streets after having been dumped by her lover thereby getting arrested for public drunkenness. It was also where The Quitters played most often.

Typhoon Frank, the most devastating storm to hit the province in seventeen years, swept thru thru the city just a week earlier. Dozens lost their lives, mostly due to flash floods, and there was heavy damage, most bars in Mellow Town had been under water and had not yet re-opened.

The mood in the evening's concert was subdued, the rock bands appeared unusually placid. It was a concert for the benefit of typhoon victims so everyone was well-behaved, there were no petty news to report, only one journalist was there, Mellow Town was unusually mellow that evening. Everyone in the city and the province was still busy counting damages and casualties.

The Quitters had an hour's slot in the concert at around 9 p.m., they had been busy rehearsing behind one of the bars since late afternoon, so Anthony had left his loyal but aging and dying mobile phone unattended inside his pocket, he did not know that he had received several text messages. He was playing his guitar, but his mind was somewhere else, sometimes in Norway where he'd never been to, and sometimes in Sitio Putak, where he thought he'd be stuck forever.

A considerable part of The Blue Cottage's roof had been blown away, Necessity's room had been generously receiving rain and sunshine and bird droppings, so she had to sleep at the tiny living room. Anthony wondered where he'd get the money for the plane ticket to Oslo when he couldn't find enough to repair the roof of his mother's house.

The Quitters played their final song, Phil Collins' Another Day in Paradise, and proceeded to the backstage to get their pay before dispersing. Anthony was walking away from the stage, tucking in the hundred peso bill he got paid with in his left shirt pocket. They were supposed to be paid three hundred, but two hundred would go to typhoon funds. Then, a tall, well-clad man in his late thirties stood in his way at the sidewalk.

The man said, Anthony? Anthony Ilaya?

Anthony just stared at the man, his face was clearly familiar, his forehead was high, his hair was wavy and he was wearing a mustache. In an instant, it evoked in him a kind of anger and hostility which he could not understand, because the man appeared gentle and very friendly. Puzzled, he asked, Yes, what can I do you for?

The man replied, I sent you a few text messages earlier this evening.

Instinctively, Anthony drew his old and dying mobile phone and scrolled thru the messages. The man's name was Renato, in the text messages he had asked to meet him at one of the cafes after the concert, and not having replied, he then proposed he'd meet him at the backstage. Anthony said, Sorry, we were rehearsing, it was too loud, I couldn't hear my phone.

The man replied, No problem, I understand. There was a brief moment of silence, then the man continued, My name is Renato, Renato Ilaya, of course, you'd never remember me because we've never met.

Anthony was dumbfounded, then after a while he tried to speak, he said, I do...remember...a little about you...

Then Renato said, Let's go have some coffee! You know a good place?

Anthony replied, There's a place called Blu Jay, they serve my favorite cappuccino.

They walked towards the cafe a block away. Renato made some small talk along the way, but Anthony was not concentrating, he was busy processing reminiscences connected to the name Renato Ilaya. His father Onyok used to mention that name a lot, that he was smart and that he was his hope for the future. He recalled that when Onyok hung Necessity on that odious fish hook, they were fighting about Renato and his mother Juliana. It finally did sink into his mind that he was walking side by side with his brother, he had no idea why he was there and what was it he wanted and what would happen next.

They went inside the cafe, ordered a cup of cappuccino each, and took a seat in a corner. Anthony was the first to speak, he asked, So what brought you here?

Renato was looking pensively at his cup of cappuccino as he stirred it with a teaspoon, he replied, I heard of the terrible storm, so I went to Balasan to check my livestock, but since they are all alright, the business trip has been turned into a charity tour. Then he told him about how he was doing, that he owned Bahaghari, one of the biggest hog farms in the

Visayas, he had his office and his main farm in Dumaguete in Negros Oriental and had several satellite farms scattered in several provinces, he'd become a millionaire already at 35, and now he's almost 40 and had established a little empire, but he was still not married. He continued, I met your mother earlier today, I received tips from townsfolk about her pochero stall so I dropped by for lunch and we talked, we talked about you!

Anthony felt embarrassed and dropped his head low, he said, There's not much to talk about me, I mean, I'm not anywhere close to what what you have become.

Renato just kept on stirring and staring at his cappuccino, then looked at Anthony and said, Oslo is a fine place, I was there in 2005, I took a weekend tour after attending a short course in wholesale organic hog farming in southern Sweden.

Anthony felt all the more embarrassed, and said in a low tone, Oh, you know about my wingless Oslo plan...

Renato replied, And the plan is going to take off now! Do you know what I mean?

Anthony got the hint, but still did not want to believe, so he pretended not to know, and shook his head slightly.

Renato continued, I will pay for your fares and I'll give you enough cash so you can pay your share according to your agreement with what was his name... Andrew?

Anders, replied Anthony, it made him laugh a little. Then there was a long moment of silence, Renato kept on stirring his cup, Anthony tried to lift his cup to take a sip but he was shaking, he had to put it down shortly after every attempt. Soon a few tears rolled down his cheeks. He said, I don't understand, my mother took all those beatings from my father because she refused to help in supporting you and your mother, why such generosity now?

Renato replied, I don't understand what you mean either, because your mother Necessity kept sending every little she could, at least once every month in high school I could buy a sandwich and soda at the school cafeteria, thanks to her!

Anthony showed some signs of surprise, and said, I never knew that, she refused to help every time Papa asked her, I remember clearly how she said no, then took the beatings...

Renato said, I'm sorry about what she'd been thru, I had an idea but I did not know it was that bad.

Anthony said, She's that kind of woman, maybe she thought it was best she said no but did the opposite, knowing the horror of the man her husband was, but still I don't understand her, how to not tell about her good deeds and take the beatings, I don't understand why she married him in the first place!

Renato said, I'm sorry, I understand if you have that memory of him.

Anthony finally raised his head, looked at Renato and asked, What's your memory of him?

It was Renato this time who looked down, a bit embarrassed, he said, Well, mostly fond memories, I mean, he was always happy when he was with us in Miag-ao, he was sweet and kind to my mother and my little sister, he never beat anyone of us, and we always played together, and he told me about all the things I could achieve, he had big dreams for me. But of course, he came to visit like twice a year so maybe it was easier to play nice every time...

What Anthony heard ought to have set him in a rage, but the thought of Renato reaching out to help him all but neutralized it. All he could say was, I see...

Renato said, Look, if I had known earlier how he treated you and your mother I would have despised him too, but I had been given another picture of him, I'm sorry about that.

Anthony said, Why be sorry? You did nothing wrong!

Renato replied, Because I was angry at your mother for a time, because it was she who said it was best we didn't attend his funeral, and I resented it deeply. Had I known the extent of the monster in our father I wouldn't have harbored that anger all these years, I would have been there in your greatest hours of need.

Anthony said, Oh you never had to, life made us find a way out of those trials, or at least a way around them, I think it was best it happened that way.

Renato said, My mother made me promise, if ever I could pull myself out of poverty someday, to do your mother some good in return for those acts of kindness, you know, for sending us a little money every month.

Anthony asked, What happened to your mother?

Renato took a deep sigh and replied, After Papa died we moved to Dumaguete, it was the year I graduated from high school, but then I could not afford to go to college, so I worked as a farmhand, tending livestock. Two years later, I watched my mother die, we were so poor I could not buy her the mildest and cheapest of pain relievers, but she was there in bed, coughing and wailing because of the pains in her chest and back, I watched her in her agony for hours until she expired at dawn.

Anthony said, I'm very sorry to hear that.

Renato was composed and never seemed to get near teary-eyed, he went on telling his story. He said, Then I didn't know how we were supposed to bury her, we had nothing, I'd been eating wild guavas in those two days leading to her death. Then the parish priest came, he was supposed to give the last rites but he was a few hours too late, he was moved with pity upon seeing our plight, so he offered to arrange with the funeral home and they gave my mother the simplest yet very decent funeral. We were new in town, nobody knew us so well so during the funeral it was just my sister and I, then of course the priest, and two old women who attended everybody's funeral. He smiled at this point and shook his head.

Anthony said, It's amazing how you pulled thru!

Renato smiled weakly and said, Well, the priest was quite odd, he thought of raising livestock, you know, poultry, hogs, cattle as some kind of an income-generating project for the parish, so he hired me, and realizing I had a knack for numbers, he sent me to Siliman University where I got my college degree in commerce. His tiny hog farm grew while I was in college, then a few years later, he was transferred and the bishop did not allow him to take the business with him, so I took over, but the wise guy sold his share, of course, and hopefully brought it with him to heaven. Bless his soul, without him I'd still be gnawing wild guavas right now somewhere in Negros Oriental!

They both laughed lightly. Then Anthony tried to look serious as he asked, When do you expect me to pay you back? I mean it might take a couple of years before I...

Renato replied, Look, this is not a business deal! In business deals I expect return of investment, not otherwise!

Anthony said, Someday, I'll repay you in any other way possible...

Renato said, I don't expect you to, or to put it clearly, I demand that you don't pay me, otherwise it would be a mere business deal, like what I just said.

Anthony said, Then this ought to be the start of a lasting friendship between us, brothers, I'll come and see you whenever, if ever I'm back in the country!

Renato sighed and gave him a warm smile, he then said, Would you mind if I said no to that one too?

Anthony could not quite understand, and felt embarrassed about being too enthusiastic about friendship too soon.

Renato continued, I mean, this is the finest moment between us brothers, I think we should always remember it this way, don't you think? It has deleted a great deal of pain, I think this moment is more than enough!

Anthony said, Maybe you're right, but you can't stop me from dragging you into my thoughts and prayers.

Renato said, Alright, done deal then!

They rose, not realizing they never drank a drop out of their cup, for anyhow they did not know it was not really coffee they wanted there, what was needed to be said was said. Renato drove Anthony to his boarding house. Anthony was teary eyed, he felt the need to thank his brother some more, so as soon as he got off the car, he walked over to the driver's side and said, You know, I can never ever thank you enough…

But Renato interrupted him, in a quick manner and in a loud voice he said, Don't forget to see the Fjord, and the mountains in the north! And of course the northern lights! Drive down the west coast of Sweden in summer, and all the way to Copenhagen, there's so much to see! He then closed his side window and drove off. Anthony watched the car disappear, Renato was also watching him getting smaller and smaller in the rear-view mirror. All their lives they thought of each other's names as some mere words which evoked a faint memory of resentment, but that night they finally became brothers, and they were not to see each other again.

14

August 6, 2008, the sunny afternoon was fading too quickly into a dark grey evening. Anthony thought he'd take a walk by the shores near the village. He was painfully aware that it was to be his last afternoon on the shores of Sitio Putak, perhaps for a very long time, if not ever. Burog Bay had been cleaned up a few years earlier, the government installed privies at both Sitios Putak and Paka, heavy fines were in place for anyone trying to make a latrine out of the Pacific Ocean. Burog Bay was declared the cleanest area in Iloilo Strait, so he was not worried about getting diarrhea if he kissed the waters. He took a knee by the shore, scooped seawater with his right hand and kissed it.

He hated cliches. He always thought that the phrase - a dagger thru one's heart, was a another one of those made-up cheesy cliches everyone used to make a prose or a poem sound more complicated than it actually was, but at that point he began to understand what the phrase meant clearly well, as he was definitely going thru it. He looked around, there were a few pump boats with outriggers passing by going both north and south, there were seagulls in small flocks mocking each other, he saw some small crabs cautiously creeping out of the tide pools, and at a distance some children playing hide and seek by the big rocks. He could hear people at the nearby Sitio Paka intermittently erupting in screams while playing mahjong, and one or two among them could be heard shouting a swear-word. He could smell the stale, salty odor of loam in low-tide.

These things had been there all his life, but now he could see, hear and smell everything, because he was aware that these things were to die from him, and only at that moment did he know that a big part of him was to die when they died, frivolous little things that he never even cared about before.

His feet finally grew tired by dusk, so he decided to retire to The Blue Cottage, one final time. He found Necessity sitting on a bench made of used steel pipes which she'd put up right in front of the house after the storm. He could see her face clearly, aided by faint orange sunset rays coming from the hills at the west. She had turned 61, she had a lot more grey hair than black, her face was all-worn, and its expressions showed like it had been a constant battleground of hope and despair, but still it radiated some kind of peace. He sat beside her, it was getting dark, and from nearby talisay trees the cicadas were commencing their evening symphony. Neither mother nor son spoke a word for almost ten minutes.

Then Necessity spoke first, she said, Never forget this place, wherever you go, no matter how humble it may look like, no matter how humble it may make you look, do you understand?

Anthony replied, I promise, Mama.

Necessity said, Because if you forget this place, you will forever be lost!

He began to cry quietly and thought, How can I ever forget this place? To his right he could see the rock that had a little protrusion, looking like a human hand making a thumbs-up sign, it was sitting still upon some heaps of mud, totally visible in low tide. He recalled when he was eight, Onyok and Necessity had one of those fights, Necessity was taking a good beating though she was fighting back, Onyok was hitting her hard on the face as if it was a fair boxing match, and she was eventually knocked out of consciousness.

It was extreme horror for Anthony to witness this, he was unable to eat and sleep for two days and two nights. That was a horrific memory to recall, but there was a fond memory attached, because a few days after that, he thought of a way for his mother to escape in case such beating occurred again. He built a raft made of cardboard, its skeleton was made of acacia twigs which they gathered for firewood, and he bound everything altogether with thin ropes made of straw. He tied his raft to that rock that looked like a hand making a thumbs-up sign. The next morning, Onyok came home drunk and began throwing things at Necessity - jars, spoons, shoes, picture frames, and everything he could get hold of. Anthony took his mother by the hand and led her to the Thumbs-up Rock, he told her to board the raft he made and urged her to escape to the nearest island.

Necessity thought it was cute and endearing, her terror-stricken face quickly turned into an amused one. Realizing that Onyok had passed out, she decided to recognize Anthony's efforts by boarding his raft. She then told him, Come with me, we will sail to the island of my fairy godmother, where no one intends anyone any pain or harm! Anthony boarded the raft too, and it did float some five feet before it capsized, mother and son were laughing as they waded ashore. Soon Jeremy joined them, they played sharks and dolphins and sailors and pirates, they knew Onyok was to remain unconscious for the rest of the day so they were basking joyously in peace and freedom, however temporarily.

Anthony turned to his left, he could see an area in the beach were there used to be a big mound of mud, he recalled the day when his father Onyok gave Necessity a beating with his leather belt and she retaliated with fish hooks. He was rolling there in pain as he had about five hooks clinging to the skin of his butt, and Necessity saw to it that they were evenly distributed. His loyal thugs Dodong and Totong were taking turns in pulling out the hooks, but each having only one arm, they were not doing it properly, they were pulling out the hooks as they would pull out a straight pin, it was too painful that Onyok kicked and punched them both in the face each time a hook was pulled out, partly to drown his own pain, so by the time all the hooks were pulled out, Dodong was lying unconscious and Totong, though still standing, was having a temporary retrograde amnesia. The memory usually made Anthony laugh, but this time, nothing could keep him from crying.

When she realized that Anthony was crying, Necessity said, I always hate to see you cry, but not today, yours tears are an affirmation that this place will always be with you wherever you go.

Anthony glanced at his mother. He loved that face, no matter how worn it had become, and there were too many memories, and he intended to cherish every single one of them, happy or sad.

He recalled the times she was hurt because he and Jeremy were embarrassed of her. He recalled that Christmas Family Day at Santa Helena when he was in the second grade, Jeremy did not want to talk to Necessity and even denied knowing her before his friends because her dress was quite shabby and her hair looked like a typhoon just made landfall and caught her outdoors. He warned Anthony not to talk to her or else he'd get a fist straight to his nose. Anthony forgot about this warning and had a nice chat anyway with his mother while they were eating ice cream in front of his classmates and their parents. Jeremy saw this and was furious, he dragged Anthony to the toilet and gave him several punches on the belly until he'd vomited everything he'd eaten for lunch. That made Anthony follow suit in treating their mother like air the rest of the day. Necessity was too hurt to stay there, she went home two hours before the affair was to end, she asked her brother Percivale to fetch the boys later in the afternoon.

But Anthony could not place all the fault on Jeremy, for there were instances when he acted all alone in hurting his mother. It was the evening after the final exams in their junior year in nursing, it happened not so long ago and Jeremy had already long been sitting in jail.

The class was celebrating the end of the school year at the elegant home of a classmate named Alice Rovet in Jaro. Anthony had a big crush on the girl but he felt too poor to even strike a conversation with her, he had resigned to the fact that she was way out of his league, but that night he was partying in her house and she was treating everyone like a fellow nobility, she talked to him and even danced with him a couple of times. He felt grand, he wanted to forget that feeling of being impoverished at least that night, and he wanted to forget that the night wouldn't last forever.

Then thru the window on the second floor of the house where the party was being held, he saw his mother standing outside the gate, she had with her a laundry bag full of clean clothes which she had washed a few days earlier. It was a Friday night, everybody in Anthony's boarding house was out somewhere, even the landlord of the boarding house himself was dining out, so he locked the place, and Necessity did not have the keys, she was supposed to leave Anthony's clean clothes there. He had told her earlier where the party was, and the Rovets' house was almost like a landmark in Jaro.

He felt like his mother's presence reminded him too soon of the reality about who he was, something he'd like to avoid at least that night. The sight of her annoyed him, so he ignored her and hoped she'd just give up, go away and leave his clothes at his Uncle Percivale's or come back another day. Half an hour later he looked out again, and she was still there, waiting patiently. After another half an hour he looked out again, she was still there, and it was 10 pm. By that time he was drinking his fourth can of beer and was already cursing and was not listening when talked to.

A few minutes later, a maid in white and blue uniform entered the living room-turned- dance floor, took the microphone and interrupted the music and the dancing, she announced, Is there an Anthony here?

Anthony muttered a barely audible, Oh no! Then he found his way thru the little crowd and said out loud, It's me, sorry, sorry everyone, you just go on with your dancing, don't mind me, it's just one of those days!

As he got out of the party room, the maid approached him and said, At the hall downstairs near the piano, you'll find your laundry bag there, someone left it there for you!

Anthony asked, She left the bag? Is she gone?

The maid replied, Yes, she said she had to catch the last jeepney to where was that, Batad? Burog? At eleven thirty! Very nice laundrywoman you have there!

Anthony was perplexed, looked at her straight in the eyes and asked, Laundrywoman?

The maid replied, Yes, that was how she introduced herself! Why? Was that a mistake? Don't you have a laundrywoman? Check if those are indeed your clothes!

Anthony felt like collapsing, all of a sudden the beer tasted bitter he had to throw it away. He sat on the very soft sofa and sank low, wishing he could sink even deeper. He realized that Necessity knew what was in his mind and what he needed that night. He knew she was quite numb when anyone tried to hurt her, but not when it was he, he was certain she was badly bruised.

He looked at his mother again, it was already dark, he could see her face aided by the light from scattered lamps in the village, he was soaked with tears so he could only mumble a little, Sorry.

Necessity asked, What are you sorry for?

He replied, Many times... a lot of things!

He kept reminiscing, thirty long years with her, her name, how it was a burden to her and those who needed to say it.

214

He recalled that it was not before the second grade when he was able to say and write her name. It was worse for Jeremy, he was already in the fourth grade and still did not know exactly what his mother's name was.

Their fourth-grade civics teacher Mr. De Gracia, known for his pungent criticisms, read out loud randomly picked pupils' homework one day, it was Jeremy's he picked first. The homework was about family tree, they were to map out their family tree from their great grandparents from both sides. The teacher removed his glasses and said, Mr. Jeremy Ilaya, what's this? Neseng-Sity? Are you sure this is your mother's name and not the capital of Zimbabwe?

The entire class roared in laughter, Jeremy was looking around, trying to find out who had the most annoying face among those who laughed, he thought of giving that classmate a hard punch on the nose come lunch break. Then a bespectacled girl named Luisa who was vying for the top honors raised her hand, stood up and said, No Sir De Gracia, the capital of Zimbabwe is Harare!

Mr. De Gracia looked annoyed, he said, And nobody asked you, Luisa, I know! Take your seat! His annoyance stemmed from the fact that he actually did not know what the capital of Zimbabwe was, and was unsure if Luisa indeed gave the right information.

Tagalog was used as the medium of instruction in civics class, so Jeremy could speak fluently. He sensed the teacher's unease and doubted if he really knew what Zimbabwe's capital was, so he planned to retaliate. He asked the teacher, So Sir, what was the capital of Zimbabwe again?

Mr. De Gracia froze, then got infuriated because he could not recall what it was, he huffed and said, Didn't you hear what Luisa just said?

Jeremy replied, I didn't, sir, won't you just enlighten us this once?

Mr. De Gracia said, Why don't you look for it and come back with the answer tomorrow? That would be your extra homework!

Jeremy sported a triumphant smile and said, Alright Sir, I remember now, it's Harare, isn't it, Luisa?

Luisa replied, Yes, it's Harare!

Mr. De Gracia chided them, saying, Quiet, Luisa! Speak only when asked or spoken to by the teacher! Be quiet the two of you or I'll send you both to detention!

Jeremy said, Sorry Sir, but I just forgot again, what was Zimbabwe's capital again?

Mr. De Gracia was beginning to grow furious, he slammed the bunch of papers he was holding on his table and said, Before I answer, let me ask you, what was your mother's name again?

Jeremy replied, I'm not really sure, Sir, that one is hard to pronounce and write!

Mr. De Gracia said, Oh you're not sure? You cannot say or spell your mother's name yet you concern yourself with the capital of a country whose paths will almost never cross with those of the Philippines? You have to know your mother's name, boy, it's a necessity! He used the word necessity in English and not Tagalog in order to make a point in a mocking manner. A few who already knew Jeremy's mother's name laughed audibly.

Jeremy said, It's difficult, Sir, her name is like a word you'll never find in the dictionary!

Mr. De Gracia said, Oh yes, Mr. Ilaya, I know her name, it's in the dictionary! The problem is, you've never opened a dictionary your entire life, I can tell by the way you speak and write! And by the way, you don't look for names in the dictionary, boy!

Jeremy asked, So how did you find hers there?

There was an audible laughter from the class, Mr. De Gracia was fuming, he yelled, You get out, Mr. Ilaya! Get out! Go to the detention room!

Jeremy asked, On what grounds, Sir?

He replied, Grave disrespect!

Jeremy picked up his bag and happily trotted out of the room, and as soon as he reached the door, he turned around and said, It's Harare, Sir! The entire class laughed loudly.

The teacher yelled louder, Out!!!

Jeremy did not go to the detention room, he went straight to the public market and played taksi with some street children, it's a kind of game with coins and and small stones, the earliest form of gambling a child in the streets could learn. After winning a few coins, he went to a corner where there were a couple of Atari devices, and he played there for two hours.

Necessity was stroking Anthony's left arm to comfort him. She too, was reminiscing. She never found a way out of the country, not even out of Burog, because she never actually wanted to, it felt like someone else's dream, and her hometown, by hoping she would not succeed, made her feel the weight of their expectations that she ought to fulfill that dream. That was what she thought, but their resentment actually had its roots on her being exceptionally smart and apparently ambitious. So it was like that, the human mind loves to see imposing structures crumbling, imposing structures like a big dream and a big promise, it could happen to anyone like her in any small town. For her, Anthony's departure was some form of closure to everything that happened to her since she was given that name, a name which she had borne like a cross.

She recalled walking with her grandfather Jose Cañosi Baydadong one late afternoon when she was seven, in a meadow near the rice paddies which he rented. It was also in August, it rained in the morning, but the sun shone bright in the afternoon, harvest was nearing and the fields had begun to take up bright yellow colors.

She could clearly remember how her grandfather was like - dark and quite taller than most adults, he used to be plump but was slowly wasting away some muscles as the years passed. He wore a sparse, all-grey beard and his forehead stretched to the southernmost tip of the back of his head. He always had on his white trousers and white jacket no matter how hot or cold or wet or dry the weather was. He always had with him a black wooden cane which he claimed was carved out of hardwood from the hills of California and was given to him by a veteran of the Filipino-American War. She recalled those shoes, old, brown, muddy with holes that exposed parts of his toes. She recalled their conversation that afternoon, how they seemed at times not to make sense.

She exclaimed, Look at them, Lolo, look at them!!! She was referring to a small swarm of grasshoppers which seemed to hop in unison away from their direction as they approached.

He replied, Ah, Necessity, my Necessity, someday when you go to America in Yoyork you'll see grasshoppers many times as big, and you'll see them hop from the sidewalks up to the top of The Emperor Building!

She stopped walking, sighed and asked, When will I go to America, Lolo?

He replied, When you're a big girl and ready with your career, and when your big table on top of The Emperor Building is ready!

She said, Can I not stay here with you until I grow old? I like the meadows here, I want to be with my friends too!

He replied, No, no my girl, you can't stay here, it's no place for you, and I won't be around long enough to see you grow old!

She asked, Where are you going?

He replied, You see, like the grass and the flowers which die, we too die! You know that, I suppose?

She said, I think we should make an agreement, I won't go to America, and you won't die, how's that? In that way we will always be here, happy you and I!

His knees were stiff and aching, but he tried to take a knee so he could talk to his granddaughter face to face, because he wanted to sound like he meant business. He took a deep breath and said, Look Necessity, if you don't go to America, I wouldn't be happy, and I would die early because I'd be unhappy. You like ice cream, right?

She replied, Yes I do, very much!

He asked, And how often do you eat ice cream here? Barely once a month right?

Right!

Think about that, in America, there's a button in every lamppost, just press it and you'll get all the ice cream you want!

Really?

That's right! And that thing you ate when you went to the movies in the city last week, siskarls?

Yes, cheese curls!

That's right, siskarls! Do you like it?

I love it, but it's expensive!

Right! So think about that! In America, they sweep siskarls at the sidewalks because they are overflowing, you can fill your bed with buckets of siskarls!

Wow! And Coca-Cola too?

Oh yes, Coca-Cola! Some wells are filled with just Coca-Cola, you can fetch buckets of it, no one will stop you, if you're busy you can get Coca-Cola out of the tap!

That's amazing!

So now, do you want to go to America?

Necessity paused for a while and thought hard, then said, Do they have arupi there?

Oh, forget arupi, my girl, they have chocolate cakes there a hundred times sweeter than arupi!

But I like arupi!

I heard that Americans have learned to make arupi after the war, all sorts of flavors! Chocolate, milk, apple!

That's nice! I'd like to try those!

That's my girl! So now, would you like to go to America?

She paused again and thought hard, then asked, Can I bring my friends along?

He replied, If your friends are as smart as you, maybe they can follow later, but I don't see anyone of them getting close, so if I may answer you bluntly, I don't think so, I think you'll be going alone!

Well that's sad, I'd like to bring Rowena along!

Rowena who? Ah, you mean Sese?

Her name is Rowena, Lolo!

But the whole town calls her Sese! Ha! I don't think she can go to America, she can't even say a word in her own language, how do you expect her to speak English?

She's doing fine, she's studying hard, by harvest time she'll be speaking English like she's from New York!

Haha! When that day comes the guava trees will bear apples!

Can that happen?

Of course not! My point is, my girl, Sese will never be able to speak English, unlike your Lolo!

You know Charlie Chaplin Lolo? He's in America, he doesn't say a word but he seems to be doing fine!

Haha! You're a funny girl! That's because everyone else around him doesn't talk either!

Then we'll live in that place, where no one else talks! Rowena and I!

You wouldn't like it! They all move too fast there and everything's in black and white! Besides, you were born to talk! You're on top of your class in English!

But I don't think I'll go without Rowena, she'll be scared and lonely!

Look, Necessity my girl, think of the nastiest, meanest boys and girls in your class or in your school, do you have them in mind right now?

Yes, I do, there are about five or six!

Right! Many years from now they'll still be here, doing laundry all day by the river, planting rice under the scorching heat, feeding their ducks in the afternoon, borrowing money at the lender's to buy rice for dinner, while you are there on top of that Emperor Building, sitting by your big desk, everyone brings to you all the ice cream and siskarls and Coca-Cola and apple flavored arupi you want!

I think I can handle all six of them without going to America!

Jose Cañosi Baydadong just laughed, gave his granddaughter a playful rub on the back and patted her head, and said, You are a smart girl, how can I ever end an argument with you?

It was dusk and it was beautiful, she recalled, the sun gave out those golden orange rays because the earth in which it was trying to hide for the night had been earlier soaked by the rain. The church bells tolled, it was 6 pm, they prayed the Angelus, then she got her grandfather's blessing by placing the back of his hand on her forehead, as millions of other children around the country were doing with their parents or grandparents at that same moment. Then he said to her, Let's go home now, your Lola is cooking pochero!

Necessity said, Wow, I love it! Lola is teaching me how to cook that!

Jose said, You don't have to, no one will eat that in America! In America you'll eat jam-bur-jer!

What's that?

Oh, just wait, and you'll learn! And you know why they'll gladly welcome you to America?

Why?

Because the first lines of their national anthem begins with your Lolo's name!

Is it the English version of Bayang magiliw perlas ng silanganan?

Haha, oh no! He then sang his name in the tune of the first line of The Star Spangled Banner, Jo-ho-se Caño-si, Bay-da-dong Ernie Night!

Necessity asked, Who's Ernie Night?

He replied, I don't know, must be some American hero, but he belongs to the second line, your Lolo's name occupies the first line! Great isn't it?

That's amazing! She said. Then they both went inside the house where a large cauldron of pochero and a pot of hot rice were waiting.

Anthony had packed everything for the trip, all he had left to do the rest of the evening was think about the life he was about to leave behind, and cry. He had all the evening for crying, it seemed as though he couldn't stop and it could go on until morning. He sat beside his mother on that steel-pipe bench for almost an hour, crying most of the time. Then she rose and went inside the house. She returned after about a quarter of an hour, and she was carrying an old bamboo culm, it was quite thick and was roughly half a meter from node to node. Anthony quickly recognized it, it had been beside Necessity's bed for many years, he was not so certain as to what it was for, but countryfolk used it for two main purposes - as a coin bank or as a bamboo percussion instrument. He had lifted that culm recently when he cleaned the room, it didn't seem to contain any coins, and Necessity was never known to play any musical instrument. There must be something else in it.

Necessity was moving sluggishly, her left hip ached. She handed Anthony the bamboo culm and said, There you go, it's for you!

Anthony tried to shake the culm, he could not hear any sound. He said, I've always wondered what's in this one, now I'll get to know!

Necessity said, I always knew this day would come, and that coins would surely be an unnecessary heavy baggage, so I put only peso bills in it!

Anthony began to cry again and said, Oh Mama you didn't have to!

She said playfully, Oh don't get too excited about it, they're mostly ten and twenty-peso bills, and rarely, so rarely that I can still recall when, I placed fifty and hundred peso bills in it too! I started the day you agreed to take up nursing, even before you took the entrance exams!

It made Anthony laugh briefly, then he resumed crying and said, I have enough as of now, I think you'll be needing this more!

Necessity said, You'll break my heart if you leave out a single peso bill!

Anthony understood, he nodded. They ate dinner, then he opened the culm, it was full of peso bills, and they all totaled roughly 4,000 pesos, eight years of Necessity's thoughtfulness and hope.

They were at the Iloilo Airport in early afternoon the next day for his flight at 4pm. They sat there at the cafe outside the departure area, Sese was with them, they ordered La Paz Batchoy, but only Sese was busy eating. Both mother and son barely touched their bowls, and they were silent, both found it too painful to speak. Then Anthony rose, as it was time to go.

Four members of The Quitters then arrived to see him off, and then two other friends from the nursing school. Sese gently placed a rolled 500 peso bill in his shirt pocket, kissed him and then wiped her own tears. He walked towards the door, showed his passport and his ticket to the guard, and went inside that door, formally considered to be a point of no return. He waved but did not look back, because he was still considering staying put and giving it all up, at least at that moment, and it was all but natural. He was afraid that if he looked back he might just run back to his mother and stayed put. Then Necessity watched as he disappeared.

His flight was for Manila, he was to stay another night there, this time, in an apartment room owned by a couple from Burog who owned a retail store for mobile phones, quite ironic, because the first time he was there in the capital city his host was a mobile phone snatcher.

The plane lifted, he was sitting by the window. It was only the third flight of his life, he had flown back and forth to Cebu before as a nursing student representative, so it ought to have thrilled him, but it didn't. He looked out of the window, the plains and hills of Iloilo were vast and green, the afternoon sun created golden edges among the scattered rainclouds, it was majestic. Soon, Iloilo was out of sight, and all he could see outside was his mother's face.

15

October 2009, the digital world had gone that far, but still Necessity had not overcome the fear of laying her hands over computer keyboards and ending the digital-free era of her life. She needed Sese to accompany her to the public market where there was a tiny computer and internet station flanked by a dried fish stall on the left and a bicycle spare parts store on the right.

Sese had put up an e-mail account for her. She actually still preferred to get letters from Anthony in the traditional, tested and proven way, but it took the letters weeks to get from Oslo to The Blue Cottage in Sitio Putak and back. She had received an e-mail from Anthony dated October 29, 2009, and that was two days earlier, still she was amazed on how fast it got to her - two days. It was more or less an hour's walk from The Blue Cottage to the public market, she thought if she had the time it would have gotten to her in an hour, and if she had internet and computer at home it would have gotten to her in seconds. But given a choice, she still would have preferred the old snail mail. Sese opened the inbox and then the message, Necessity had her hands tightly clasped together under the table and over her lap, she made it clear to Sese that she was not touching any key or any part of the computer, she was just there to read her son's letter.

A group of kids from ages five to twelve thronged behind them the moment they logged in, all were in a curious, dropped-jaw stance quietly and patiently probing the screen over her shoulders. Soon they realized that she wasn't there to look at pictures, and obviously, with her age and her hands stiffly bound under the table by imaginary handcuffs, she never looked anywhere near playing video games. The children slowly dispersed, Sese tried to shoo away a couple of small ones who looked like they were staying put just to stare at the screen no matter what was in it. They did not budge at all and Sese did not bother pressing further, she thought, the entire letter was in English, if she herself could not understand more than half of what was written there then she was certain that neither could they.

Ant78berkid
To: neneseng1947@yahoo.com
Thursday, October 29, 2009

Dear Mama,

It's past midnight and they are all asleep, it's deafeningly silent here, the sound I make with the keyboards are as loud as footsteps. You asked me in your recent letter if it's lonely here. Don't worry, it is always lonely here and I hope you understand what I mean when I say that feeling that kind of loneliness is such a privilege, it is a kind of loneliness like no other, it has made me wise and strong and see the world in angles I thought were never there. For every drop of tear of loneliness grows an inch of fortitude.

In September I was a week shy of saying to immigration "I don't know" in case they asked me how I was to planning to support myself if they extended my student permit for another year. Then just like that, a lady named Birgitta Aaker called me, she is the chief of this psychiatric home I'm working in. I sent dozens of emails to chiefs of different departments and different companies, even moving companies and warehouses and only one responded - Birgitta Aaker, and I got the job, though I'm just a substitute nurse assistant paid by the hour in case they need someone to fill in, and they have been needing me almost everyday, I don't mind working everyday, I've had a lot of free time in the past year, I don't miss being off from work.

In January I will begin a fast-track course at the university, for two terms it will be intensive language, theory and clinics, and by December next year, God willing, I will be a registered Norwegian nurse! They say I can even secure employment at some hospital or home already in the second term, so the immigration can approve my permanent residence by September next year.

I'm more than alright, though the first two weeks was tough. I cannot speak the language that fluently though I try hard like no one else, and they just all talk too fast, think if we all talked to Anders Bjorge in crisp Hiligaynon at the clinics in Iloilo, I don't think he'd have lasted two hours on his first day!

The telephone scares me, I think my comprehension of Norwegian drops 90% on the phone. I make sure whenever I pass by the tiny office where the telephone is that another colleague is nearby, so she or he will pick it up. In other areas I'm quite good, and it's about cleaning the patients' flats, doing the dishes, there's a big dishwasher here and you don't need any college degree to figure out how it works. I set the table, sometimes I cook, sometimes I accompany patients to the grocery store and it's quite a challenge. I give out their pills too, morning, noon, evening and before they go to bed if I take day or evening passes. But I usually work at night, so the task is easier, that is, if I can put them all to sleep and if no one freaks out. I attached some pictures of the place here, ask Tita Sese to open it. As you can see the house is very old, it was built in 1750, a century before Jose Rizal was born, but I've never once felt that it is haunted, I fear the telephone more than any ghost. The house has 12 rooms made into apartments, and right now we have 10 patients, most of

227

them schizophrenics and mild psychotics who have been stabilized, so don't worry, if they had the tendency to be violent they wouldn't be here. Each of them has a room, a furnished apartment and we personnel help them with the cleaning, the rooms are so well furnished it reminds me of standard rooms at five-star hotels in the Philippines, if I may exaggerate a bit.

I have a lot to tell you about these patients. I'm not even two months on the job but I've already felt some kind of attachment to some of them. Secrecy is a strict code here, I cannot reveal their identities or their real names, breach of secrecy is one of the most serious crimes here.

There is a man in his late sixties, let's just call him by our native term, Bugok. He's a paranoid schizophrenic and an outspoken white supremacist. He ran amok the first time he saw me, he kept saying that the lower races managed to lure Birgitta Amok, I mean Aaker to hire me so they can poison him thru me. He never assaulted me physically, but he poured a barrage of racist insults, the kind never lobbed at me my entire life. He refused to eat and take his pills whenever I was on duty, so he worsened and got confined at the hospital for a week. There was trouble with the taxi when he was discharged, so he came home late in the afternoon very hungry and had no choice but to eat the lunch which I cooked. It was some kind of codfish gratin, and he ate a whole platter. The next day he requested the same dish, and it was granted, he ate three portions. He requested it again the next day but was denied, as the other patients complained about eating fish for two consecutive days. A few days later, he started to converse with me. He said he never knew I could talk. He said he believed that those of the "lower races" should be kept on the other side of the planet so the caucasian race wouldn't be diluted, and if the lower races insisted on coexisting with them the caucasians had no choice but to put them in gas chambers. Imagine how scared I was when he said it, we were eating breakfast together at one corner of the long table and he sat between me and the emergency exit, he is 6 feet tall, typically overweight from antipsychotics and he has that long Viking beard that touches his groin when seated. But then he assured me, if that time comes I will

228

*be spared, he said he'll testify that I'm his kitchen slave. Such
thoughts are never tolerated here, but then he's excused a bit because
of his diagnosis, but each time he makes racist remarks he's being put
in his place by the personnel. And don't worry about him, he asks for
me a lot and seems to be worried when I'm not on duty, and everyday
he calls Birgitta Aaker requesting my codfish gratin for lunch.*

*There is this lady, an older one, she's over 70, still unclassified
type of psychosis. Let's call her by our native word, Taray, like your
old housemaid, God rest her soul. Her hairdo looks like an inverted
Eiffel Tower, all gray, and she has this very coarse voice she would
have been an easy pick for witch hunters in medieval times. I saw her
first on my second day when I gave out her evening pills. She
quivered upon seeing me and went down on her knees, then she
kissed my feet, well of course I had my shoes on. Guess what? She's
been to the Philippines when she was a teenager, her father went on a
hunting expedition in Masbate in the early 50's, she said she'd been
to some of the neighboring islets around Masbate and had heard of a
local folklore about a prince named Poldo who, as a toddler, was
snatched by a big eagle and taken somewhere far. The islets suffered a
dip in their fishing catch and their harvests and the locals believed it
would go on until Prince Poldo returned. She said the locals saw
thru her eyes that she was the chosen one, the one who'd find Poldo
one day. And from the moment she saw me she's been calling me
Prince Poldo, to everyone's amusement. She's been here for 10 years
now and she's been talking about the legend everyday, especially
during breakfast, so everyone who's been a patient or a personnel here
for at least a day in the past decade knows the story of Poldo. Birgitta
Aaker knows about it and I wonder if it was why she hired me, maybe
not. Taray put an abaca necklace around my neck, its pendant is a
small bunch of tattered bird feathers which have been spray-painted
blue, she said it was Prince Poldo's necklace, and Birgitta wondered
if it was alright if I wore that whenever I knocked on Taray's
apartment, and I said it was not a problem. They noticed that Taray
has been happier in the past weeks and the psychiatrist just reduced
the dose of one of her anxiolytics. Mama, you have to travel with me*

someday! The biggest, most elating element of surprise in traveling is finding some fragments of home somewhere far away!

There is another patient here in her early thirties, let's call her by our native term, Ugak. She's so laid back she cannot harm a fly. She's the only one without the sleeping pills because the only thing that can put her to sleep is the film Braveheart. Yes, it's one of your favorites but you'd learn to hate it if you lived near her. Because of that she was placed in a room far from the others, but exactly near the night personnel room, it's where I am at this very moment. She plays the film loudly every night at around 8 clock, I can hear each and every word being said in the film, my relief comes at around 10:45 when it finally ends. Real freedom!

Then there is this Swedish guy in his 40's let's call him by our native word Topak. He laughs all the time, it's his only reaction to everything. He told me about how his parents died in a skiing accident when he was a child, and he just kept on laughing as he told it. Last month I caught him rolling in laughter in the living room while watching BBC and they were featuring Typhoon Ondoy. I was pissed, well, at least only at that time, otherwise I think he has the best medicine innately installed in him.

I cannot tell you about all of the patients here as of now, I need to end this letter before someone freaks out from sleep, I'll be back with some more colorful characters later, I'm so fond of them! Sorry I seem to have gotten lost here, I've written too much about my work, I just wanted to tell you that I'm doing fine. Please don't withhold anything from me, especially about your health and finances, I'd appreciate it if you were as open as I am. In trying to keep me from worrying by not telling me about your problems you might make me worry all the more.

You asked me if I was lonely, I have to tell you, I am, and I'm proud to feel and say so. It's a strange new kind of loneliness, I feel like a sapling trying to regrow roots fast for my own sake! Then of course I miss a lot of things I never once thought I'd miss, small things I took for granted, like that fountain in front of the Provincial Capitol, that rapidly returning tide in early evening near our little Blue Cottage, those kids playing at the plaza and the drunks at the karaoke bars, and how everyone stands in attention like startled ducks when the bells toll at 6 P.M., the jeepney ride and how you can just ask the drivers to stop to alight anywhere, the lively news in the evenings, the fishballs on sticks and sodas poured in clear transparent cellophanes which we suck out with a straw.

Of course your pochero, but I knew long beforehand that I was gong to miss it, even in the Philippines there's nothing like it. I miss these things so much that it hurts. We may not be together for two more Christmases! But hang on, as soon as I get stable here I will get you a plane ticket, hopefully by December 2011, and we will have a very merry Christmas. You asked me in your letter last Christmas how the snow felt, well, keep hoping, you will have the answer in two years, and it will melt in your hands! Maybe, who knows, we can fly to New York City? Things will be good, Ma. We have squatted all our lives on those rocks by the sea, we have been living at the mercy of the tides of life, as soon as I can I will buy a piece of land of our own, and build a bigger blue house there.

We need to keep hoping, Ma, it's all we've ever got and somehow we have weathered life's harshness. You know I keep praying, I know you keep praying, though we are not as vocal and as loud about how we communicate with God like most of our townsfolk, you and I and God know we communicate, and I think that's enough. No one has hoped all her life more than you and I'm almost there, someday in the near future you'll wake up and say, "I don't want anything more." And then we will eat breakfast and forgive the past. On my way to work today I saw two deer prancing in the wet fields, you know these creatures mystify me, to locals here they bear ticks that bear Borrelia burgdorferi and tick-borne encephalitis, but for me they bear some message, whenever I see them I feel like God is wishing me well. If He initiated the entire universe with a single phrase, imagine how powerful His wish can be. We will get to that day!

Please write, if possible here, it'll get to me faster and I cannot wait to hear from you. You may ask Tita Sese or her granddaughter to type it for you. If you are ready enough, then sign up to Facebook, it will bring us ten times nearer each other. You have missed an entire Friendster era, now is the time, Mama!

Love,

Ton-ton.

A little less than a year later, on September 14, 2010, they saw each other's faces thru Skype. Sese's eldest had found work as a repairman in Abu Dhabi and he made sure that she was having quite a comfortable life. She got a laptop and had an internet installed in her house recently.

Necessity moved into one of the rooms in Sese's house that morning, and by noon they were ready to call Anthony, and it was 6 a.m. in Oslo. Two nurses and three nurse aids had to help Necessity on a stretcher from the ambulance. She had been confined at the University Hospital in the past two weeks and it was time to go home, everyone agreed.

She'd felt a lump on her left breast as early as 2007 and she had been seeing Madame Tisay, a local herbalist in the neighboring town of Banate who had been applying all sorts of wild leaves and saying all kinds of pseudo-Latin formulas to drive away evil spirits that did not mean her well. She did not tell anyone, not even Anthony. By the time she saw a surgeon in April 2010, her breast was all swollen and sore, and the cancer had spread to her lungs.

Anthony sent every money he could spare for her treatment, her brothers and Renato Ilaya helped too, so she got to be among those private patients with the privilege of comfort and superior care. In July she had seizures, and they found out she had metastases in her brain. And so the once brave and indomitable Necessity Berano Ilaya was lying there in bed wearing a pretty green gown, the top of her head was covered by a flowery pink bandana, she turned her head to the left when they told her Anthony was to appear on the screen anytime. There were four rosaries of different colors and different sizes and materials hung around her neck. A small patch of the Sacred Heart, a button of St. Martin de Pores and a small chopped piece of ginger were pinned on her gown on the left side of her chest, a healing cocktail from ancient Filipino animism and Roman Catholicism. She could not say a word anymore, she was being fed thru a nasogastric tube, she could only communicate thru the movement of her head and eyes, her left cheek and her right arm.

Anthony had shaved and put on a sleek grey sweater, he had about an hour to see his mother on Skype, he had to leave at 7 am for school to take an important term exam. As soon as his face appeared on the screen there came a loud, high-pitched scream, it was from Sese, as usual, uncontrollably excited, Aaaaaayyy!!! Ton-ton! Look at your Mama Seng, she's so pretty, pretty Mama Seng, Ton-ton is here, say hi! Mama Seng, look at your Ton-Ton he's so gwapo, all the way from Norway!

For more than two minutes, all that could be heard was Sese, screaming, until her husband tapped her on the shoulder, signaling it was time for mother and son to try to communicate. Sese shrugged her shoulder but kept quiet anyway. Anthony was devastated, he broke down in tears. Johanna, Sese's twelve year old granddaughter, was handy with the laptop, she managed to focus the camera on Necessity's face, it soon filled Anthony's screen, and he could clearly see her eyes, she stared at the screen and tears rolled down. Don't worry about me Ma, he said, I'll be doing fine, I'm doing good, everything will be fine!

Then nothing was said for a long while. Sese came up with something again, she said loudly while sobbing, You know Ton, we have to accept this, it is the will of the Lord Gee-sas, the Lord Gee-sas will take care of your Mama Seng! He loves your Mama Seng! Sese had been pronouncing Jesus that way since she was a child.

Necessity shook her head a bit, her left cheek moved, she seemed to smile. Anthony asked, Are you sure she is not in pain?

Sese replied, Oh the nurse just gave her a dose of morpain!

Anthony was bothered and a little annoyed, he asked, What did you say? More pain?

Johanna interrupted and said, Lola meant morphine!

Anthony said, Whew, that's a relief!

Sese was never a bit embarrassed about mispronunciations, she just went on with another agendum. She drew a piece of paper from her handbag and said, Oh your brother Jeremy, guess what? He wrote a letter to your Mama!

Anthony said, Well, that's a surprise!

Sese said, Your brother is a good boy now, he's among those who joined The Reformed Alleluia Gang in prison and he wrote your mother!

Anthony tried to process what he was feeling upon hearing that, he instantly recalled all sorts of pain associated with the memory of his brother, it then turned into some kind of joy, a kind that still hurt, it all felt like it was leading to a closure. He asked, What did he say?

Sese cleared her throat, and said, You know, my granddaughter Johanna is the top student in her English class, so she can read it to you! Come dear, read to your Manong Tonton, come, read Manong Jeremy's letter!

The letter was in Hiligaynon though, not in English, otherwise Jeremy could not have written it that well. Reluctantly and shyly, Johanna took the letter, Sese focused the camera on her but her husband instantly shifted it back to Necessity. Johanna read the letter out loud.

August 15, 2010

Dear Mama,

Praise the Lord Jesus Alleluia! I am writing you from my cell in Bilibid prison, Amen, and I praise the Lord and not question my

234

presence here, Alleluia, Amen, because I know I more than deserve it, so I accept it in Jesus' name, Amen!

I am deeply sorry in Jesus' name Amen, to hear about your cancer, Alleluia! May the power of the Lord Jesus bring you to healing in Jesus' name Amen!

Yesterday I fasted in Jesus' name, Alleluia, I gave my share of linugaw in the morning, Alleluia, to an inmate, Amen, who was badly battered in a brawl the other night in Jesus' name, Amen! We had lina-gang langka for lunch yesterday, Alleluia and Amen I gave my share to an elder who's had diarrhea for weeks in Jesus' name Alleluia! Praise the Lord I gave my dinner to another younger but depressed inmate Amen! I'm very hungry Alleluia upon writing this letter to you Amen, but praise the name of Jesus Alleluia I'm doing it all for your healing, Amen!

I wish in Jesus' name Alleluia that someday when you are healed Alleluia you may be able to visit me again, Amen, because Alleluia I know I should have talked to you when they took me away in Jesus' name Alleluia Amen!

I'm not in any way hoping to be released Alleluia, Praise the Lord Jesus I am just waiting for the day that you will be brought back to health, Amen Alleluia, and we can hold each other's hands again, Amen! I heard about Anthony, Amen, Praise the Good Name of Jesus Alleluia he is doing well abroad, Amen! Please tell him to just accept Jesus Christ as his savior and everything will go fine for him, Amen, and someday we will see each other again too Alleluia! I have accepted Christ as my savior, Mama, Alleluia, and I hope you do too, Amen, so you will be brought back to health Alleluia Amen! Please write back, Alleluia, if you can in the powerful name of Jesus, Amen!

In Jesus Christ,

Jeremy

Everybody in the room then exclaimed, Amen!

For the remainder of the time, Anthony was only crying, not much words were said from both rooms, most were occasional bursts from Sese who said things like, It's okay to cry, it's okay to cry! Or, Gee-sas will take care of Mama Seng!

It was all too painful, Anthony had sent all the money he could spare, he had been finishing the nursing course at daytime and worked at the psychiatric home at nighttime and on weekends. He'd been virtually subsisting on instant noodles, canned tuna and rice in one of the world's richest countries. Needless to say, he did not have the dough for the plane ticket home to see his mother, even if he did his future would be compromised if he flew home, he would have to drop the course and the employment which was to be signed the following week, thus his permanent residence would go up in smoke.

Still he had that choice, and he could opt to give it all up if some angel from somewhere, like Anders Bjorge, Renato Ilaya, Bobby Hong or some Norwegian bank could make it possible. But no, he thought, they had helped more than enough, except of course the banks. He thought at that moment about giving it all up just to be with his mother in her final hours or at least to attend her funeral. But then on the other hand, he looked at his mother's eyes staring back at him, the eyes that never told him at any point in his life to give up on what would have given him a bright future.

He was being torn to shreds. It was 7 am, he had to leave, a hectic day at the university awaited him. He was to make another excruciatingly painful choice - he had to sign off.

Goodbye Ma, I have to go, he said.

Necessity was staring at him, almost never blinking. Then she lifted her right arm, to say goodbye...and a thousand more beautiful words.

Epilogue

Necessity died later that evening, they laid her in a fine white coffin lined with golden paint. Sese never had second thoughts about hosting the wake at her house, as The Blue Cottage in Sitio Putak was too small and had not been attended to for many months. They said the heavens could not aptly decide on the day of her funeral, sunshine and showers took turns several times when they took her from the church to her final resting place beside her parents, her little sister Daisy, and the great Jose Cañosi Baydadong. She planted daffodils that bore white flowers with faint hues of purple in scant soil between the rocks outside The Blue Cottage the day she moved in there many years ago, and they bloomed every year in May when the rains came. She asked Sese to dig up some bulbs there and plant them by her grave.

Her brothers Arthur, Lancelot and Percivale and their families were present during the wake and the funeral. Geronimo and Leonora Balbago were at the funeral mass and surprisingly, their son Bryan Balbago was with them, he was now an adult, though he was not fully aware of the event, the time, and the place. He had a long, hearty talk with the flowers and the empty pews inside the church. Two unfamiliar faces came on the last night of the wake - two old ladies who introduced themselves as Margareta and Josefina, two of Onyok Ilaya's sisters, the ones who refused to live in the house he built out of smuggling money, and who were absent during his wedding. They said their prayers by her coffin, and it was like the past was to be forgiven that day. Renato Ilaya did not come, but he sent truckloads of flowers.

The line in the funeral procession was not that long, it was barely a fourth of the usual in town, but people who knew her at least stood and paused and either made a sign of the cross or bowed their heads as the procession passed by their homes. Whatever her memory evoked in them - disdain, pity, envy, admiration, or even just some faint, scattered reminiscences which did not stir any affect, she was still a daughter of the town, and she was not coming back.

And I, Anthony Berano Ilaya, was not there. My mother and I faced the jarring winds of life side by side almost never blinking, and when her eyes finally closed I chose to stay far away. It's January 5, 2015, it's been more than four years now since she died, I might just agree to start judging myself less harshly for that decision, for life has finally presented itself to be kinder, just as my mother had wished for me.

I am living alongside what the world calls the happiest people on earth, people who'll never have to sign a paper to waive away their lives because they cannot afford treatment. I ought to be persistently grateful and happy, but still I hold the right to allow sadness to visit me, because I miss my mother. I am going back to visit, for the first time since I left, my home country and my hometown. I saw some pictures of my mother's grave last May, it was flanked by dozens of white daffodils with faint purple hues, and it was like I could hear her calling me to come home. I think of The Blue Cottage in Sitio Putak, I always think of it whenever I feel lost, no matter where I roam it will lead me home, like how it led the fishermen back to shore at daybreak. I've never forgotten it, as I had promised my mother.

She slipped into one of my books that old picture of The Empire State Building which her grandfather gave her, and at the back of the photo is written a crooked line in blue ink, and it must have been written by Jose Cañosi Baydadong himself. It says, My Dear Necessity, Get there!

Impeccable English! But I believe it's his words as it certainly looks like his handwriting - all in capitals on an uneven base. I think I've stained it with chocolate from my fingers as the stains look fresh. I was eating Butterfinger and Mars a while ago, and I am holding the photo right now.

I am right now on the 102nd floor, the observatory deck of the Empire State Building, I thought I'd drop by before going home, to see for myself so I'd have something of a surprise to say to my mother by her grave. Oh my Great Grandfather Jose Cañosi Baydadong, I don't know in what manner he looked into the future, but to the best of my knowledge, no one else has ever been named Necessity, not in my hometown Burog at least, nor in the nearest ten towns. And if he only knew, one could not mount a big desk in this cramped room on top of the world, it would have been such an uncomfortable office for his little Necessity. If only he knew, she would have been spared that dream, the dream she never harbored herself, and I'm not so sure, but I still believe that life then would have been a bit kinder to her.

It was she who surprised me though, she did not seem to pursue that ambition herself, as if she had been here in this tiny room all the while, and had seen for herself that it was not really worth all those troubles. It is just right now, right here, that I've come to understand what my mother had in mind all along. This country is great, it had colonized then liberated us at the other end of the globe, but true liberation comes when we learn to let go of the need to put this country at the center of our universe, the need to make it the focal point of our hopes and frustrations, of our love and loathing, of how we see and judge people. America was born out of love of liberty and she is still finding her way, and we shall find our way too, and we cannot find it without true liberation, and true liberation is something which we have to dig up from deep within us, something which my mother found without leaving Burog.

I still have not come into terms with me leaving the country, something which my mother dreamed for me later on. I'm not sure whether we were right or wrong about it, whether I should have stood by my country and helped her find her way to a better state, or left like I did, to pursue a better life for myself. It's an ongoing debate in my mind, but it does not plague me that much. Time will tell, and hopefully, time will tell me kindly, regardless of me having been right or wrong. Let it unfold.

I have to go now, two ladies await me on the 86th floor, one is Signe, Anders' younger sister whom I married. She is a CEO of a robotics company in Sweden, a strong woman who wouldn't bow to anything except heights. The other is our little girl Ann. I gave her one of the most common names, as I must have learned. She has Necessity's eyes, though they are a bit hazel, and she has her sturdy spirit too.

I just need to gaze at the big city from here one more time, as I am not keen on coming back, I've finally seen what it was all about. In a short while I will descend what my great grandfather called The Emperor Building, to go on and face the life I've chosen. I'm still struggling to be at ease living in relative affluence, something which eluded my mother her entire life. It's a cold, still night and the moon is shining bright, and I'm finally shaking hands with the past. I can feel my mother's presence from all directions on top of the world and she's wishing me well, telling me to do my best and to be strong whenever I feel frail. If there is a spot in this world where hope never dies, it must be somewhere inside a mother's eyes.

ACKNOWLEDGMENT

Since my mother's, my two sisters' and my wife's names are already written somewhere in this book, I'd like to acknowledge the rest of my closest family members here, for their patience and understanding when my thoughts were wandering far somewhere else while writing.

Pacifer Y. Ticao, my good father who is the complete opposite of Necessity's husband. My brother Bisoy Ticao, his family Lyndel Grace Acovera Ticao, Charlize Ysabelle Ticao, Chelsea Anne Ticao, my sister's cowboy Joe Abanes and their talented pearl Pio Ticao Abanes, Emma 'Taray' Ticao, my in-laws Dan Emil Vilhelm Pettersson, Siv Pettersson, Lourdes Lasaleta Pettersson, Karl Albin Pettersson, and the people who gave me a family far away from home: Anne Haby, Staffan Haby, Zandra Hansson, Mads Olsen, Lisbeth Skoglar, Hannelore Buyle, Douwe Mol, Jacob Risholm, Homan Naevee, Reidun Strömberg, Johnny and Kristina Carlsson, and of course, The Biggest Apple of My Eye, Julia Ticao-Pettersson.

About the Author

Mark Ticao has written several literary fiction manuscripts, some of which he lost, some are locked somewhere and cannot be retrieved, but most of which he never intends to publish, as he writes largely for his own amusement.

However, a promise made to his mother on her deathbed that he'd publish at least one compelled him to publish Necessity, as his promise made it feel like a necessity to do so. The manuscript was written in the summers of 2017 & 2018 on the Greek Islands of Samos, Patmos and Cephalonia.

In 2004 he moved to Sweden where he currently works as a district physician, but his thoughts have never left Panay Island.